The Cornermen

BY JOHN GARDNER

The Cornermen

JOHN GARDNER

DOUBLEDAY & COMPANY, INC.
Garden City, New York
1976

Library of Congress Cataloging in Publication Data

Gardner, John E
  The cornermen.

  I. Title.
PZ4.G2312Cq4 [PR6057.A63] 823′.9′14
ISBN: 0-385-00525-3
Library of Congress Catalog Card Number 75-150896

For the other Edmund

Corner . . . 3. Buying up whole of any stock or commodity, so as to compel speculative sellers to buy from one to fulfil their engagements; (loosely) any combination to raise prices by securing monopoly. . . . **Corner man,** end man of a row of minstrels, usu. playing bones or tambourine and contributing comic effects.

The Oxford Illustrated Dictionary

The Cornermen

Prologue

IT HAD BEEN A HOT DAY, and now the stretch of motorway running from Heathrow Airport into London took on the vague dreamlike quality of dusty twilight. Anthony Chassen smiled at his own reflection in the window of the Daimler hire car as it slid neatly up the Hammersmith flyover, in the fast lane, overtaking the other traffic. He considered that it seemed longer than three years since he had last been in this city.

On that previous visit the name on his passport had been Anthony Champion, not, as now, Anthony Chassen. But that was purely academic, for Chassen was used to wearing different names, like suits, none of which reflected his true origins. Within him the facts did not alter. He had been born Antonio Campelli, and this last change of name, from Champion to Chassen, arose from the fact that, as Champion, he had been forced to leave London in a hurry with half of Scotland Yard on his tail, close enough to smell the sweat.

That was the time of the Wexton fiasco, he reflected, when Al Vescari was anxious to make a foothold in Europe by financing profitable operations. Chassen himself had been under a cloud for some time after, because Wexton had proved to be a bad choice.

The Daimler nudged into the heavy evening traffic, creeping towards the West End.

To Chassen that last visit seemed a hundred years ago. For one thing Al Vescari (Don Alberto) was dead. Chassen had only been back in New York for just over six months when it happened. There were rumours, tension, talk of yet another war within the families. He had gone, with two of the other trusted *capi,* to Don Alberto's apartment to discuss strategy (Alberto had given up his substantial home in Long Island two years before, after his wife

1

had died of cancer, preferring to live in the smaller apartment with close members of the organisation).

On that evening Vescari was as cool as ever, talking quietly in his soft-accented voice, the two bodyguards, one at the window and one sitting near the door, remaining silent as the executives spoke of the possibilities of having to go to the mattresses again and their chances of sitting out a long siege.

They all had drunk a little and smoked too much. Then, around eleven o'clock, Don Alberto had become restless, as though he found the surroundings claustrophobic, insisting, against their advice, on going down the street to Frazzelli's, his favourite restaurant.

"I have survived the bombs and bullets for a long time, Tony." He had smiled warmly at Chassen. "I do not fear them any more."

Chassen had rung down to Michael, asking him to bring the car to the rear entrance. They had taken all the usual precautions, which were almost automatic to them. But, as Albert Vescari had stepped out onto the sidewalk, moving quickly to the car, there was a burst of fire from a window high in the building across the street.

In a second, Don Alberto lay dead in a pool of pumping blood, only a couple of paces from the car door, two bullets in his neck, a third and fourth in the stomach, while one of the bodyguards rolled in the gutter, screaming, trying to hold his guts in. Chassen always held this picture in his mind: the sprawled body of the don and the stubby man writhing with his hands over the ripped abdomen, fingers desperately wrestling with hanging entrails.

It was no wonder that Chassen's previous trip to England seemed so long ago. Much had happened. Reorganisation, the war among the New York families, the sense of bitterness and anger, later tempered by vengeance after the don had died. The chaos and turmoil, which had already existed before the shooting, magnified and intensified through the closing months of the sixties.

The pattern of life among the organisations in New York was changing beyond recognition, so that the family areas became less well defined; the characteristics and leadership altering; the old values of honour, loyalty and courage seeming to mean less, so that the weaker families in the city appeared to be failing, dying,

2

falling apart, split by indiscipline within and pressures from without.

The older, respected, men reached for the mantle of prophecy, saying "This thing of ours is finished," going on to explain that, just as they had taken over from the Jewish and Irish gangs, so the blacks and Puerto Ricans were now taking over. Younger members counselled that they should admit blacks and Puerto Ricans, an idea which scandalised the rigid, inflexible older men, causing more bad blood.

Yet, as far as the fragmented Vescari family was concerned, the harbingers of doom had reckoned without Don Alberto's son, Giuseppe.

A short, muscular young man of twenty-eight with strong, good-looking features inherited from his mother, Giuseppe Vescari was, to the bulk of the members, a man apart, living in another world. Educated in the Midwest and at UCLA, Giuseppe appeared to be carving out a career for himself far removed from the complex web of kinship which bound the brotherhood to past, present and future. True, he was a member of the family by birth rather than sponsorship, but, like many third- and fourth-generation Italian-Americans, his interests seemed to be centred more in the growth of his country of birth than in the country and traditions of his blood. He had taken courses in business management, was a skilled company lawyer, even though he did not practise law, and could negotiate the dangerous shallows and depths of accountancy.

Few had banked on Don Alberto's shrewdness. Since Giuseppe had left UCLA he had been rehearsed in the ever changing fortunes of the family. With the help of his *consigliere,* the wise seventy-year-old Vincent di Prizzi, Don Alberto had schooled his son, with much secrecy, in the family business of real estate, trucking, olive oil and cheese, the garment industry, restaurants and bars on one hand; extortion, gambling, prostitution, narcotics and hijacking on the other.

When Alberto died on the sidewalk on that chilly evening, Giuseppe knew the exact financial state of all the family interests; he knew most of the *capi* personally, and the soldiers at least by name and distant sight, he was aware of those who could be trusted and those who were borderline cases; he knew how each intricate operation worked and who was responsible; the structure, how the squads were formed under the *capi* and how the complicated communications system functioned, involving literally hundreds of pay phones throughout the city and its environs. What was more, the young Giuseppe had discussed in detail, with his father and Di Prizzi, how the legal business could be handled with greater efficiency and profit, and how the illegal could work with less harassment and smoother cash flow. He also foresaw a more ideal future for the family, involving bloodless takeovers of territory and businesses, accomplished with the pen, adding machine and smooth tongue, rather than the bomb and machine gun.

Within twenty-four hours of Alberto's assassination, there was whispering among the family, and so outside to the wider area of the other families. Giuseppe was in New York, planning to step into his father's shoes. The rumour grew and was received with scepticism within and without the Vescari family.

On the day before the funeral, the most trusted capi were called to a meeting with the consigliere, whom they all respected as being one of the lifelong amici of the late Alberto Vescari, and a trusted friend and adviser to the former don. Also present at the meeting were the Vescari underboss, the number two of the organisation, Joseph Bertel, and Don Alberto's son, Giuseppe Vescari.

In the Vescari family the consigliere had always been the one closest to Don Alberto, combining the classic roles of his position as adviser, friend and confessor. Now the grey-silk-suited Di Prizzi took the floor and spoke to the assembled eighteen capi. He talked with controlled emotion about Don Alberto, finally swinging his panegyric in the direction of Giuseppe. Without giving away the full facts of Giuseppe's long training and preparation, he hinted that there was more to the young man than most of the family knew or realised, a truth which became apparent as soon as Giuseppe took the floor.

For half an hour the young Vescari spoke with quiet authority, assuming without question that he was the natural heir to his father's place of honour. Even with his stocky stature, Giuseppe conveyed a certain elegance and style, a hint of the courtliness of the old dons, displaying once and for all that his knowledge of the family and its affairs was deep and detailed.

It was a scene which Chassen would long remember; the well-known faces of his brother capi relaxing as Giuseppe talked

4

quietly of the future, of how he would expect the loyalty and discipline of former days (obedience, he said, was the key to survival); his plans for strengthening all their areas of business; that violence for its own sake would not be tolerated; that there had to be a return to the traditions of their brotherhood.

From this launching platform Giuseppe moved to the first vital question: honour. His father, their don and the godfather, the sponsor, of many present, had died at the hands of the Vizzinis, that was no secret. There had been bad blood between Alberto Vescari and Luigi Vizzini for many years, and it was an open secret that Vizzini, now nearing sixty years old, had set his heart on a final desperate bid to become the *capo di tutti capi,* the boss of bosses, with control of all the existing families.

"There are those, even within our family, who would help Vizzini and his degenerates." Giuseppe's voice dropped, almost to a whisper. "I think of one in particular who has met with Vizzini members many times in the last three months."

The men showed no emotion. Chassen recalled that, from where he sat, he had a diagonal view of the whole gathering. The faces set like granite. No eyes sneaking looks at each other. No tics in the face muscles. It was as though the entire group had been turned into effigies.

In retrospect it had seemed as though this state hung, suspended in a mental time lock, for an age.

Giuseppe broke the tension and spell. His body shifted slightly, turning on the balls of his feet to face the Vescari underboss, Joseph Bertel.

Bertel, now in his early forties, had been invited to join the family by Don Alberto personally ten years before, and had made a rapid climb to his position as the family's number two man. They all knew that he had often disagreed with the don over many things, and it was also obvious that he was a man of much ambition.

Now, as Giuseppe turned to face him, Bertel showed no emotion.

"I speak of you, Joseph." Giuseppe still maintained his quiet manner.

Bertel opened his mouth as though to defend himself, but Giuseppe cut him short.

5

"It is useless. I have names, places, times, dates."

Bertel again opened his mouth, poised as though to take a pace forward, when Giuseppe's voice changed to a hiss, as though his whole being was charged with hatred.

"Be missing," he said. It was a phrase which conjured the whole past of the brotherhood into the room. Two words of almost sacramental value.

Again there was a pause. Once more the suspended animation before Bertel turned on his heel, face drained, and walked slowly to the door.

On the following afternoon, the afternoon of Alberto's funeral, the body of Joseph Bertel was discovered sitting at the wheel of his Ford Mustang in a New Jersey parking lot, one bullet neatly splitting his heart. It was later established that he had been dead for nearly fourteen hours.

After the Vescari funeral, Chassen returned to the late don's apartment with three of the capi. Di Prizzi and Giuseppe were also present together with their bodyguards. There was no panic, only a sense that speed was needed. The FBI would soon start looking and there would undoubtedly be a grand jury waiting to ask questions about the don's death and the murder of Bertel. There would also be Vizzinis watching and waiting.

It was time to take to the mattresses: to hole up in already arranged hideouts. Giuseppe was packed and ready to go, and, as he went through the final preparations he turned, almost casually, to Chassen. "Tony Campelli," he said quietly (only rarely after that did he ever use one of the aliases), "there is a vacant place of respect in the family. My father trusted you; was fond of you. He was your sponsor. I want you to be the family underboss. Next to me. Vincent has also advised it." He gestured towards the old consigliere.

So Chassen came to his high position. In the following week two Vizzini capi were eating lunch in a seafood restaurant in Queens when three men entered, walked up to their table and shot them dead, leaving the restaurant without any move to stop them from the other diners or waiters.

Two days later a Vescari soldier was shot leaving a drugstore, and, on the following afternoon, Rocco Gallimo, who managed one of the Vescari shirt factories, was gunned down as he walked from his car to his own front door.

It was war, though war was the wrong word. War was the word used by newsmen and TV commentators. The old words were vendetta and feud. It lasted for the best part of a year, and in that time there were about seventeen deaths.

In spite of being in hiding for most of the time, Giuseppe Vescari moved forward with his plans, negotiating takeovers and reorganising the family affairs, inspiring loyalty and demanding obedience.

Giuseppe was always in a stronger position than Luigi Vizzini, for he had no great aspiration to become capo di tutti capi, a title which in private he scorned. His goal was that the Vescari family should be unified, strong and expanding daily.

By the end of that warring year, nobody doubted that the Vescaris were the strongest and most financially secure of the New York families, nor that the relatively young Giuseppe Vescari could be accepted as a don, a fact quickly confirmed by the National Commission.

It was about this time that Giuseppe (Don Peppe as he became known) spoke with Chassen and Di Prizzi about his further expansionist aims. This was the reason that Chassen now sat in a car threading its way through the London traffic.

The Daimler came to a smooth halt in front of the Mayfair Hotel, a uniformed commissionaire opening the rear door with a flourish.

Anthony Chassen stepped out onto the pavement, sniffing the air. The leading emissary had arrived, safe in the knowledge that his other executives were already in the city.

The Vescari family was expanding into a new territory, on the edge of making their largest takeover yet, changing the pattern and history of the brotherhood.

I

THERE WERE THREE INCIDENTS within forty-eight hours, though, to begin with, it was not plain that the first two had any connection with the third.

It started at Dover Harbour.

The morning was warm with a slight southeasterly wind, veering southwest; visibility good, sea calm.

At twelve forty-five, right on schedule, the car ferry from Calais, *The Lord Warden,* dropped her ramp and began to disgorge the cargo of cars which crept, like multicoloured beetles, into the light, crawling up the ramp, turning left along the quayside, edging, one by one, into the big customs shed, their steady progress regulated by a quartet of uniformed policemen.

There were watchers waiting. Two parties. Each group unaware of the other.

They all saw the Bentley, grey and dusty, as soon as it hit the quayside. One squad of men had been waiting and watching for that particular car since the previous evening, when the tip came, unexpectedly, from London. For the past two hours, since the telephone call from the *douane* at Calais, they had known that it was aboard *The Lord Warden.*

The Bentley carried no passengers, only the driver, a young, fair-haired man, his face pink and healthy from the sea breeze during the crossing.

It took ten minutes of waiting in line before the Bentley hissed softly into the customs shed. A smiling officer in shirtsleeves flagged it down at the first bay and approached the open window.

"You mind stepping over to the office for a minute, sir? Just bring the documents with you; leave the keys in the car, Mr. . . . ?"

8

"Terrice. Robert Terrice."

"Mr. Terrice."

"Nothing wrong?" A moment of hesitation, the merest flicker of apprehension in the young man's eyes.

"Nothing to speak of." The officer appeared to be in good humour. "Except in our planning department. You get 'em in every organisation, sir. We've got to stop every twelfth car today. Not tenth or thirteenth, but twelfth. Document examination by a senior officer. Bleedin' marvellous, isn't it? Every twelfth car. Next week it'll be all the red cars, I shouldn't wonder, and the week after, all drivers with Zapata moustaches." He grinned. "All zapata the service."

Terrice winced at the pun, climbed from the car, clutching a fat leather travel wallet, followed the officer across the wide shed towards the cluster of doors which marked the executive offices. He was tall, well-built, with a gait and manner exuding confidence.

From another part of the shed Terrice's progress was being observed by a large young man who somehow seemed out of place in the casual sport coat and slacks he wore. His eyes followed Terrice in an absorbed, almost fanatical, act of concentration, noting the small details of the driver's dress and appearance; things like the Scholl driving shoes and Graham Hill gloves, the dark blue cord battledress and the easy, relaxed grace of his walk. A natural, concluded the young man, one who could be counted upon to drive an expensive vehicle with precision over a long distance under strict orders.

The uniformed officer with Terrice tapped punctiliously at the door marked SENIOR OFFICER HM CUSTOMS AND EXCISE, before opening it and standing to one side with a slightly exaggerated deference, allowing Terrice to step into the room in front of him.

The moment Terrice disappeared and the door was closed behind him, two officers in the uniform of HM Customs, who had appeared to be lounging idly near the first bay, walked unhurriedly to the Bentley and slipped into the front driver and passenger seats.

The engine started and the car rolled smoothly forward, gathering speed as it reached the exit doors, other traffic being held back until it passed out of the shed.

The observer in the sport coat and slacks turned towards the telephone at the third bay, nodding to a customs man who was in the process of showing the inevitable declaration form to a worried-looking man, the owner of a dark blue Volvo.

The observer's finger rotated the telephone dial and waited. He spoke three brief sentences into the mouthpiece before returning the instrument to its cradle. Nodding to the customs man again, he began to walk quickly in the direction which had been taken by the Bentley.

In a garage, about a quarter of a mile up the quayside, a big man, who might have been taken for an ex-boxer, replaced his telephone. "On the way," he said to his companions.

There were three of them, leaning against a wooden bench which ran the length of the rear, whitewashed, wall. There were also ten mechanics in the garage, all in white coveralls, five standing against each of the long walls on either side of the hydraulic jack.

The three men by the workbench had constituted one of the waiting groups which had watched the Bentley disembark from *The Lord Warden*. Now they watched with a grim pleasure as the car slid into the garage and the technicians went to work.

The mechanics were precise and fast, like a racing pit team. In a matter of seconds the Bentley was raised on the hydraulic jack and the ten men fell upon it like vultures swooping upon a carcass. The agitated whir of compressed air guns filled the garage, working on the wheel nuts, door panelling and the small Phillips Screws inside the boot.

One man went straight into the back of the Bentley to lift out the rear seat squab. It was there that they found the first bags: polythene sacks weighing between ten and fifteen pounds. There were smaller packages in the door panelling; a long cylinder had been substituted for the inner tubing of the spare tyre, while more were found in the area around the petrol tank directly behind the boot.

As the packages were exposed, the mechanics removed them to the bench at the far end of the garage where one of the three plainclothesmen carefully went through the process of weighing them on platform scales, while another opened up one of the smaller packets. Like the others, it contained a fine white powder.

The third officer opened a slim, oblong case and started removing bottles, setting up his equipment on the workbench. He was the thinnest of the trio and the only one who wore spectacles, which gave him a constantly worried expression. All three handled the packages and powder with immense care: they could have been explosives experts dealing with an unstable composition.

The man with the scientific equipment began his ritual: scooping out a small quantity of the powder, spreading it in a shallow porcelain dish, measuring the exact 3cc of concentrated sulphuric acid needed for the Marquis Test, adding two drops of formaldehyde solution, stirring it with a slim glass rod and then touching the powder with the rod. The white particles changed colour, a magician's trick—purple-red, shading to violet and then to blue. The worried man, who was from forensics, looked at his companions. He had a voice which suggested a most serious attitude to life.

"Diacetylmorphine," he said.

"Shit," breathed the taller of the other two.

"Yes, heroin," the forensics man said in agreement. "I'll have to complete the other tests, but it looks top grade in this packet."

"What's best to do?" asked the man who had been concentrating on the weighing. He did not seem to expect a reply.

"How much?" the tall one asked.

"We've got around a hundred and fifty pounds, if it's all the same garbage."

"Jesus Christ."

"Instant shit."

"Instant horseshit. Just add water. Around twelve million pounds sterling on the open market." The tall man was undoubtedly the senior. He turned to the forensics officer. "Can I leave you to get the other tests done and then secure this filth in a bonded warehouse while we talk to chummy?" He paused, brow corrugated. "We should charge him here, but I'd prefer to get him up to the Smoke."

The forensics man pursed his lips. One could have taken him

for a prissy schoolmaster. "It'll take time. You'd better leave me here. I'll come back by train or cadge a lift."

"Okay, whichever way you want to play it, but I want all this secure. We'll see what this son of a bitch has to say for himself."

"I doubt if he even knows he's carrying it."

"He'll fucking know when I've got through with him."

II

THE SENIOR OFFICER of HM Customs and Excise (Dover Harbour) was essentially a mild, quiet man; an administrator, a keeper of ledgers and personnel files rather than an interrogator of those suspected of dealing in contraband.

It had been an unpleasant hour, spinning out the checking and rechecking of the Bentley's documentation, which appeared to be normal—insurance, logbook, international driving licence and the rest.

Terrice had left England exactly one month previously, in the same vehicle, the Bentley S3, registration number GXT 1567A, and the car had undoubtedly spent the intervening four weeks in France, as had the driver, according to his passport.

The senior officer now racked his brains, desperate for a subterfuge which would allow him to keep Terrice in his office and follow the instructions that had been given to him: keep the driver until the police officers return to question him, or until you receive a telephone call from them allowing you to release him.

There was a great sense of relief when a tap came at the door, heralding two of the three policemen who had arrived so unexpectedly on the previous evening.

The senior customs officer noted that the pair looked tough, grim and heavy. The taller man spoke first.

"We take over now, sir." A statement, in response to which the customs officer nodded, rose to his feet, handed the documents to the police officer, and quietly left the room. He was not surprised to find a pair of uniformed constables outside the door.

The larger plainclothesman eased his bulk onto the corner of the senior customs officer's desk, his eyes scanning the documents. His partner slumped into the chair opposite Terrice, whom he regarded with disdainful eyes, traversing the driver from head to foot, finally settling his gaze steadily on the Scholl driving shoes.

"You are Robert Eric Terrice?" the tall one asked, his voice hard, unfeeling.

"Yes." Direct but perturbed.

"You are the owner of a light grey Bentley S3 motorcar?"

"Yes, but . . ."

"Shut your bloody row." His hand held out a warrant card. "Mann. Detective Chief Superintendent Mann. C1, Scotland Yard. That mean anything to you?"

"What?"

"C bloody one."

"Should it?"

"It fucking well will. My friend's from C1 as well. Detective Inspector Robins."

Terrice made as if to rise, but Mann leaned gently forward and pushed him back into his seat with the flat of his hand.

"Not yet, lad. You are the owner of a light grey Bentley S3 motorcar . . ."

"I bloody told you, yes . . ."

". . . with the registration GXT 1567A?"

"Yes, it's mine. Paid for, taxed, insured, the bleedin' works."

"And you entered the country in this vehicle from *The Lord Warden* this morning, place of embarkation, Calais."

"You bloody know I did."

"Sparkling repartee." Mann turned to his DI. "For a young man who sports a Bentley and has time to tour the Continent he has a fucking fair turn of wit. Been on holiday then, Terrice. Been on a swan in your Bentley?"

"So?"

"So where've you fucking been, lad?"

"France, but I don't . . ."

"I don't care what you bloody don't. Where in France? You been exploring the magnificence of the Loire châteaux? Or the rich natural beauty around the vineyards of Burgundy? Or were you, perhaps, copping yourself a bit of genuine Parisienne brass?"

"And copping himself a bit of genuine Parisienne syph at the same time," grinned Robins.

"I was in Paris."

14

"In, or through?"

"Couple of nights on the way down. Couple on the way back. No, one on the way back."

"Playboy of the bleeding Western world. Down to where and back from where?"

"Do I have to answer your bloody questions? What am I supposed to have done?"

"You don't have to answer my questions, and I haven't said you've done anything yet. But if you don't answer, Mr. bloody Bentley-driving Terrice, I'll stuff your arse with applesauce and roast you. Then serve you up for Sunday dinner in the coppers' canteen."

"I don't need to answer."

"Putting it another way, I would advise you to answer. In your own interests I would advise you to cough the lot."

"He means that if you don't you'll end up with your balls in your throat."

"Where in France?"

"Nice. I went to Nice."

"Which way did you go?"

"Straight over. Grenoble; Grasse."

"And on the way back?"

"Along the coast. Marseille, then up the Rhone Valley."

"And what did you do in Nice?"

"What do you think?"

"Sun, sipping and screwing."

"Something like that."

"You stay the night in Marseille on the way back?"

"Just the one night. What am I supposed to have bloody done?"

"You really don't know?"

"No, I bloody don't, and if there isn't a charge I want to go. Otherwise charge me and I'll make my one telephone call to my solicitor."

"Your solicitor in London, is he?"

"It's where I live."

"You stayed one night in Marseille?"

"I just bloody told you."

"And I suppose you garaged the car?"

"How . . . yes, I had some trouble with the headlights."

"You had it in a garage overnight?"

"Yes."

"Just long enough."

"To get the lights fixed, yes."

"Long enough to pick it up."

"Pick what up?"

"Never mind. How did you spend the night in Marseille?"

"Restlessly."

"You could prove where you were?"

"Yes."

"How?"

"I was with a girl, wasn't I?"

"You tell me."

"I've told you."

"A girl you brought up from Nice?"

"No."

"A whore?"

"A bird. Just a bird."

"I said, a brass?"

"I got her number from a bloke in Nice."

"What bloke?"

"A bloke I met. Said she was good. I was going through Marseille and I told him. He gave me her number, the bloke."

"What bloke?"

"Bloke I met in a frigging bar."

"And you spent the night with this bird?"

"All night."

"You think she'd swear to it?"

"I don't know. I expect so."

"You left the car at a garage to get the headlights fixed?"

"I told you. At a garage."

"You got a receipt for the work?"

"No. I just paid the man the next morning."

"What garage?"

"Christ, I don't know the name. Near the hotel. I could take you there."

"Fat bloody chance. You expect taxpayers' money to take us all on an outing to Marseille so that you can show us the garage?"

"You going to charge me with something?"

"You'll have to be charged with something. Eventually."

"For what? For screwing a bird in Marseille?"

"For driving a Bentley into Britain with every crevice stuffed with shit."

"With . . . ?"

"With one hundred and fifty pounds of heroin."

"You're fucking mad. Heroin?"

"That's called being in possession. Possession, Jesus, your car was constipated, lad. What did they tell you it was going to be? Money?"

"Nobody told me anything. I don't know anything about heroin."

"I believe you, Terrice. You'd have to be either mad or desperate to waltz into Dover with that sort of load. You co-operate, cough the lot and everything will work out. Who paid you? Who set it up?"

"Nobody set anything up. I was on my holidays."

"You must take me for a shithouse inspector not a copper. Terrice, my bet is that you were paid to drive to Nice and give yourself a good time. You were paid to drive back through Marseille. You were told to have a little headlight trouble and garage the car. You were given a telephone number which in turn provided you with a bird. You pulled the bird all night long while some fancy gentlemen filled your motor with shit. Who paid you, Terrice? Names."

"Nobody sodding paid me. I don't know a bloody thing. I want my solicitor."

"He's up the Smoke yes?"

"Yes."

"Then we'd best take you there. We can charge you in comfort. Don't screw me, Terrice. I'll get the names from you, lad, if I have to use red hot irons on your tackle."

"I want my solicitor."

"You'll want a fucking doctor if you're not careful. Get the car, Mr. Robins. The deluxe pushers' tour to Scotland Yard."

III

THEY TRAVELLED in the black Zodiac, the one from C Department's motor pool in which they had come down to Dover. A uniformed driver and constable in front. Terrice, white, shaken, sitting between Mann and Robins in the rear.

Clocking an average seventy, they were three miles up the motorway when the driver caught the tail.

"There's a white Jag behind. Persistent. Been holding station for about a mile."

Mann swivelled to look out of the rear window.

"Push it."

Their speed increased, but the Jag maintained its position.

"Maybe we should've stayed," muttered Robins. "Twelve million's enough to have the heavies out in royal flushes. They might even think we're carrying it."

"Not a chance. Sons of bitches."

The Jag had begun to gain on them. When Mann spoke it was with urgency. "Put out a call. There must be some mobiles around. We need them here fast."

The constable reached down for the handset. He started to talk but did not complete his first sentence.

The Jag thrust forward into the fast lane as though overtaking the Zodiac. For a few seconds it rode alongside, too close to the police car.

"Mad bastards. Pull over. For Christ's sake pull over."

The noise of the engines and tyres drowned the metallic thump on the rear of the Zodiac. Mann only had time to turn and look back over the boot, the Jag accelerating forward and away as the police driver braked.

"What the fuck? There's a circular object sticking to the . . ."

18

The chemical fuse operated in the magnetic explosive device, packed tight with plastic composition, and the blast ripped through the Zodiac.

The rear of the vehicle was torn apart, Robert Terrice receiving the main force of blast in his back, leading to near total disintegration. Mann, on his right, and Robins, on the left, were almost literally torn in half, wrapped round with metal and hurled sideways. They felt nothing. The front section of the car, engulfed in flames, careered forward, hitting the hard shoulder and fusing itself into a tangled block of metal, the driver and constable pulped and burned within.

Later, an eyewitness told of the Jag suddenly overtaking the Zodiac, which seemed to slow, braking violently, trying to pull over; of a man in the rear of the Jag pitching a circular object with great accuracy onto the Zodiac's boot before the Jag pulled away at high speed. ("It was like a large biscuit tin, greyish colour I think.") The same man estimated that the white Jag had covered between 100 and 150 yards before the Zodiac exploded, ". . . like a great orange blossom. The rear just turned into this ball of fire and the front shot away like a bloody rocket."

The blast smashed through the windshields of three cars travelling between one and two hundred yards behind, causing a miraculous minor collision in which one driver was taken to hospital, suffering a fractured arm, while two passengers had minor lacerations of the face.

The northbound carriageway of the M2 was closed for the best part of three hours, the local police clearing the mess and checking on information regarding the white Jaguar, while, in London, the whole of C Department became alerted. Four police officers had lost their lives in the bombing.

Automatically, behind all major enquiries, up and down the country, officers were conscious of the brutal and senseless action on the motorway. They all instinctively wanted to know why and whom?

At Scotland Yard, Detective Superintendent Tickerman of Crime One spent considerable time talking to his Detective Chief Superintendent, known to all members of C1 as The Guv'nor.

"It must have been a contingency plan thought out well in advance." The Guv'nor stared down from his window at the late afternoon's seething traffic in Dacre Street. "It was bloody professional. We're not dealing with part-time idiots."

"Full-time idiots," murmered Tickerman. "The lad Terrice had no form. It doesn't make sense. We're checking local knowledge, circulating the description and all that." His face showed disgust. He had known Mann for a long time. They had been beat coppers together. "Poor bastards. They were hard men, sometimes too hard, but . . ."

The Guv'nor made a growling noise at the back of his throat. It was as near as he ever got to showing emotion. "I still can't understand Terrice coming straight into Dover with such a large cargo."

"Well he didn't, did he?"

"Didn't what?"

"Come alone."

The Guv'nor thought for a moment. "No. As soon as Mann felt his collar and put him in the open, they got rid of him."

"And a pair of good coppers with him—four good coppers. That leaves us with a hundred and fifty pounds' weight of heroin."

"And that frightens me."

"What? The amount?"

"Come on Ticker, who imports that sort of bulk?"

"Nobody over here."

"Quite. Only one outfit in the world."

"Precisely, and this isn't their style, even if they had begun operating that market over here. You've had all the information. How often does an innocent bystander get hurt when they're around? How often do they hit a police officer?"

"Very rarely. It's not their style, I agree; like this kind of bulk isn't anyone's style over here. In New York, yes, but here . . . ?"

They were both silent for a moment. Then Tickerman said, "Mann called his office before they left. He said that he didn't think Terrice knew what he was carrying, but he was convinced that the lad knew who was behind it."

The Guv'nor grunted. "Always the same. Large amounts only get nicked if there's a tip. Without the word out we'd never have touched the bloody Bentley, and if those boys were pulling a stroke like this Terrice wouldn't have known a thing. There wouldn't have been a contingency plan involving police officers and the general public. There'd have been so many cutouts that Terrice wouldn't have known who he was driving for, let alone what he was carrying."

"Torry would know all about the way they operate."

The Guv'nor bristled. "Yes, I suppose he would." He did not sound impressed.

Tickerman was referring to Detective Inspector John Derek Torry of Crime One who, in spite of a splendid record was not altogether trusted by senior officers like The Guv'nor. It was not a question of jealousy—most police officers have nothing but admiration for a good colleague. It was something in Torry's make-up that they mistrusted. Perhaps the fact that he was a man who seemed to have done too much and a man whose experience had taken him along different paths from the traditional road followed by coppers like The Guv'nor.

The Guv'nor was a hard, tough man who had risen slowly from being a beat constable to the position of responsibility which he now held, clawing upwards through a long series of promotions and experiences wholly concerned with the Metropolitan Police. His manor had always been the sprawling dirty mass of London: he knew its pavements, buildings and villains at close and detailed contact.

Torry, on the other hand was young, smooth, a corner-cutter when he wanted to be. He had also risen swiftly and his past was packed with a great deal of experience, the like of which The Guv'nor and his contemporaries could never have had.

Torry, for instance, was the product of two societies. Born in London of a cockney mother and an Italian father, he had a combination of those two strong and emotional race qualities blended within him.

There was also the fact of Torry's American education. He had been evacuated to the States at the start of World War II, eventually studying law at Albany, changing his nationality and becoming a patrolman with the New York City Police Department.

That change of nationality irritated The Guv'nor. Perhaps you could trust a man who did it once with conviction, but the older policeman found it difficult to accept Torry's double change.

Torry's real name had been Torrini, and, after his father's death, when he returned to England, he had resumed his British nationality, done some time with the Special Air Service and then changed his name by deed poll to the more anglicised Torry before applying to join the Metropolitan Police. A lot of experience, a sharp mind and a heavy paradox for The Guv'nor to accept. While he appreciated Torry's knowledge and brilliance, the man still remained a personality which irritated.

One night passed with activity, both furtive and open, bringing no new evidence: not a word about Terrice, nor any information regarding the white Jaguar.

The minutes of another day clocked by with nothing but minute droplets of fact. A man came forward to say that he had seen a white Jaguar in Dover on the previous afternoon. He thought that it contained four men, though he could not describe them, nor had he even glanced at the number plate.

Robert Terrice, or at least his ghost, yielded little at this stage. He seemed to have come from nowhere; nobody claimed either friendship or kinship.

Then, later in the day they found his address.

Since January 1970 Terrice had lived, in reasonable luxury, at a service apartment in Notting Hill Gate: four rooms, leather furniture, all the advertised electrical gadgets in the small kitchen, a beautiful set of Georgian silver cutlery, good heavy glasses, expensive modern china. In the wardrobe there were a dozen suits, most of them off the peg from Harrods; shoes mainly by Bally, except for two pairs of Scholl driving shoes; casual gear miscellaneous, but bought with flair and an eye.

The squad which descended on the apartment had no prints of Terrice so the fingerprinting was obviously going to take time. A detective sergeant began to sift patiently through the books and papers. They yielded little, certainly no reference to relatives, friends or the dead man's bank. Most of the books were predictable, either concerned with motorcars or motor racing; the remainder were thrillers and popular fiction.

A detective constable questioned the porter with few results. Later, a detective inspector called Berry had a go. Still only tiny fragments. Yes, Mr. Terrice always seemed a nice, easygoing young man, mad keen on cars and racing, motor racing of course.

No, he did not keep normal regular hours. No, nobody knew who employed him, or, for that matter, what he did for a living, though he always seemed to have plenty of bread.

The Bentley had arrived on the scene about six months ago. It had surprised the porter because it replaced a Jensen Interceptor. He really did not regard the Bentley as Mr. Terrice's kind of car.

Very few people visited him at the apartment, though there was one young woman; he did not know her name, but she was pretty, had dark hair and a good figure. She often stayed the whole night. Yes, Mr. Terrice did spend long periods away from the apartment.

By the early hours, the late Robert Terrice was still something of an enigma.

The squad checking out Terrice and his living quarters worked on through the following day. Throughout the country there were still no fresh leads. Although everything was going on, nothing happened. Not until the small hours of the following morning, and then, unexpectedly, at the Dorchester Hotel.

IV

THE HOTEL BEDROOM was like a slaughterhouse. You could smell the blood mixed with the tang of powder. It was sickening; blood spattered on the walls, a lot on the ceiling, around a blackened spread gouged out by shotgun pellets.

The two things were in pyjamas, one covered by a green silk robe, sprawled on the floor.

The body nearest the door was intact, laid out like a puppet, the only part missing being the bulk of its head, the remains of the chin visible from the pulp.

The other, on its side at the end of the first bed, still retained the back of its head, but the entire face had been blasted away, as though someone had positioned a shotgun upwards and pulled the trigger.

Derek Torry, Detective Inspector, Crime One, mentally made the sign of the cross and dragged his eyes away from the corpses, momentarily wondering what he was doing there anyway. He seemed to spend a lot of time looking at things which had once been human beings, alive, vital, now turned into rubbish. Sudden death was one of the principal preoccupations of Crime One.

Torry was C1 night-duty officer, and, in spite of the motorway bombing, things had been quiet. It was a breathing space, a time for catching up on the eternal paperwork, and the large, bare office on the fourth floor of Scotland Yard had echoed to the duet of typewriters (Sergeant Hart had been at the other one).

Torry was at full stretch, dealing with four major enquiries, and, until tonight, the paperwork lagged. There was the girl who had been found in Kensington Gardens, not yet identified, huddled under a tree, around nineteen or twenty, strangled with her own tights, the maniac bites all over her shoulders; and the lad from

Bermondsey carved up in Soho, bleeding to death before anyone found him. A young man up West for a Saturday night spree ("He never looked for no trouble," the father said). A nasty, straightforward battered wife, at least a week dead in her flat overlooking Baker Street, husband missing, leaving a trail which could be followed by a boy scout. They would catch up with him in a matter of days, but the written word and building of evidence took time and patience. There was also the shooting of the night watchman at a department store, but that was routine and really being handled by the local station.

The call came through at four minutes past three. Serious shooting incident at the Dorchester Hotel: West End Central were dealing with it and at the scene. Torry telephoned Tickerman, who sleepily acknowledged and said that he would like a full report on his desk in the morning. Hart rang down for the car and they were out into the chill darkness of the city.

It was the low ebb of early morning, the time when you are most easily dropped into acute depression, and the streets whispered violence.

In spite of the time there was still traffic around Park Lane. The driver put on the klaxon and they weaved through at speed. Outside the once imposing hotel façade a large knot of people pressed forward. There always seemed to be more people around these days. Torry could remember a time, in his childhood, when you could walk down Oxford Street and not have to elbow your way through the crowds.

"Don't they ever bloody sleep?" Hart grunted to himself.

Torry remained silent. He did not really like Hart and the feeling was mutual. It was as though they recognised the similarity of approach and character which was in each other, and the dislike bred, strangely, a kind of healthy respect.

In front of the hotel there seemed to be enough uniformed officers to quell a couple of major demonstrations. From two police motorcycles the crackle and chatter of the operations room provided a background as it filtered from the radios. A lot of coppers, thought Torry. Old habits died hard, money still talked. Torry supposed that there were a lot of rich and famous people inside the hotel.

25

They flashed their warrant cards at the uniformed men by the glass doors and headed across the foyer towards the elevators.

A uniformed sergeant told them that it was on the third floor, giving them the room number. They rode up in uneasy silence. Now they faced the carnage.

A squad was starting the painstaking, careful work of scene-of-crime routine. At the far end of the room, by the windows, Torry spotted a detective super and a younger inspector from West End Central. He did not know their names, but the faces were familiar.

The super looked across and identified Torry. "Crime One to the rescue." It was muttered with a shred of sarcasm.

Torry, followed by Hart, made a wary and ginger journey towards the super.

"Thought we should look in, sir. Can we help?"

The super had a grey complexion, brought on, Torry thought, by the time, place and circumstances.

"We could do with half the Met. Who's your super?"

"Mr. Tickerman, sir."

"He'll want it on paper then. I'll give you the story."

A flashbulb exploded as one of the team started taking the pictures.

The super talked fast and gentle, like a doctor with little time to spare, trying to give relatives the immediate facts.

The two bodies on the floor had been Americans. Businessmen, listed in the hotel register as Paul Denago and Richard Fantonelli. They had been guests at the Dorchester only once previously, some three months before. Already some of the hotel staff had volunteered that the two men were good tippers, and the clothes in the wardrobes were expensive. They seemed to have lived well.

On the earlier visit they gave the impression that they were combining business with pleasure.

On this present trip they had arrived only three days before, and appeared to be totally engrossed in some business deal. There had been comings and goings, a lot of telephone calls and meetings. The super had six officers checking the staff at this moment, seeing if they could place any of the business contacts, while descriptions of the two dead men were already on their way to Washington. Within a few hours they would be processed by the FBI computers.

26

On the previous evening, Denago and Fantonelli had dined alone in the hotel and taken their room key from reception just before eleven.

The shotgun explosions, which wakened the guests and night staff on the third floor, had blasted off at two thirty-three. In the foyer there had been no unusual occurrences, no incidents. No suspicious persons had been seen going up or coming down from the third floor. For all they knew, the killers might still be in the hotel. They might even be checked in, and the guest list, as Torry suspected, included a number of influential people. The area was as sensitive as a lanced boil. It was little wonder that the super looked grey and concerned.

"What sort of descriptions have we?" Hart inclined his head towards the cadavers.

"Their passports." The super motioned to one of the plain-clothes team who came over with the two passports, opened within plastic envelopes. "They're listed as business executives," he said.

You could see the passport photographs clearly through the plastic. Both men looked to be in their middle forties. Heavy Italianate features, faces which you might see in any city in Europe or North America.

Torry's finger stabbed out towards Fantonelli's picture.

"That one I know."

"Yes?" The super looked hopeful.

"I know the face, but he was younger then. I'd lay money that he's Mafia. You'll get something back from Washington on him." He combed his mind, stretching back to his days in New York. No details sprang easily into the present, simply the knowledge that this face had appeared on some file at some time, and that the connection was Mafia.

Torry and Hart stayed on for the best part of an hour, noting details, before leaving to return to the solitude of the duty office to write up the report for Tickerman. In the docketed maze surrounding police work, facts on paper are essential. It is the most laborious part of the job, checking and rechecking times and tiny facts, details on the obvious face of crime. In his report, Torry made a brief mention concerning his recognition of Fantonelli's photograph from his time in New York and his memory that the man had Mafia associations.

Both men checked off duty at eight, Torry returning to his flat in the Cromwell Road: the two rooms plus bathroom and kitchen on the second floor of one of the many converted houses in the area, dotted among the one-night private hotels and guest houses, and exactly 220 regulation paces from the BEA Terminal.

Returning on that morning, with the depression of the night's events still heavy in his mind, Torry felt the apartment was more sparse and uncluttered than usual. It was eight weeks, almost to the day, since Sue had broken off their engagement, a point in time which he associated with finding his domestic surroundings drab.

It came as no surprise to Torry that the engagement ruptured. There had been many differences of opinion, not least his own inability to express his strangely paradoxical feelings concerning the Roman Catholic faith in which he had been brought up and which clung to him like an old coat steeped in familiar, if not pleasant, scents of the past.

As a policeman he had been taught to be precise and logical. As a schoolteacher, Sue Crompton had the same attitude to facts, but she found his arguments and actions regarding religious matters an irritating complexity which finally led to an immovable barrier, an obsession.

"Derek, I'm sorry," she said on that final night, the thrust of her breasts through the black turtle-neck sweater arrogantly appealing. Torry remembered that she stood with one booted leg forward, the thigh straining against her red skirt, so that he felt the old despair of desire clash again with the strange sense of family, tradition, religion and the whole mess of background which forbade the consummation until blessed by the Church.

"I know you don't believe in those things any more than I do. We've had it over and over so many times." Her eyes moist, tears near to the surface. "It's simple. I don't understand you; I don't understand why you cling to things which you admit are outdated superstitions."

"But when we're married . . ."

"They would become bigger barriers. They're bloody great rocks, Derek, damn great minefields which would do for us. It's

not that I don't love you—Christ, you must know that. It's just un-
bearable. We're so far apart on this thing."

He tried to argue once more, but, as on so many occasions in
the past, the exchange became explosive and she finally left at the
apex of a wounding shouting match.

"Mama's right, Derek," his brother, Roberto, told him when
Torry confided that the marriage was off. "You should get a good
Catholic girl, like I did. Therese and I have been happy from the
start. We understand each other. It's dangerous to marry out of
your own kind."

"I'm not you, Bobby. And what kind are we? Mama's the biggest fake in the business. The most lovable fake there ever was but
still a fake. She's a cockney through and through, yet she thinks
like an Italian half a century, two centuries, ago. We're an
anachronism."

"You still go to mass, still see Father Conrad."

"But I'm no more a Catholic than Chairman Mao. It's habit,
symbols to ward off the evil eye, Bobby. I drive myself crazy. Sue
wanted us to sleep together. Two years she wanted it and I refused. She was to be my bride, and, against all inclinations I
treated her with a bridegroom's respect. I don't even understand
myself. I'd go with other girls, I think she knew that, but I
wouldn't touch her. It's background, family, the old ways, they
have you trapped like a lifer in his cell. The background has your
balls in an ecclesiastical vice."

Torry heard the conversations with Sue and his family echoing
in his head as he stood, now, alone in his living room, the repro-
duction of Hieronymus Bosch's "The Haywain," bizarre and disturbing above the fireplace and he was conscious that through the
door, in the bedroom, the symbol of his private anachronism, a
large brass crucifix, hung over the bed.

Sue was strong in his mind, yet there were none of the emotional surges within him, none of the "if only" or "if it could have
been" feelings one was supposed to experience at the collapse of a
relationship. Simply a void that needed filling.

His mind flicked back for a second to the more recent violence,
the picture of the two bodies at the Dorchester—the splintered
bone and blood: the mess of violence. He shrugged and walked
slowly to the bathroom.

V

THERE WERE THREE CARS. One above the pay phone booth and one below, pulled in tight to the curb. Another was across the street. Up towards the intersection the traffic still roared in late night New York.

Don Peppe glanced at his watch. Three minutes and the call should come, all part of the communications system. Anthony would be in his hotel room in London waiting for the operator to link his call to the number of the pay phone in the centre of Manhattan. There would be no problem with the London telephone.

It was the only way to be sure that the conversation was not tapped and taped by the FBI or another of the government agencies. Only the most innocuous and innocent calls could be made in and out of the Vescari apartment in the high East Forties off Madison. That was the reason why all the men carried plastic containers stuffed with quarters, nickels and dimes in their pockets, and a list of pay phone numbers and locations in their heads.

In London, Anthony Chassen sprawled on his bed in the hotel room. His jacket was neatly folded over a chair and he had taken the links out of his cuffs. The telephone was within easy reach and he watched it like a rattler poised to strike, his face anxious, his eyes deep and flat.

Don Peppe leaned forward and spoke softly to the men in the front seat of the car. The driver flashed the headlights once quickly. An answering flash came from the car across the road, while the car in front, on the far side of the pay phone, winked its brake lights. The heavy man beside the driver in Peppe's car slid his stubby revolver from its shoulder holster and placed it carefully on his knees. The men in the three cars were alert. Don Giuseppe Vescari was about to leave the car, and, during the next few minutes, would be in the open, at night, in that most vulnerable of places—a lighted telephone booth.

Peppe slid from the rear seat, closed the door quietly behind him and walked slowly towards the booth. As he reached the upright glass oblong the bell began to ring.

In his room at the Mayfair Hotel, Anthony Chassen reached for the phone.

"Your call to New York."

"Okay. Thank you."

A whisper of static and then Peppe's voice. "Anthony?"

"I'm here."

"How is it with you?"

"Not good. You're not going to like it."

"Speak."

"They've reneged."

"How?"

"It got blown for them. The whole consignment and the driver."

A sharp hiss of indrawn breath from the New York end.

"What happened?"

"The driver and four cops killed. A bomb in the car I think."

"Piromani."

"There is worse."

"Yes?"

"Paul and Ricardo. They got hit."

"Eh." A keening. "In London? *Non. Non.*"

"In their hotel room."

"Paul and Ricardo. *Non è possibile.* What kind of pigs are we dealing with? They are moustache Petes, these men. They know you are in London?"

"I think not."

"And they refuse to honour the agreement?"

"That is implicit in what happened to Paul and Ricardo."

"Ricardo was married to my mother's sister's child. Can you manage them?"

"You want a contract?"

"Not on them. On someone close to them. You make it hurt. Then reopen negotiations. Call me in two days. The fourth number."

"I've got you."

"Do it well."

"Don't worry. I believe they think Paul and Ricardo were here on their own."

"Show them different."

The telephone rang just as Torry, bathed and shaved, was drawing the curtains to blot the day from his bedroom. He knew that he could forget about sleep the moment the bell began its clatter.

Tickerman was on the line.

"In the land of nod were we, Derek?"

"Not quite, unless you happen to be a particularly bad dream."

"You're not as ill-tempered as young Hart anyway. I think he must have had a bird with him."

"He's young and attractive like I used to be."

"A long time ago," Tickerman laughed.

"Last week."

"It happens to us all."

"What's up?"

"Your presence is requested."

"Now?"

"Ten minutes ago. You're off the duty roster as well. The Guv'nor has work for us to do."

Torry smiled wearily to himself. "Because I opened my big mouth and said I recognised Fantonelli?"

Tickerman chuckled again at the other end. "He called you our expert in American affairs."

"Then I won't have to disappoint him. I'll be over as fast as I can go, Tick."

The Guv'nor stood behind his desk. Before him, ranged about the austere office, sat Tickerman, Hart and Torry. Torry slumped arrogantly in his chair, the other two bolt upright, sitting to attention.

"I'm sorry to have recalled you two from normal rest and put you on full duty at such short notice." The Guv'nor sounded as though he begrudged those few words of apology, sweeping his eyes first towards Torry, then Hart. "You're all up to date with the narcotics' squad's trouble? The heroin haul at Dover and the subsequent murder of four officers and one suspect, Robert Terrice?"

They nodded. Almost in unison, Torry thought. Nodding pigs.

"And I've read your reports on last night's shooting at the Dorchester Hotel." The Guv'nor paused. "We have info. Through local knowledge, by which I mean a pair of detective constables with ears very close to the ground in Notting Hill, we now know that Robert Terrice was a close associate of Peter and Paul Magnus. He drove for them."

The news was like an electric charge in the room. The Magnus cousins, Peter and Paul, were a pair that any dedicated London copper would give his pension to nail. They were vermin, scum, and fireproof.

Typical of the cunning villains spawned out of the chaos of wartime childhood, the Magnus boys had risen from being hellraisers, doing their fair share of time for Grievous Body Harm and obtaining money with menaces, into hardened men working in a more sophisticated area. There was little substantial proof, they were well versed in the art of hiding facts and evidence, but you did not have to be a clairvoyant to know the names of four clubs run and owned by the Magnus cousins; nor that they had the arm on a number of smaller clubs, and took a heavy percentage from quite large coveys of call girls in the West End. Getting the evidence and bringing them into court was another matter.

Torry had read the files and heard the whispers, but his first reaction was that, up until now, there had never been a rumour of the Magnus cousins operating in the narcotics field. That was new.

The Guv'nor went on talking. "There's another interesting fact come to light. We've yet to have anything from Washington on the Dorchester victims, but four members of the hotel staff—one hall porter, two waiters and a lift operator—claim that during Fantonelli and Denago's visit three months ago, they twice met and entertained two men in the hotel. They met and entertained the same two men only three days ago, on the night of their arrival. The two men have been positively identified as Peter and Paul Magnus."

"You know that action should be taken on this matter by Tintagel House." The Guv'nor paused once more, he was heavy on the dramatic effects this morning. Tintagel House was the headquarters of the Serious Crime Squad, the men known by the press as the Gang Busters: the men who had toppled the Krays, the Richardsons and others. They were the most natural enemies of people like the Magnus cousins.

"Tintagel House has its problems," The Guv'nor continued. "They've been working on Peter and Paul Magnus for some time and with little effect. Like all of us they're short-staffed. We discussed the problem at the Commander's Crime conference this morning, and he has agreed to a deployment of forces. I am to set up a special operation from this Department. It will cover the whole area now opened up by the latest information. Mr. Tickerman will be in charge and directly responsible to me. You are to have two officers on detachment from the Drug Squad. Mr. Tickerman has asked that you, Mr. Torry, and Sergeant Hart work with him. You'll gather your own team together and I will see that you'll get office space and facilities . . ."

"I might feel happier working outside the Yard sir. Can you give me a day or two to make up my mind?" Tickerman was looking up from under his heavy brows, pipe firmly planted in the corner of his mouth, one hand on the bowl.

Torry felt that Tickerman had all the appearances of a friendly uncle. It was a good mask. A lot of villains had coughed to Uncle Tickerman, your friendly local policeman.

"You must be your own boss, come back to me in a couple of days by all means." The Guv'nor nodded. "What about staff?"

Tickerman reeled off a few names and then turned to Torry. "Anyone you specially want, Derek?"

"Only on the clerical side. I've carried the cross of Sergeant Dumphy for a long while. He's an old mother, but he knows my habits and he's damned efficient."

Tickerman gave a curt nod and turned to Hart who had nobody to add to the list.

34

"Any more you want to say, sir?" Tickerman asked The Guv'nor. Nobody had any doubts that the super wanted to get on with the job.

"Just nail 'em, Ticker."

VI

It WAS DECIDED that Tickerman, Hart and Dumphy should get the team organised, arrange for the Magnus files to be collected from the Serious Crime Squad, while Torry would go down to Notting Hill Gate and look over the work being done at the Terrice apartment.

Within half an hour he was on his way.

The hoardings for the *Evening News* and *The Standard* both said the same thing in different ways—POLICE HUNT FOR DORCHESTER HOTEL SLAYERS . . . DORCHESTER HOTEL: POLICE IN KILLER HUNT. Torry saw them from his seat in the back of the car and knew what the papers would say. He could see it without even buying either tabloid: *Early today detectives from Scotland Yard, and a special force, were combing London for the killers of two American businessmen shot to death in the early hours in their luxury suite at the Dorchester Hotel.*

The apartment block where Terrice had lived was considerably more plush than Torry had imagined. The Magnus cousins obviously paid well. They could afford it.

Before leaving the Yard, Torry had called Notting Hill and was told they would co-operate in every possible way. A DI called Berry was at the Terrice flat with a scene-of-crime investigation team, and he was being informed of Torry's impending arrival.

A young uniformed constable stood at the door to the block and hurried over when Torry's car came to a standstill.

"Mr. Torry of the Yard, sir?" It sounded like something out of bad television.

Torry confirmed with a sharp affirmative action of the head.

"Mr. Berry's up there now, sir. I think I should warn you, they've got a young woman up there."

"On the firm's time? Some people," shouted Torry as he headed for the lift.

The small, compact flat seemed to be crowded with young detective constables, all hard at work. The incongruous presence was a woman of about twenty-two, looking as though she had collapsed in one of the big leather chairs, the thin sunlight shafting through the main window picking up the contrast between the black leather and the girl's smart purple midi dress.

She had a face which looked too young for her body, cheeks drained of colour, the eyes red-ringed, a hand—long, slim fingers and a Greek puzzle ring—clawing through the short dark hair.

Standing over her was a tall plainclothesman in his early thirties; a heavily jowled face and tired eyes. He looked across the room at Torry, the question framing on his lips.

"Mr. Torry?"

"Yes."

"I'm Berry." He turned to one of the young DCs. "Keep an eye on her for a minute." Then, again, to Torry: "A word I think. The kitchen?" He nodded towards the door. Torry beat him to it.

"I'm sorry about this, we've got a female officer on her way over." Berry leaned against the stainless steel sink unit.

"What's up?"

"The girl. Terrice's girl. Claims she hasn't had time to read the papers or watch any TV in the last couple of days. Had a long-standing date with Terrice for this afternoon. Just turned up out of the blue. One of those idiots told her." He inclined his head back towards the living room.

"She looked shattered."

"No doubt. I was there, mate. She's in shock and I doubt if we'll get any joy there for a while. Name of Peterson, Jenny Peterson; lives in Richmond; works for a publisher. Straight as the distance between two points I'd say."

"What's the drill?"

"I'd like her out fast. Take her back to the nick and make a short statement."

"I'd be grateful if they didn't let her go until I get there." Torry switched on a quick smile. "I'd like to be the guardian angel who drives her home. Right?"

Berry nodded. "Consider it done. Better get back in there before the Junior Maigret Club perpetrates a disaster."

"One more thing."

"Yes?"

"Have you had the word on Terrice?"

"What word?"

"Come on. It came from your nick."

"You mean that he was one of the Magnus's drivers?"

"Yes. How strong is that?"

"Absolutely full strength. I know both the boys who passed it, they're hot as fresh horseshit."

Torry gave a sharp nod. Low in his guts he felt the tingle of excitement. The same electricity he had sensed in The Guv'nor's office. He hated lawbreakers, particularly men like the Magnus cousins.

Run-of-the-mill coppers did not approve of that kind of emotion on the job. You had to be like a lawyer, they held, playing the game so that people became counters and numbers, ciphers. It was something Torry could never do.

When they got back into the living room the DCs were still going through their routine, scouring every nook, cranny, book, paper. One had the contents of a vacuum cleaner spread out on two sheets of newspaper, rummaging through the matted dust and hair with his fingers and a pair of tweezers.

The woman detective constable had arrived, a short, dark girl with heavy calves and a face which made Torry think that her father was probably a weight lifter. Like many of her colleagues, she looked butch. Berry went over and spoke to her quietly, occasionally shooting a glance towards Torry. The WDC looked over once, her face showing interest.

The girl, Jenny, was even more white, bleached parchment replacing her skin. She had been crying again. The WDC finally turned towards her and Torry was relieved to see that the policewoman visibly softened as she bent over the girl.

Berry was at his shoulder. "All fixed. What do you need from here?"

"What've you got?"

"Sod all. No links, no connections. So far it's a place lived in by a young guy who loved cars and driving, had a healthy attitude towards his bird and lived well."

"What do you mean by a healthy attitude?"

"She kept some clothes here. A couple of dresses, nightdresses, underwear, three pairs of shoes, tights, some make-up and a month's supply of Minovlar."

"Minovlar?"

"A contraceptive pill. There were three missing from the one month's supply. He played both ends against the middle, by the way. One packet of multicoloured French letters, minus two, very definitely hidden away in a drawer."

"Nothing to connect him with Magnus? Either Magnus?"

Berry shook his head. "Not yet. We could still turn something, but I doubt it. This one was an expert. Nothing to connect him with anything or anybody, except the girl."

Torry stayed for about half an hour, made some notes, chatted with Berry, who promised that all detailed information would be sent direct to Tickerman.

The chill of late afternoon hit Torry as he emerged from the apartment block to find his driver deep in conversation with the uniformed man on duty on the main door. Without comment, Torry told him to drive to Notting Hill Police Station.

The station did not appear to be in a whirl of activity, but the WDC was peering anxiously out of an interrogation room doorway. She hurried up to him, her voice quite soft and pleasant, belying her appearance.

"I'm glad you're here, Mr. Torry. I've run out of excuses for keeping her any longer."

"You get a statement?"

"Short and very general. I had a carbon done for you." She handed him the sheet of foolscap. Short and general was an understatement. It gave Jenny Peterson's name, age (twenty-three), address, telephone number; place of occupation and telephone number. She had met Terrice about a year ago and was having an affair with him, seeing him perhaps twice a week. She knew he drove cars for a living but had no information about who employed him, though she had got the impression that he was a freelance, and thought he sometimes tested racing cars. Apart from that he did not talk to her about his work.

They always met at his flat and she gave a list of about a dozen restaurants to which he took her—not exclusive but pricey. She also gave a list of films and shows they had seen together in recent months. He often had to be away for a week or so, and, in the last instance, she had known he would be away for around a month. He had asked her to come to the flat today for their reunion, and in the previous month had received three postcards from him. One from Paris, one from Nice and, the most recent, last week, from the Marseille area. It had said, *Looking forward to next Thursday as arranged. Wear the blue.*

That was all.

"*Wear the blue?*" queried Torry. "She's wearing a purple dress."

"Not underneath, sir. I checked it out. It's not a code. She got quite coy."

"What do you make of her?"

"Nice girl. Lonely. Straight."

"Thank you. Okay, let her out."

She had got some of her colour back, the WDC having persuaded her to repair the make-up. Torry, who had dismissed his driver when they arrived and taken over the car himself, went straight over to her.

"I was at Robert Terrice's flat with the others this afternoon. Remember?"

She gave a tight little nod, biting the upper lip.

"Like a lift home?"

"Thank you. Thank you very much. Everybody's been so . . ."

"Kind?"

"Yes." She sounded surprised. "Kindness isn't a word that you associate with the police."

Torry registered that she called them the police. Not the fuzz or pigs.

They got to the car and Torry helped her into the front passenger seat before going around and sliding in behind the wheel.

"You okay?"

She gave another little nod, the eyes brimming. Now that he was close to her, Torry realised what a little dish she must be when not in the full shock of grief. Whatever else, Robert Terrice had known how to pick birds.

"Yes, I'm okay." Quiet and fighting for control. "It's just the sudden . . . It's unbelievable."

"I know. In my job we face it every day."

"It happens to other people."

"Never to you. I know that too. But it always happens to you, it's the first thing you learn when you become a copper."

She shifted her body as though to get a better look at him. "You don't sound English. What did you say your name was? You sound American."

"I'm a mixture. Spent a lot of time in the States. The name's Torry. Derek Torry. Detective Inspector doing hire car work for Miss Jenny Peterson in my spare time."

"Oh, I'm sorry. You must want to get on."

"I've got all the time in the world for you. You want to go home?"

"Not really, but there's nowhere else."

"When did you last eat?"

"I had a sandwich for lunch. A sandwich and some coffee."

"Then I'll buy you a meal. After that you can go home. Anyone else there? At home?"

"No. I live alone."

"No parents?"

"Yes, two. One of each sex. They live in a place called Evesham."

"The Vale of?"

"That's it."

"Tourists riding the blossom route every spring."

"Smallholders, markets and tittle-tattle."

Torry looked at her hard. "Not your scene?"

"Not my scene."

"Your parents meet Bob?"

At the mention of the name she seemed to close up again, an automatic gesture of protection. "They didn't even know he existed."

"Generation gap?"

A sigh. "Not really. Communications. Lack of communications."

Torry put the car into gear and pulled out into the traffic. "Your fault or theirs?"

"Both sides. People who want their daughters to get on, have the education and goodies they never had, don't always realise that it means altering their children out of recognition. The parents have to grow as well. Oh, that sounds terrible. It was as much my fault as theirs."

"So parents are out. Any close friends? Close girl friends?"

"At the office, yes."

"Can you get one to stay with you for a couple of days?"

"There's Mary, she's always said . . ."

"We'll telephone her. I don't want you left alone."

She nodded, quiet acquiescence. "I understand, but I'm not the suicidal type. Anyway, Bob and I weren't hallo young lovers. We had a relationship, but I wasn't in love with him, whatever that means."

"But you spent time together. You went steady."

"We screwed steady."

There was something brazen, out of character, in her attitude.

"About twice a week," the girl continued. "Sometimes three times, and the occasional weekend. Our bodies had a relationship, not our minds. You couldn't get into Bob's mind. He didn't open up."

"You found that satisfactory?"

"It was a relief. Someone to be with. He was good in bed. We fitted one another and it broke the routine: getting up, going to the office, the same work every day; and then Bob twice a week. It was something I could look forward to."

"I would have thought working for a publisher . . ."

"It's like working for anybody. I'm an editorial secretary, and it's like being anybody's secretary. Right?"

"If you say so." Torry saw the place for which he had been looking, across the road to their right. "Fish and chips do you?"

"Oh great."

"Sorry it's not the fancy kind of joint you're used to."

"I'm not used to any kind of joints. The kind of places Bob took me made me nervous."

Torry pulled up in front of the fish and chips restaurant: big windows with unlikely coloured fish transfers on them. Inside there was a long serving counter and a wide area with about two dozen tables, each covered by a chequered plastic cloth, green and

42

white; menus, bottles of sauce, salt, pepper and the inevitable vinegar.

The only other clients were a couple with a child of about four. He was in his middle forties and looked harassed; she was much younger, about twenty-three. The child whined and would not eat, while the father looked near to exploding. Torry's mind played for a second, wondering about the pressures which surrounded that situation.

They sat down at the nearest table and he passed the menu over to Jenny, who seemed to have got herself together. A tall, tired, sloppy and angular waitress approached without much interest. Taking the mood from her they ordered in the same desultory way —cod and chips twice, bread, butter, coffee.

"Am I going to be hounded?" Jenny asked after the food arrived. The fish and chips were good but the coffee was like hot coloured water. Torry had never readjusted to English coffee.

"How hounded?"

"Police grilling me? They were all . . ." She corrected herself. "You were all so kind this afternoon. Will the honeymoon end?"

"It doesn't have to. You mind if I ask you a couple of questions?"

She raised her eyebrows, a gesture which Torry took to mean that he could go ahead.

"Where and when did you meet Bob Terrice?"

"About eighteen months ago. At The Bear Hotel, Esher, one Sunday morning. Mary, the friend I told you about, has a Triumph Spitfire. We used to go out for runs on Saturdays or Sundays. That morning we went to Esher. We met Bob in the bar."

"He was by himself?"

"Yes, alone. Just started to chat. Mary went to the loo and he asked for my telephone number. Called me the next day. There was nobody special around so I went out to dinner with him, then back to his place. That's how it started."

"Just like that?"

"Exactly. It was nice. I felt that I belonged to someone. Not love, like I said. Affection and belonging. There hasn't been anyone else since, not for me. Though I'm pretty sure he had one or two other birds."

"What makes you think that?"

"Your way; by being observant. Scratch marks on his shoulders that weren't made by me; a bottle of scent that wasn't mine"—she gave a giggle—"there was even a pair of knickers that I certainly did not own—in his bed, how about that?"

"Did you ever meet any of his friends?"

"Never." Firm but probably true.

"He ever have telephone calls while you were there?"

"Not that I remember."

"If you do remember, will you tell me?"

"Yes."

Torry gave her the office number and his home number and address. "You said in your statement that you didn't know about his job, and you've told me he was close. Did you ever pry?"

"No, there wasn't any point. I told you, he made it quite plain. He'd talk about motor racing and cars, but he told me, right from the start that when he was with me, it was time out, time away. I took him at his word."

Torry understood the situation, yet something worried at the back of his mind. She was an attractive, intelligent girl who had left home to come to the big city, possibly after a rift with her parents. London gave her what every big, overcrowded, polluted and stinking city had to offer. Anonymity. Loneliness. To quench it there had been Bob Terrice. Yet she seemed so easy to get along with, so nice (that was the wrong word, Torry knew). Why not a steady bloke, with an eye to marriage? Perhaps that did not attract her.

He drove her back to Richmond and home: a big Victorian house now segmented into neat sets of rooms and bed-sitters for working girls and men. The old Queen would not have been amused.

"You want to come up?" Jenny asked. Torry was not certain, but there seemed to be more than a hint of sexual invitation in her voice.

"No, I'd better be getting along. Will you call the girl—Mary?"

"Yes."

"Promise. I don't want you left alone."

44

"I promise. But why don't you stay? Nice little wife to go home to?"

"I'm not married. I was going to be, but she called it off a few weeks ago."

"That makes two of us, though I never intended marriage. So why don't you come and keep me company?"

"I have a detective superintendent waiting up for me."

"Yes, I've seen you all on television, slaves to your jobs, like doctors."

"And priests." Torry did not know why he had said it.

She gave him a lopsided look. "I shouldn't think there's much that's priestly about you."

"I'll call you tomorrow and make sure you're all right."

"Please, and thank you for the fish and chips. Thank you for everything." The invitation was definitely there this time.

Tickerman was just leaving when Torry got back to the office.

"There's an outline file on your desk. The bare facts. You'd better read, mark, learn and inwardly digest," Ticker told him after hearing the brief report on the Terrice situation and Jenny Peterson.

"Young Hart's gone over to put a little pressure on the Magnus boys. I gave him the most villainous bunch of coppers we could muster. They'll be expecting a call and it'll be nice to get their reaction."

A good touch, thought Torry. It would be considered an insult by the Magnuses, having only a detective sergeant call on them.

The file was on the desk they had set aside for him, and he put it to one side while he made up his notebook and typed a report on Jenny Peterson. Thinking about her gave him a hard. Sue flipped into his mind and then out again, quickly, like a flashing sign. It was disturbing.

He sat back, rang down for coffee and opened the buff folder and began to read the précis on Peter and Paul Magnus.

VII

THE FILE on the Magnus cousins gave only the brief facts, the first sheets concerning the time they had served—from borstal for both of them at an early age, through to the individual sentences following the end of World War II: obtaining money with menaces, pimping—the usual hellraising run.

There was a particularly nasty incident which put Paul Magnus away for seven years in 1950: a bloody assault on a club owner. The case got wide publicity if only for the facts that it had involved a pair of tailor's shears and sparked a sensation in court when, after sentencing, Paul shouted loudly, "I don't care. It's cheap. The bastard'll never screw my girl again. Or any girl."

In the following year, Peter Magnus went down for five years on a charge of Grievous Body Harm, the victim being a prostitute, Anna Paulik, who ended up with both arms broken, three ribs cracked and a hairline fracture of the jaw.

At this time the cousins were working for Joseph Drummond, a smooth, sharp, violent man who, after dabbling in professional prize fighting, had turned to the more lucrative byways of crime— the strip, near-beer and clip joints, and other pastimes including protection and long firm fraud.

Drummond's "firm" had carved itself a large manor which covered a slice of the West End, and the Magnus boys were both important factors in his organisation. There were many stories, almost legends, concerning their ruthless violence.

Extortion and the enforcement of discipline was their speciality and there were few in the criminal fraternity who doubted that both men had killed on a number of occasions.

It was said that they were both implicated in the now famous case of the Greek coffee-bar owner whose little shop was gutted one night, its owner found dead in the rear alley. That was at a time when the Magnus cousins were still unsophisticated in the ways of their trade. A pianist in one of Drummond's clubs had his hands smashed with a mallet; another, suspected of operating a long firm fraud for Drummond, literally got his fingers stuck in the till—both his hands were, in fact, found chained to the heavy till when he plunged onto the pavement from the sixth storey of an apartment building.

The two jail sentences in the early fifties seemed to have a sobering effect upon the cousins. Peter Magnus came out of prison in 1957, his cousin a year later, and since that time neither of them had spent a single night in a cell or police station.

Joseph Drummond, however, disappeared on a November night only three months after Paul was back in circulation.

There were what the law calls "suspicious circumstances" about Drummond's disappearance, and there was one witness: a nervous bookie's runner, Bob Proctor, a small, sharp-faced man with a pronounced tic in his right cheek. Proctor was known to his friends as The Jockey, not that he had ever had experience in that profession, but because of his stature and appearance, which was similar to those actors who played jockeys in the Hollywood films of the thirties and forties.

Proctor had been with Drummond on the night in question, drinking in an Islington public house until about ten. Joe Drummond offered him a lift home, and it was as they were walking to his car that a maroon Hillman pulled up beside them.

In his statement, Proctor told the police that there were four men in the Hillman, one of whom called out to Drummond, "Joe, we want a word."

Drummond walked casually over to the Hillman, leaving Proctor on the pavement. In the next minute, Proctor saw two men leap from the rear of the car and drag Drummond, struggling, inside. The car then took off at speed.

The police took Proctor through the heavy books containing photographs of known criminals and the bookie's runner tentatively identified Peter and Paul Magnus as being two of the men in the Hillman.

On the following morning, the Magnus cousins were invited to attend an identity parade at which Proctor failed to point the finger at anyone.

"None of them looked like any of the blokes I saw," he commented to the uniformed super after it was over.

The police were not surprised. Detectives keeping Proctor under surveillance noted that he had had a visitor in the early hours of the morning of the identity parade. Proctor claimed that the man who had called was his brother-in-law, who corroborated the story.

But two of the detectives were certain that the night caller was Ben Doffman, an associate of Drummond and friend of the Magnus boys.

But Doffman had witnesses to swear that he was in one of Drummond's clubs, The Naked Statue, from midnight until around four in the morning. There was also a girl, one of the club's hostesses, to affirm that Doffman was with her for the remainder of the night.

It was watertight and the police could not break the chain, even though they knew Doffman was the man. They also knew that, in the circles in which he ran, Ben Doffman boasted a sinister nickname. He was known as "The Dumper."

The facts could not be changed. After that November night Drummond was neither seen nor heard of again, and the police brought no light on the case. It was later evident that a week before his disappearance, Drummond had legally signed over his clubs (The Naked Statue, Harmony House, The Buff and Dotheboys Hall) to four independent businessmen; there was no reason to doubt that, after all the requisite documents were there for anyone to see.

Drummond had disappeared and, slowly, the Magnus cousins prospered. They kept out of court, yet openly associated with men and women who had previously been close to Joseph Drummond. With the years they became more sophisticated, well-groomed, driving in style with a uniformed chauffeur and dressing with flamboyant taste.

The names of the four clubs were changed to The Statue of Eros, The Graven Image, Boy Meets Girl and Winner Takes All. There was a note in the file concerning the last two names. Even though there was no legal evidence that the Magnus cousins had any financial interest in the clubs, someone had noted that the names—Boy Meets Girl and Winner Takes All—were titles of James Cagney movies, adding the fact that both the cousins were ardent fans of James Cagney and Humphrey Bogart films.

Torry knew that it was common knowledge that the two men often arranged screenings of old Cagney and Bogart films at The Statue of Eros.

He flicked through the file. As well as the brief summary of facts and police knowledge, there were the guts of psychiatric reports, notes by prison governors, and remarks from three senior police officers who had all made determined, and lengthy, attempts to bring solid evidence against the cousins.

One section concerned the private habits and sexual tastes of Peter and Paul Magnus. Neither of the men were married, though each carried on associations with various women, mostly club hostesses and fringe girls. Some of these relationships lasted for as long as three or four years, others only a few weeks.

Peter preferred quite young girls, often in their mid-teens, whom he liked to take when they were dressed up—as schoolgirls, nurses, even nuns. He told one doctor that he kept a special wardrobe at home stocked with the necessary costumes and underclothes.

There is little doubt, one psychiatrist wrote, *that this man is subjugating a deep-seated desire to deflower young girls, the dangerous urge being kept at bay by the dressing up and play-acting. One should, however, be aware that his problem could become acutely difficult if a girl refused to co-operate, or should he become unbearably frustrated.*

Paul Magnus was more straightforward, his tastes revolving around relatively normal sex. But he was an emotional man with a strange touch of romanticism, and his girls were required to stay utterly faithful to him while they were in favour. Even then there were difficulties, for he was consumed by jealous fantasies, often founded on tiny pieces of insubstantial evidence, which, to a normal man, would mean little. A psychiatrist described it in his report as *an Othello syndrome.*

The cousins were inseparable, often showing the mental attitude of identical twins. They shared a house in Islington: a large, expensive old place bought in the name of Harriet Magnus, Paul's mother.

Known as Big Harriet, Mrs. Magnus was a character, still a fine-looking, tall woman with striking golden hair and a turn of phrase which could wither strong men.

For all practical purposes the house was divided into four separate apartments and a communal ground floor which they shared as a family. Peter, Paul and Harriet lived in three of the apartments, while the fourth was inhabited by Raymond Tobin, a young man now in his early twenties, whom Big Harriet had almost literally picked out of the gutter when he was barely a child. Indeed he had become another son to her, the relationship subtly changing as he grew to manhood.

At sixty-two, Harriet Magnus was still very much a woman, having retained her sexual needs and a fair proportion of sensuality. In short she was an amazing example of bodily survival. Nobody dared to say it out loud, but most of the Magnus associates knew Big Harriet's thing was young men and that Ray Tobin was her private screw, and if either of the cousins harboured any moral disgust over the situation they kept it well hidden.

Since his first appearance in the Magnus menage, Ray Tobin was accepted as part of the family. Peter and Paul always treated him as a younger brother, lavishing more affection on him than they ever gave to their girl friends, doing their best to give him the kind of education they had not experienced, and keeping him apart from their business dealings. It was as though Tobin filled a special need in them: a focus of their love, a human idol whom they used to appease the gods, or devils, of criminal guilt.

The cousins spent much of their time in the four clubs which had once belonged to Drummond. Mostly, Torry noted, they were to be found in The Statue of Eros, the largest of the clubs, which they used as a kind of headquarters.

It was to The Statue of Eros that Hart had gone with his heavy squad.

VIII

THE LEGAL OWNER, and manager, of The Statue of Eros was a plump, bald man with the face of an ageing cherub; his skin was pink and incredibly smooth, and on the pudgy third finger of his right hand he wore a heavy gold ring, inset with a diamond. His name was William Shaw and he was known to the Magnus fraternity as Bill the Statue Man.

The title referred to his front position as operator of the club, but it had other implications. Despite his weight, William Shaw had remarkable control over his muscles and had been known to stand for as long as an hour, watching over some part of the club's activities, without moving any part of his body.

The habit, he maintained, was a form of relaxation learned early in life when employed at a waxworks exhibition as an attendant, playing the old game, used to great effect still at Madame Tussaud's, of appearing to be a waxwork which came to life at regular intervals, often causing much amusement.

In spite of police opposition, The Statue of Eros had been granted a gaming licence in 1968. Its premises were situated in the heart of Soho, off Wardour Street, and ran to three storeys. The gaming rooms were on the ground level and above them a bar and strip club flourished. The second floor housed the club's restaurant, while the top floor was given over to offices and a small cinema, the one in which the Magnus cousins viewed the work of Messrs. Cagney and Bogart. At other times it was used to screen more bizarre items, mainly imports from the Scandinavian countries which could not be bought in the open mushroom market of sex boutiques which flourished in the area.

When Hart arrived the club was quiet. It was early evening, and the big spenders, intent on satisfying their addiction for the green baize or the soft sight of naked flesh, were not yet out and about.

Bill the Statue Man was talking to his head croupier in the club's foyer when Hart entered, backed by six muscular plainclothesmen.

William Shaw stood stock still and looked, his face impassive, at the warrant card in Hart's hand.

"This is a private club. I need to see your authority." He thought it was a raid but could not figure the reason for such an early call.

"No authority." Hart looked calmly into the club manager's eyes. "We just want a word with a couple of your regular members."

"There are few members in."

"These two are here. Their Rolls is in the Dean Street car park and Chung Yin's sitting in it ponced up like the sweet-and-sour faggot he is." Chung Yin was the Magnus chauffeur, a cockney Chinese boy with a penchant for his own sex, which was indeterminate.

"I'm not with you."

"You'd better be." Hart's smile was unpleasant, a cross between a snarl and a leer.

The Statue Man regarded Hart with dead eyes. In the one quick look at the warrant card he had taken in everything. The copper was only a detective sergeant, young, flashy, not dry behind the ears. They did not send detective sergeants if it was really heavy, though the sextet of constables backing him looked unfortunately intimidating.

"Come on," Hart barked. "We haven't got time to fuck around all night. I want a word with Peter and Paul Magnus."

"I'm not sure . . ."

"Well I am. The area car fingered them coming in over an hour ago, and unless they've got mystic powers they're still here, old son."

The "old son" sparked anger in the Statue Man's blood. The young copper could have been his own offspring, yet he was calling him "old son." Arrogant bastard, thought the Statue Man. Without a trace of rancour in his voice he said, "I'll see if I . . ."

"No, you bloody take me to them. Even if they're screwing your hostesses end to end you take me to them."

"I don't . . ."

"If you don't, old son, then I'll leave my chums here and be back in half an hour with some real legal muscle. We'll turn this place over like it's never been turned before. You'll think you're on an electric spit."

"This club's strictly legal."

"Yes, as legal as a prospective rapist's prick. West End Central turned you over a couple of years ago. But you're not dealing with them now. A word with Peter and Paul Magnus. This minute."

The Statue Man remained unruffled. "I'd rather not have all these gentlemen tramping through the club. It's not nice for the clients."

Hart grinned and turned to the constables. "You outside. You two stay here. You, you and you with me."

The little procession followed Bill the Statue Man up the staircase.

Torry turned the final page in the Magnus file, pushed it away and leaned back in his chair. Sergeant Dumphy, who had been pottering around the office, had brought him coffee before going off duty. Torry swilled it back. It was almost cold. He pushed the cup away in the direction of the file.

He closed his eyes and thought about the Magnus cousins: their power, cunning and ruthlessness, wondering about their rise from the raw edge of semi-poverty.

The key to the characters of Peter and Paul Magnus lay in their early background, in the climate and teeming insecurity which, through circumstances, had shaped their mould.

It began with Elsie and Harriet Wise and Bernard and Cyril Magnus.

Elsie and Harriet Wise had known Bernard and Cyril Magnus since they were kids: known them in the most fundamental way that people knew one another in the old East End of London—through the crowded proximity of their schools, streets and homes; the feuds of their families and neighbours; their common causes and that incredible old East End camaraderie which ranged from great bouts of emotional generosity to sudden changes of mood leading to knock-down-drag-out fights and vituperant shouting matches.

In 1927, in the aftermath of the General Strike, Bernard and Cyril were nineteen and twenty respectively, big, fine-looking lads, working, like their father, in the East India Docks.

In the same year, Elsie and Harriet Wise were seventeen and eighteen: Elsie taking after her mother, dark, willowy, with a superb figure; Harriet unusually tall, like her father, Big Jim Wise, but with a marked sensuality in the way she moved, her ample hips swinging almost in a grind as she walked with firm, wide strides on long, slim magnificent legs.

They were bright girls, chirpy, always with a sharp answer for the boys who chi-iked them on the street corners.

Watching the girls trip past on a warm summer evening, Cyril observed to his brother, "Those Wise birds're real sprauncy. They're ready for it, Bern. Bloody asking for it. Lovely bits of grumble."

The fact that neither of the girls had been strangers to it since their sixteenth birthdays did not enter Cyril's mind. The boys plainly fancied the handsome sisters and did not hesitate to show it.

In September, the Wise and Magnus families found themselves, together with hundreds of their friends and neighbours, in the heady hop fields of Kent, the traditional holiday resort of the prewar East Enders.

Few would consider it a holiday today. The work was hard and the hours long—hop picking was never regarded as the easiest manual labour, but, for that particular group of city dwellers the yearly trip to the hop fields was a change of pace, a refreshing, different way of life among the open spaces and burgeoning fields, a distinct contrast from their brick- and dust-lined lives.

There were unpleasant aspects: the bugs, rough sleeping, primitive lavatory arrangements, but these were outweighed by the whole experience, the sense of holiday and the magnificent, boozy, song-wrung and fornicating nights.

On their second evening of hopping in the September of 1927, the Magnus brothers set their sights at the Wise sisters, made their first advances at The Bull Inn, and bore the girls off to a friendly and secluded coppice where Elsie teamed off with Bernie and Harriet with Cyril, each giving the other the fervent, delighted and feverish use of their bodies.

It was one of those unlikely chemical fusions, the odds against which are impossible to determine. Yet, either on this night, or one of the many following evenings in Kent, caution was thrown off with their clothes and both sisters became pregnant, the error of their ways being just apparent by Christmas.

The double wedding was held in early January, following protracted recriminations and loud argument, which included Big Jim Wise taking his belt to both of his daughters and the Magnus brothers forcing their way into the Wise home to do Big Jim.

When it came to the nuptials nobody knew whether they should laugh or cry. In the end most of them got drunk instead and life continued in its set pattern.

In May, both of the young brides gave birth to baby boys within a week of each other. Bernie and Elsie named their son Peter, while Cyril and Harriet's boy was christened Paul.

So began the lives of Peter and Paul Magnus.

They grew through their baby- and early childhoods in much the same way as other East End kids, though by the time they were eight years old they both demanded a marked respect from their contemporaries.

Physically they were big boys for their age, with more than the normal aggressive instincts, not an unusual occurrence within the society into which they had been born. As they grew, however, it became apparent that the aggressiveness was deep-seated.

In plain language, Peter and Paul Magnus were a pair of bullies —and it was a time when physical courage, toughness and fitness were at a high premium. They were both good at games, excelling at football and boxing, in which they were coached at a Church of England boys' club.

In 1939, when they were eleven years old, the war came and with it the first rift. Peter and Paul Magnus found themselves among the first of hundreds of children scheduled for evacuation to safer country areas.

There were tearful good-byes, made worse by the fact that their fathers were preparing to leave home and the docks to serve in the armed forces—Cyril and Bernard seeing in the war a chance for action, new experiences, and, to be fair, an escape from the daily round and the now familiar presence of their wives.

Peter and Paul were taken by train, with their string-slung cardboard gas-mask boxes and cheap suitcases, to a quiet market town eighteen miles from Oxford, where a kind-hearted billeting officer, feeling that the boys would be happier together, foisted them on an unsuspecting draper and his wife.

Plumped down in strange surroundings, with people whose values were alien to them, Peter and Paul stayed sullen for a couple of days. The eruption soon followed.

Within the month the cousins had been moved from house to house no less than three times, attempts to split them up resulting in uncontrolled outbursts.

Efforts by their teachers, the harassed billeting officer and other locals, had little effect. The boys were constantly in trouble, fight followed fight and they were the cause of much damage, within their foster homes and throughout the local countryside.

As the months passed the situation became worse. Finally, in a last-ditch attempt to bring reason to the boys, their parents were summoned. Bernard and Cyril were given compassionate leave and they prepared to make the trip to unfamiliar Oxfordshire.

By this time it was late 1940, and the problem of the Magnus families was a minute pinprick compared to the concern which immersed the nation as it stood alone against the might of the Third Reich.

The Battle of Britain was being fought high in the southern skies and the first bombs had fallen on London. So, it was with some sense of respite that the two worried Magnus couples set out to try and talk sense into their children.

They arrived on a beautiful morning, the sky cloudless and temperatures soaring into the eighties. The adults became hot and sweaty as they listened to a catalogue of their sons' misdeeds, so that Bernard and Cyril at least were exceptionally irritable by the time they faced Peter and Paul.

"I'm just telling you one thing, you little buggers," Bernie said, his clenched fist inches from their noses. "If we hear another word about you two getting into trouble, we'll be down here so fast you won't be able to shit with fright and neither of you'll stand up straight for a month." He was convincing and the cousins paled.

"You might get away with it here, with these bloody hayrick Charlies," added Cyril, "but my Christ I'll tan the arses off both of you if it happens again. Then I'll pass you over to him," he nodded towards his brother, then looked at Peter, "And you know what that means, lad."

Peter knew what it meant. He wanted to lash out with rage.

The charade of threatened violence over, the two families went off for the day to enjoy a makeshift picnic in the local fields.

Travelling back to London that evening, the parents felt heady and rejuvenated by the day in the country. It reminded them of Kent in the September of 1927, the fresh air and fields being a stimulant which spoke of erotic sexual promise once they were back in their respective beds that night.

They got into Paddington just after eight and into their street at nine-thirty. The Brewer's Dray, their local pub, was open and they opted for a couple of pints before the forthcoming connubial pleasures.

The air raid warning went as they were entering the public bar and the first bombs fell three minutes later.

There were forty men and women in The Brewer's Dray when it received the direct hit. Only one was pulled out alive—Harriet Magnus.

The news sparked a great spasm of bitterness within the cousins. The bitterness coagulated into a hard venom. The boys wanted to wound, hurt and maim. The object of their anguish was to punish whoever was responsible for the deaths of Peter's parents and Paul's father. The local curate, who broke the news made the error of saying, "We must remember it is the will of God."

The following night, the boys descended on the local parish church, a beautiful fifteenth-century building much loved by the faithful.

They set fire to the altar linen, smashed the heads from three carvings, tore down the large crucifix and trampled upon it, shattered the bowl of the font and were trying to break in the vestry door when they were caught.

The townspeople were incensed, not even considering the events which led to the outburst.

No relatives appeared at the hearing in the juvenile court—Harriet Magnus was in hospital for three months—and the town breathed a sigh of relief when the two boys were removed for their first taste of the penal system at a borstal institution.

The key, thought Torry, was there, with the background and the Nazi bombs. Everything which had followed was inevitable—the violence, power, sadism; their hidden uncertain and jealous sexual desires. But it did not matter now who was at fault: society, politics, individuals. Peter and Paul Magnus had to be put away for good, before they destroyed any more lives.

Torry glanced at his watch and wished Tickerman had sent him with Hart. He looked forward to meeting the Magnus cousins.

IX

IT WAS ONLY A YEAR since The Statue of Eros had undergone a major interior face lift. Grudgingly, Hart had to admit that it did not seem half bad. Glass chandeliers glittered overhead and the deep-pile carpet was soft under foot: at each step you felt that you might sink in up to your armpits.

As he stood and talked with the Statue Man in the foyer, Hart could see through into the gaming rooms, the decor of which was unexpectedly elegant—velvet draperies, a quietly efficient atmosphere right down to the pair of heavies standing near the door. They were neatly barbered, tanned and punctiliously tailored in dinner jackets; only their build, watchfulness and the way in which they stood, betrayed them as muscle-men.

The sprinkling of women in the rooms, obviously provided by the management, were a cut above the scrubbers one often got in the clubs of Soho. Hart had found his mind wandering as he watched. There was a particularly attractive dark beauty, sheathed in a white dress, who took his eye. Hart had never paid for it in his life, but, for a second he wondered if, on his salary, he could afford the girl for a few hours. It was distinctly unnerving and he had to re-enforce mental discipline and drag himself back to the matter in hand.

As he followed the Statue Man up the white-banistered stairs, the three constables a pace behind them, Hart felt what he could only diagnose as a tweak of envy. The club was plush, sensually exciting, exuding at least a veneer of luxury, not falling prey to the trap of flash vulgarity.

Whereas the ground floor had been almost noiseless except for the evocative sounds from the gaming rooms, the steady voices of the croupiers and the click of the spinning ball, once they reached the first floor, Hart noticed a change of mood: piped music flowing through the upper rooms. Quincey Jones sang "Smackwater Jack" in a soft, hoarse voice with a firm downbeat. It was not Carole King, but the effect was slightly more soothing.

They passed the restaurant on the second floor, where early diners were already being served by white coated waiters who moved like acolytes at a religious ceremony. The Magnus cousins certainly knew how to put you on. Hart also decided that the cousins were greedy. He knew that a year's membership subscription to The Statue of Eros set you back twenty quid, and there was rarely any difficulty about being elected a member, even if you just wandered in off the street, an overnight business tripper who would probably not use the place again for a year. The overheads would be heavy, yet the profit had to be big. The Magnus cousins must be coining money on this operation alone.

They reached the top floor and the Statue Man tapped at a heavy door marked PRIVATE. That was another thing about the club, the doors and fittings had a solidity, not the plastic and disguised hardboard one often saw in Soho.

Now in their mid-forties, the Magnus cousins could easily be mistaken for brothers, even twins. They were both big men, topping six feet, with broad, muscular shoulders. Even a superficial glance told people that they carried no flabbiness or extra weight; under their fashionably cut suits there was hard, controlled muscle, and the decisive way in which they moved left nobody in doubt that they were both in exceptionally good physical condition. The similarity did not stop there: their faces had matured into cognate hard good looks—identical clear blue eyes, the same bone structure including the short, straight nose inherited from the Wise family. From the Magnus side they had acquired the thick, sandy hair which they both wore in a well-trimmed cut, brushed over to the right with neat left-hand partings, neither showing any signs of thinning or baldness.

There were differences, however. Paul's left cheek was marked by a two-inch crescent scar which showed white, even through his healthy sun tan, and Peter's jaw line was unmistakably weak, his mouth more full than that of his cousin, with heavy, sensual lips which looked almost negroid.

Peter was standing by a serving cart, about to pour vodka into a

60

Stiegel-type glass, as the Statue Man entered with Hart and his men. On the other side of the room, Paul lounged in a large black leather chair of Scandinavian design. There was another man with them, leaning over Paul's shoulder reading something which the cousin was pointing out in *The Evening News*. This third man was a little older than the Magnus men, shorter, more weathered, yet, like them, impeccably dressed in a dark blue business suit.

There were also three girls present: a very young blonde seated on the floor at the foot of another chair near the serving cart. Hart thought she could be no more than seventeen years old. The other two, a striking redhead and a slim, insipid blonde, sat on a couch set under the window.

"I thought I said we wasn't to be disturbed." Peter Magnus' eyes flashed dangerously as he looked up at the Statue Man, the bottle and glass poised in mid air. Then he saw Hart and his party. "What's the filth doing in here?"

"They insisted. I'm sorry, Pete." The Statue Man had moved forward into the room.

"They bleeding would." He turned his gaze onto Hart. "If it's West End Central, we've already contributed. This is a private club; you couldn't afford a bag of crisps here."

Hart held out his warrant card. "It's not Central. Eric Hart. Detective sergeant, Crime One."

"Who you looking for then, Sunny Jim?" Paul's arrogant manner ignited a small flare of fury in Hart's guts.

"Peter James Magnus and Paul James Magnus."

"You're looking at them, aren't you?"

"Both of them." Peter went on filling the glass. He dropped ice cubes into the vodka and topped it with tonic water. "What's your problem?"

"My Guv'nor had a bilious attack this morning. Your names came up."

"Very bleeding funny. We got the laughing policeman here, Paul."

Paul grinned unpleasantly. "You after an audition for the cabaret, son? Sorry, we don't use drag queens here; try the vice squad."

Hart held on to his cool, lapsing into official language. "I am enquiring into the deaths of four police officers and one civilian,

Robert Eric Terrice, on the M2 Motorway on Monday afternoon."

"Read about that," Paul's eyes did not flicker. "Some people didn't ought to be allowed out. Bloody hooligans."

"Nasty." Peter passed the vodka to the young blonde and sat down in the chair at the foot of which the girl crouched. His movements reminded Hart of a graceful animal.

Hart swallowed. "I am also looking into the shooting of Paul Denago and Richard Fantonelli at the Dorchester Hotel in the early hours of this morning."

There was a subtle change in the atmosphere. The girls looked uneasy; the youngest plainly frightened. Peter Magnus stroked her hair. "Yeah, that figures," he said, unsmiling.

Paul shifted in his chair. "We was going to call the nick ourselves. Bit of a shock that one."

"They was mates of ours. Bleedin' outrageous." Peter continued to stroke the girl's hair, his movements becoming perceptibly faster.

"We hoped you'd be able to help us. You knew Denago and Fantonelli?"

"You know we bloody knew them. You wouldn't be here if you didn't, would you?"

Before Hart could answer, the third man behind Paul's chair straightened up. "You want me to take the girls downstairs, Pete?"

Peter Magnus gave him a thin smile. "Why? We're all friends; all mates. The law's doing the asking, least we can do is help them. It's getting to something when your mates can't sleep safe in the bloody Dorchester." He switched to Hart. "You lot're slipping up on the job letting people get blasted in a place like the Dorchester."

Hart ignored him. His attention turned to the third man. "Just for the record, your name?"

"Talisman." A minute pause. "Arthur Talisman."

"You are a member of this club?"

"He's a friend of ours," Paul cut in.

"A business associate perhaps?"

"Just a friend."

"And you knew Mr. Denago and Mr. Fantonelli?"

"I never had that pleasure, no. Peter and Paul mentioned them a couple of times. We talked about them today of course, after the news. Peter and Paul were distressed. Shocked."

"Peter was very upset about it this morning." The young blonde had a voice to match. Hart saw Peter Magnus's fingers tighten on the hair at the back of her neck and then relax quickly. There was a brief flash of pain across the girl's face.

"How well did you know them?" Hart threw the question towards Peter.

"Not all that well, really. We had an introduction to them, or I should say they had one to us. Mutual friend in the States."

"What friend?"

"Bloke called Mallinari. Eytye bloke."

"His address?"

"Jesus Christ, you expect miracles. I'll have to look it up."

Paul grinned. "Pete doesn't carry numbers in his loaf. One-two-five Madison Avenue, New York, N.Y. That's his offices anyhow. Clubs and restaurants, that's his business."

"When did either of you see Denago and Fantonelli last?"

"Bleedin' spooky that." Peter Magnus's face took on the expression of an innocent and puzzled child. "We had dinner with them on Sunday night. To be honest we've only met them two, no, I tell a lie, three, times. We had dinner with them last time they were over."

"Twice we had dinner with them then, Pete."

"That's what I said, didn't I?"

"So you knew them socially through this Mallinari?"

"You might say that." Peter Magnus still toyed with the girl's hair. "Mallinari was looking for properties over here. Wanted to set up a couple of class nosh houses in the Smoke here. Asked us if we'd have a rabbit with them. Suggest things, perhaps. They was nice fellas. I felt real sick, wanted to throw up, when I heard the news."

"Yeah, me an' all." His cousin nodded gravely.

"Did you know if they had any enemies? Did they say anything about that?"

"Hang about," Paul frowned. "We only got the social chat with them. Didn't even get round to the business thing."

"I think I suggested a couple of possibilities." Peter was still giving the innocent look.

One of the constables behind Hart shuffled, turning the pages of his notebook, in which he was taking down the conversation.

"Can you help with Robert Eric Terrice?"

"Never heard of him, son. Not till we read his name in the paper." Very quick from Peter.

"You're certain about that?"

"Certain as a straight tenner."

"And you?" Hart flicked his eyes towards Paul.

"Don't know nobody called Terrice. I know a bookie name of Ferris, but no Terrice. You're asking a lot of questions, cocker."

Hart nodded. "It's the job."

"Don't know how you put up with it."

Hart paused. "You planning to go out of the country in the near future?"

"What's that supposed to mean?"

"What I said."

"Me, him, or both of us?"

"Both of you."

"That sounds like a dead bloody liberty to me. But no, we don't plan to go away. Not till later in the year when we go on our holidays."

"And where're you going? Marseilles?"

"You're bloody stupid."

"Why?" asked Peter Magnus, the innocence gone.

"Because I expect one of my superiors will want to talk to you about Denago and Fantonelli."

"It'd *better* be one of your superiors and all, son. We don't usually chat up the errand boys."

Hart ignored it, even though his inclinations were to play it as tough and heavy as he knew. He found the Magnus cousins too much; their confidence, arrogance and attitude of disrespect to the law was something which was hard to stomach. He had to ask a few more routine questions before being escorted, by the Statue Man, down the stairs.

Several members were checking in when they reached the foyer. Among them, Hart saw a face he recognised. He did not pause, but went on walking, taking in the face as he went, his brow furrowed by the time he reached the street. It was a face he had seen before, yet he could not put a name to it. Warning bells were ringing in his memory bank, and it worried him that he could not match face and name. All he knew for certain was that the face was not local.

Back in the foyer, Anthony Chassen signed in, checked his coat and a brown paper parcel, then sauntered into the gaming rooms. He was a stranger to The Statue of Eros, though his name had been on their list of members for three months.

X

EARLIER IN THE EVENING, Anthony Chassen had faced two men across the table in his room at the Mayfair Hotel. The men's names were Enrico and Carollo, and they were trusted members of the Vescari family. Chassen had worked with them many times in New York, and they were both now thoroughly acclimatised to London, having been in the city for the past four months.

Chassen had summoned them by telephone, giving certain specific instructions which were to be carried out before they came to meet him. With them, Enrico and Carollo had brought an oblong parcel, wrapped neatly in heavy brown paper. The parcel lay on the table while Chassen gave the men his further orders. They stood and listened with respect.

"I want no mistakes," he said finally. "He is the one, and that is the way Don Peppe wishes it to be."

"Only him?" Enrico looked angry. "Why not the two degenerates?"

"Because that is how it must be for the present. On no account will you touch anyone else. This will cause them much pain, as Don Peppe has been caused pain by the deaths of Paul and Ricardo. It will cause pain, it will also give us a better bargaining position." Chassen laughed. "There will be further pain when I have finished my work tonight."

"You want no help with that?"

"Carollo, I have done this kind of thing on my own many times before. I quite enjoy it. This is okay?" He motioned to the parcel.

Carollo nodded. "I fixed it myself. It will be fine until five o'clock in the morning."

"Go and do what you have to do then. I will deliver this."

After the men left the Mayfair Hotel, Anthony Chassen bathed, changed and took a cab to The Statue of Eros. He carried his light raincoat and the brown paper parcel.

Chassen was disturbed when his cab pulled up outside the club. There were two unmistakable plainclothesmen out front and a couple of police cars parked at the curb. But he had no alternative. A man, even unknown, could easily cause suspicion by rapidly changing his mind. If he told the cabbie to drive on, after seeing the police cars, the cabbie might later remember.

He paid off the cab and walked into the foyer of the club. There was another cop there, but Chassen signed in, hanging back to make sure that there were several people checking their coats in at the cloakroom, before he handed over his raincoat and the parcel.

The raincoat had no marks through which he could be identified. Enrico had bought it for him that afternoon at Aquascutum in Regent Street, paying cash. The cloakroom girl hardly looked at Chassen, taking the coat and putting it on a hanger, placing the parcel on a wide shelf upon which a number of brief cases and parcels already stood.

Men who looked and smelled like plainclothes police came down the staircase. The cop in the foyer joined them and they went outside. Chassen smiled to himself and went into the gaming rooms. He bought thirty pounds in chips, using cash, and played for an hour and a half, cashing in the remaining chips, now depleted to eighteen pounds.

Chassen was pleased that he had not won; winners were always remembered; small losers were not. He went up to the first floor bar and sat in at the strip show for a while, impressed with the kind of talent on display.

There was one in particular: a tall girl with a mane of golden hair; long, slim legs and small, firm breasts; who did not rely on the old, blatant bump and grind routine or the obscene gestures of her body. Instead, she displayed what was almost a demure modesty which she conveyed through a clever and quite believable performance which made Chassen horny—unusual for him, as strippers normally left him cold. This one gave the impression that she was a virgin bride preparing for her husband.

The finale of the show was another act of great skill: four young and lovely negresses who stripped while performing acrobatics on a pair of parallel bars. They relied on a sense of timing, the movements and undressing building from slow, controlled exercises to a high-speed frenzy in which their bodies whirled as they removed their own, and each other's clothes. The whole thing left Chassen sweating and rigid.

He desperately wanted a woman but knew that he could not risk picking up one of the club girls, or, come to that, anyone unknown. This was a bit of personal organisation which he had neglected in planning things in London. Something which he had not foreseen. In New York there was never any problem: it was something he took for granted. Here it could lead to downfall.

Reluctantly, Chassen imposed an iron discipline on his thoughts. He went down into the foyer and quietly left the club. It was just before eleven o'clock and he did not pick up his raincoat or the brown paper parcel from the cloakroom.

When Sergeant Hart left them, the Magnus cousins had an animated conversation with the man who had identified himself as Arthur Talisman.

"They got nothing. Not a bleedin' thing." Paul sneered contemptuously.

Talisman looked worried. "They got my name, didn't they? I don't like that. And you heard the bastard ask if you were going to Marseilles. What was that supposed to mean?"

"Putting the frighteners in, that's all. Jesus, they don't give me no sweat. They can't prove a bleedin' thing. No way." He turned his attention on the girls. "No way, unless someone decides to perform arias in the bleedin' nick." He looked hard at the young blonde. "You were quick enough opening your trap while the filth was here, weren't you gel?"

"I was only trying to help, Pete. Christ, I don't know anything, do I?"

"You'll know the back of my hand if you aren't bloody careful."

The girl went chalky white under her make-up. She had heard the stories, particularly the one about Peter and Anna Paulik, the girl whom he had mercilessly beaten up.

"Well, you stop pushing your oar in where it's not wanted then."

"Yes, Pete."

"I'm telling you all, there'll be no bother with the filth. All they can prove is we had meals with the wops at the Dorchester. There's nothing else for them to know, so forget it. After last night the wops won't fancy their chances any more. We've got to concentrate on reclaiming the goods now. Right?"

"That, and one or two other little matters." Paul drained his glass.

Peter still looked at the young girl. On his face there was a strange expression, a look which Paul knew of old, a mixture of lust and hatred.

"You remember, then," Peter's voice came out thick and hard, from the back of his throat. "Keep *mum* or you'll know about it."

A little later they sent the girls down to the restaurant and continued their conversation. During the course of the next hour, several men came to see the cousins, each one brought up to the office by Bill the Statue Man.

Eventually, Peter, Paul and Talisman went down and joined the girls in the restaurant. They ate with relish, as though food had not passed their lips all day—thick, rare steaks garnished with mushrooms and tomatoes, washed down with a good Beaune. After eating they wandered through the other rooms, having a word here and there with friends or favoured members.

Just before midnight, Peter left the others to go up to the office. On his way he looked in at the strip club. Whenever he could, Peter liked to watch the four spade dollies doing their act on the parallel bars. He found it supremely erotic, and there was one of the girls whom he really fancied. She was a coffee-coloured, sinuous girl with huge brown eyes, a silky skin and big nipples, like large raspberries. Her name was April and she started the girls' routine, running on, fully clothed in the claret-coloured miniskirt, white shirt and boots, which was the girls' costume.

April would grasp the bars and swing upwards, balancing on her hands so that the skirt fell back, exposing her thighs and the little tight satiny pants. Peter Magnus loved the way in which the material appeared to be moulded to the girl's buttocks and outlined her vulva.

April then walked the length of the bars on her hands, while Peter never took his eyes off her buttocks; their swelling roundness and the tight cleft between, sent his mind reeling. He thought she had the nicest arse he had ever seen. In the dark web of his fantasies, Peter saw her, usually dressed in a nurse's uniform, struggling and moaning for pity as his hands closed around the firm buttocks and his fingers moved to free them from her clothing. He was determined to have April in the way he particularly enjoyed before either of them were much older.

After watching the act, Peter Magnus, now heady with drink and the eroticism of the black girl's body, went on up to the office where he spent fifteen minutes with Bill the Statue Man, looking over the night's takings.

Chung Yin had the Magnus Rolls in front of the club on the dot of twelve-thirty. Talisman and the slim blonde went off in search of a taxi, while Peter, Paul, the redhead, whose name was Caroline, and Valerie, the teen-age blonde, piled into the Rolls and headed towards the house in Islington.

The club closed at four o'clock. Two of Peter and Paul's men arrived at three-thirty, a routine which never varied. They took turns of duty, one sleeping on the couch in the office while the other prowled the club until eight-thirty, when the cleaning staff arrived.

On this night, the Statue Man had a word with the two night men when they came on duty, did a last check of the safe and the kitchens, then walked over to the Dean Street car park, picked up his Rover 2000 and drove home to Maida Vale.

The remainder of the staff left as quickly as possible. Most of them wanted to get home to their beds. The girl in the cloakroom had special reasons for wanting to get away quickly. That night she was not going back, as she usually did, to the flat, which she shared with two other girls, off the King's Road. Instead, she was to meet Stephen, one of the young waiters from the restaurant. He had said that his car would be parked nearby and he would wait for her outside the club.

Stephen had been giving her a great deal of attention for three or four weeks now. They had twice lunched and gone to the cinema together. On the last occasion she had allowed him to fondle her breasts and the inside of her thigh in the darkness at the back of the circle.

Tonight they were going to his bed-sitter in the Earl's Court

Road, and during the entire evening, the cloakroom girl, whose name was Marylin Hughes, had thought of little else. She performed her duties automatically, her mind picturing the caresses she would receive from Stephen, the kind of response she would give, and the final pleasure. The wetness and thrilling sensations in her loins, the fevered pictures in her imagination came between Marylin and her work.

After the club had closed, she noticed that a member had left his coat behind. There was also a parcel that someone had forgotten, but it had happened before. By rights she should have reported the items to Mr. Shaw, but tonight she was too busy repairing her make-up and changing into the fresh white nylon underwear which she had bought that afternoon especially for the occasion. Customers were always leaving things behind and, from her experience, they usually came back for them on the following night.

Marylin left the club and the brown paper parcel remained on the shelf in the narrow little cloakroom.

Inside the parcel were three plastic boxes, the kind of thing one uses for sandwiches, or to protect cheese or bacon in a refrigerator. The first container was a little over a foot long, six inches wide and around three inches in depth. With this was a second container, four inches wide, seven inches long and two inches deep.

The smaller container was centred within the larger and packed tightly around with black powder. Inside the small container was a mixture of magnesium, powdered aluminium and iron oxide. The lid was sealed down with tape and an electric detonator had been inserted into a neatly drilled hole.

The wires from the detonator passed through a similar hole drilled in the lid of the larger container, this lid also being sealed down with tape. From there, the leads went through a hole drilled in the bottom of the third container which was the same size as the larger of the first two plastic boxes.

This last container was divided into three compartments, the left section holding a small alarm clock, the far right an Eveready 996 battery. The leads from the detonator were wired to the clock and battery, so that, when the clock's alarm spring unwound, a simple contact was made and the electrical circuit closed.

The centre compartment contained another mixture of magnesium, powdered aluminium and iron oxide. The lid on this container, like the others, was tightly fitted and taped. The alarm was fully wound and set for 5 A.M.

At five o'clock, Marylin, the cloakroom girl, was being had, for the second time, by Stephen the waiter: their mutual enjoyment being both passionate and agile.

Earlier, the Magnus cousins, together with Caroline and Valerie, arrived back at the Islington house. As they climbed the stairs to their separate apartments they noticed that Raymond Tobin's door was open. Peter turned and winked at his cousin.

"Your mum's at it again," he grinned.

Outside, Chung Yin powered the Rolls smoothly away from the kerb. The garage and his rooms were only half a mile away, and he felt tired tonight. He noticed there was a dark-coloured Mercedes parked about a hundred yards down the street, but thought nothing of it. The time by the Rolls's clock was then one thirty-five.

Inside the Mercedes, Enrico and Carollo watched the Rolls hiss past and they settled down for the rest of their wait.

In his bedroom in the Cromwell Road, Derek Torry slept and dreamed. There was a heavy film of sweat covering his brow. The dream was disturbing. He saw himself in the living room of his flat, looking down at a body crumpled on the floor. The head had been blasted away so that the pool of blood, bone and brains was spread, like some terrible butcher's mixture, on the carpet. The body was that of a woman and the clothes were in disarray. Torry felt strangely more embarrassed by the sight of the clothes than by the hideous mash of head. He could recognise the legs, then the torso, the breasts and arms, the clothing. It was the body of Susan Crompton, his former fiancée.

Tickerman stood in the doorway, an accusing look on his face; behind him was another girl, her face white, the eyes red with tears. She had long fingers, one hand to her head. On one of her fingers she wore a Greek puzzle ring.

Eric Hart slept on the divan under the window of his bed-sitter behind the Army and Navy Stores. He did not dream, though he had wakened twice during the night. Each time the dark girl in the

72

white sheath dress, the one whom he had glimpsed at The Statue of Eros, came smarting into his mind.

Time passed.

In The Statue of Eros, Sidney, the night man off duty, slept on the couch in the office. Harry, his mate, sat in the restaurant kitchen. He had made himself coffee and a large cheese sandwich spread over with pickles.

Five o'clock.

Inside the parcel, the alarm was triggered off, the spring winding down and making contact, closing the circuit. The bomb exploded with a dull thump, the incendiary qualities of the two containers of magnesium, powdered aluminium and iron oxide, igniting and showering out in a blazing flare.

The initial explosion blew out the cloakroom wall, exposing the girls' dressing room, which lay behind it. Peter and Paul did not allow the girls, who worked the rooms in the club, to take away their expensive dresses without express permission from Bill the Statue Man. Next to the dividing wall, between the cloakroom and dressing room, were three metal racks on which hung some thirty dresses. These took the initial impact of the incendiary.

Within seconds the whole area was ablaze, flames leaping out into the foyer. Harry did not move as quickly as he should have done. By the time he got to the first-floor landing the fire had taken hold, and, instead of making an attempt to control it with one of the many portable fire extinguishers, Harry dashed back up the stairs to wake his mate Sidney.

Sidney had the sense to dial the fire service, but by the time they descended the stairs again it was too late. Smoke and flames were rising upwards and, behind the jetlike roar, they could hear noise in the streets. The heat, choking fumes and panic, hit both men at the same time. They turned and ran for their lives through the second floor exit.

They dashed down to the nearest telephone booth, the sound of fire engines in their ears. But the booth had been done by vandals and it was ten minutes before they found another booth in operation. It took them a further minute to get through to William Shaw, the Statue Man.

The Statue Man was drifting into sleep, his thoughts on the holiday which he was planning to take with one of the girls from the club. His voice was hoarse when he picked up the phone.

"Hallo."

"Bill?"

"Yes. Whothat?"

"It's Harry, some bastard's fired the club. Going up like a fucking torch."

"Jesus Christ." Awake now.

"What we do, Bill? Like a bleedin' bonfire."

"Jesus Christ."

Silence.

"You still there, Bill?"

"Yes. The club? Jesus Christ."

"Like a friggin' tinder box."

"Harry?"

"Yes."

"Get up to the office and . . . no you haven't got the fucking safe keys. Jesus Christ."

"For Christ's sake, do something, Bill."

"You get out?"

"Course we fucking got out. We wouldn't be talkin' to you if we hadn't have got out."

"Jesus. Harry, get back there and see what you can do. I'll get straight over. We got to get at the safe."

"You'll be lucky. It's like an incinerator. It's . . ."

"Jesus. Hang on, I'll be over. See what you can do. I got to ring the cousins. See what you can do . . ."

The line clicked dead before Harry could again tell him they would not be able to do anything.

"I hope the fucking insurance is paid up," he said into the dead instrument. "You'll be for it if the insurance isn't paid up. If you arsk me you'll be out of fucking pocket."

The Statue Man did not have to be told he was for it. He knew that he was dead for it.

XI

AFTER HE HAD PUT THE TELEPHONE DOWN on Harry, the Statue Man sat on the edge of the bed in contemplation, not moving a muscle. His mind began to accelerate. Peter and Paul did not take kindly to bad news; like the kings and feudal lords of old, the cousins had a tendency to behave violently towards any bearer of evil tidings. So the Statue Man thought for a few moments, summoning his courage, getting his mind straight, arranging the words he would use to inform the Magnuses of the catastrophe. Slowly he picked up the telephone receiver and began to dial.

Peter Magnus heard the bell at a distance, through the numbing fog of sleep. It seemed that he had only just dropped into the comforting escape of darkness, and, as he struggled upwards, the events prior to slumber came brimming back into his sluggish brain.

He had glanced at his watch as he held the apartment door open for the teen-age blonde, Valerie Finch. The dial told him that it was only one-forty. Closing the door behind them, he turned, catching the girl stifling a yawn.

"Hope you're not too tired for fun and games, gel. I been raving to go all night."

Valerie put her arms around his neck. They coiled softly, like two friendly snakes.

"Course not, Pete. I'm always ready." She kissed him on the mouth, her tongue sliding lasciviously in, searching between his teeth and lips.

There were deep bags under her eyes; you could only see them at close range, under the make-up. Funny, Peter Magnus thought. Funny how all the young birds I pull and educate to my ways seem to tire after a couple of weeks. He didn't get tired. Young girls don't have no stamina these days, and they bloody should, what with all them bloody vitamin pills and that. The spade dolly, April, flipped into his mind. She'd be the next to enjoy the Magnus initiation. Bet she has stamina. He grinned, the erotic pictures clear in his mind.

"Good girl," he said aloud, disentangling himself from Valerie's arms. "You fancy being Florence Nightingale tonight?"

Valerie drooped her head, then lifted it again, looking up from under her eyelids. She had a wonderful smile; it was one of her best features; a smile which promised miracles of delight for Peter. "Florence Nightingale, Sister Anna, or Valerie Finch, Head Girl," she whispered. "Whichever you want."

"Get your lamp out then, Flo." Peter Magnus disappeared into the bathroom, re-emerging five minutes later, stripped to the waist.

Valerie stood at the foot of the bed, wearing a light blue cotton uniform dress with short sleeves and a starched white collar. Over this was a spotless white apron, her waist pinched in with a broad blue belt, her legs encased in black seamed nylon, her feet shod neatly in severe black shoes.

Peter had no idea why the uniform never failed to pump blood into his loins, feeding his desire. It was the same with the nun's habit and the schoolgirl's gym slip, both of which hung in the wardrobe.

"Nurse, I need help," he said softly.

She took a pace towards him, smiling. Then Peter moved fast, leaping for her. Valerie gave a little mock scream. "Let me go . . . What . . . ? What are you . . . ? Oh . . . Oh no . . . No . . . No . . ."

His weight carried them backwards, straddling her under him across the bed. He had one arm over her chest, above her breasts, holding her down as she pretended to struggle, still mouthing small protests.

Peter's free hand grabbed down at her skirt, pulling upwards, the rustle of her clothing driving him deeper into the familiar, wild desire. He glimpsed pink flesh and the tiny black nylon briefs above, his big hand clasping at the flimsy material; saliva filling his mouth, bubbling through his teeth, running down his chin as he pulled and ripped the thin barrier . . .

76

In Peter Magnus's mind it was the black girl, April, who writhed under him.

But that was before sleep. Now there was the ringing and Valerie lay beside him, sated by the struggle and long acts of coupling.

Peter Magnus shook his head, hard, trying to clear the dense mist as he reached for the telephone.

In the apartment downstairs, Paul Magnus vaguely heard the ringing and understood that it was the telephone. It was Peter's turn to answer. They took calls on alternate nights and the button on Paul's extension was pressed to OFF. He stirred and turned, throwing out an arm, reaching for Caroline Proctor's breasts. Sleepily she snuggled closer to him as he gently massaged a nipple between his thumb and forefinger.

In the apartment below Peter's, Harriet Magnus heard the ringing, far away. She opened her eyes. Raymond Tobin was cradled in her arms, like some oversized child. She drew him closer.

Ray Tobin was twenty-six now, and Big Harriet could hardly credit that nineteen years had elapsed since she first held the boy close to her breast. Neither could she believe that she was now over sixty years old. There were times when she still felt twenty-five or thirty, only the unwillingness of her body to do exactly what she required of it informed her that time had passed. Ray was such a pitiful, small weedy boy when she first brought him back to her home—

It happened in 1953, when she still lived in Hammersmith: the small house shared with her son and nephew—when they bothered to come home. Neither of them was home on that night in 1953, and she knew it would be some time before she would see them again, because they were both doing porridge in the Scrubs: Paul for cutting up his girl's fancy man, and Peter for doing over a worthless tom.

Big Harriet was under no illusion about the boys' way of life. After all it had its compensations, and, after Peter had gone down and Paul was awaiting trial, he told her that Joe Drummond would see her all right while they were both inside. Only Joe Drummond did not come, and it was Peter and Paul's mates who looked after her, looking in every day, slipping her the odd tenner, or leaving

77

cigarettes, legs of lamb, sides of beef, hams, fruit, tinned goods. They were all good boys.

One of the men who came over regularly was Alfred Tobin, a minder, looking after Drummond's toms, also working, when needed, at the clubs.

Alfred Tobin had two weaknesses: drink, and his wife, Christine. Married for eight years, Christine and Alf had a little boy, Raymond, who was just seven years old.

On his visits, Alf Tobin would talk to Big Harriet about Christine and all he had tried to do for her. Privately, Harriet thought Tobin's wife a common little tart, all bleached-blond hair, false fingernails, probably false tits and a deceitful nature as well. But it was no good telling Alf, who could not understand why Christine had turned cold towards him. The other boys who came around to see Harriet, knew why, and they told her.

Christine was having it away on the side. Not with one of their own lot either. The man concerned was a commercial traveller in cheap cosmetics. Nobody dared tip Alf, who was roused to anger too quickly and would certainly not believe anyone who told him the truth, his whole life being centred on Christine and the little boy. You would have to be very brave to give that kind of news to Alfred Tobin.

Yet they all knew the truth would come out sooner or later. It came sooner.

It was a classic situation. Alf was on duty at the old Harmony House one night when Drummond came in, early in the evening, just after eight. He wanted someone to take a message to Dumper Doffman who, at that time, lived in Barnes. The message was important and Drummond told Alf Tobin that once he had seen The Dumper, his time was his own.

The result was that Alf delivered the word, had a few rums, and was at his own front door by eleven o'clock, at least four hours earlier than usual.

He walked into the living room to find Christine on her back in front of the fire with the little commercial traveller screwing the boots off her.

Christine was not a bright girl. From the day she had married Alfred Tobin she had never had cause to fear him. Alf was always sweet, tender, loving and generous to her, and, in spite of the fact that she knew all about his job with Drummond, she interpreted his attitude towards her as a sign of soft weakness. She had no respect whatsoever for her husband.

Foolishly she looked up over her commercial traveller's naked shoulder and breathlessly asked, "What the hell are you doin' home at this time?"

Alfred was too shaken to reply, so she added, "Hang on a minute, we're not finished."

The shock within Tobin combined with the booze, soaring his temper well past danger point.

The nearest thing to hand was a bottle of gin standing on a side table. Tobin moved with considerable care, unhurried, but his mind magnetically fixed on what he was about to do.

He picked up the bottle by its neck, breaking it against the wall. Then, with a sob of rage, Tobin descended on the couple, grinding the jagged weapon into the commercial traveller's neck, a crag of spiked glass splitting the man's jugular. Blood spouted everywhere, pumping across the room, over Tobin, on the ceiling, walls and spattering the bleached hair of Christine Tobin, who received the next thrust, and the next, and the next.

The shock became deep when Alf realised what he had done. Like a sleepwalker, he went into the kitchen, picked up the clothesline, walked up the stairs, shooed his frightened son back to his room, telling him that the noise was only the television and everything was all right. He then hanged himself from the banisters.

Neighbours who heard the screams had already sent for the police, and as soon as the news was out, another of Drummond's lads, Billy Westlake, who lived nearby, drove over to Harriet, who returned with him to Tobin's place, loudly protesting that she was young Raymond's aunt and wanted to take him home with her.

The police did not even question the relationship, but shamefacedly told her that the boy was not there.

It was a repulsive aspect of the case. Little Raymond had not been quietened by his father and, for the second time that night had wandered from his room. Harriet was later to know, as she soothed the child from recurring nightmares over the years, what horror and shock was incised into his mind at the sight of the triple deaths, the blood and mutilation. Raymond, in blind hysteria, had left the house by the back door, stumbling out into the night.

Harriet and Billy Westlake combed the area for nearly two hours before they found the little boy, huddled up, sobbing, in a shop doorway, still dressed in his pyjamas. Harriet scooped him into her arms and bore him off to her house.

From that first night it was a strange relationship. Harriet smothered the child with love. Once they were out, Peter and Paul treated him like a spoiled young brother. At school he did not have to fight his own battles; at home there were always treats, presents and an ocean of love in which he drowned.

Harriet also formed an odd personal relationship with the boy, treating him, from their first few days, not as a child but as an equal. At the age of eighteen, Raymond Tobin still shared a bed with Harriet, who, by that time, had initiated him into the ways of men and women.

It could even be said that Raymond Tobin was never allowed to explore a free and healthy sexual relationship with any younger woman. He did it with Harriet, and to him, this was the only right and natural way.

True, when they moved to the Islington house, he was given his own set of rooms, but quite regularly he would gravitate to the older woman's bedroom. He was, indeed, a kind of prisoner, living off the love of Harriet, Peter and Paul. Not wanting any further life outside this; satisfied and content with his lot.

Now, he pushed his head between Harriet's large breasts, attempting to blot out the far-off ringing. Then, suddenly, the whole house was wakened by Peter's bellow.

"Paul, get bloody down here. The bastards've done The Statue . . . Paul. Paul, sodding move yourself."

From their vantage point in the Mercedes, Enrico and Carollo saw the lights coming on in the house.

"It's been done," said Enrico.

Paul was on Peter's landing, a towelling robe covering his nakedness. They were both red-faced, angry, shouting, when Big Harriet emerged from her rooms.

At sixty-two, few would have taken her for more than forty-five. Still tall and straight, she showed no sign of the stoop or hunched shoulders of age, and her face was exceptionally well preserved, the skin smooth, few wrinkles and a complexion unaltered. Over the years, Harriet had spent much of Peter and Paul's money on her body.

Her breasts were large and full, yet her figure retained the balance, line and curves which had been hers when she was a young woman of thirty. The most staggering thing about her was the long, seemingly undyed, mane of golden hair which swept back from the high forehead to fall softly and naturally down her shoulders.

She wore a long, fitted, pink satin nightdress, the kind of frolic beloved of movie stars in the thirties, and the whole picture of her, standing in the doorway with the sleepy Ray Tobin hovering in the rear, was one of allure.

It was only when she opened her mouth that the spell was broken.

"What the fucking hell's going on?" she mouthed. "Can't I even get sleep in my own house? You two're acting like spoiled, poxridden kids. Shut your bleedin' row."

Peter and Paul reacted as though they had been switched off.

"Trouble, Mum." Paul stood like a child.

"Trouble?" Harriet's eyes blazed. "There's always bloody trouble with you two." Her gaze fell on the two girls who were standing, white and silent, on the stairs. She had not seen them before.

"Trouble with this pair of lilies? I'm not surprised. They look as if they couldn't screw the top off a bottle, let alone you two. Where the shit'd you find them? The YWCA?"

"It's not the girls, Ma." Peter had acquired the habit of calling her Ma soon after the cousins came out of borstal. "It's the club. Statue of Eros." His face flushed with anger as he said it. "Some bleeder's bombed it . . ."

"Bombed it? I shouldn't wonder. Probably some mark who got a dose from one of those." She once more nodded towards the girls.

"It's been set on fire, Ma."

"Someone ought to set you on fire. Better still, set fire to the arses of those whores."

"Mum, The Statue's important. We got cash there. It brings in good profit," Paul mumbled.

"Well, who did it? Go and find out, sort the buggers, can't you?"

"I already sent for Chung." Peter looked surly. "It's the bloody Statue Man's responsibility. We're going to have words with him."

"Get about it then, you wet turd. Both of you get the lead out of your balls and leave Ray and I to get our sleep. I need my sleep. And while you're at it, you're not leaving those lights o' love in my house."

"They'll stay upstairs, Ma. They won't come near you. They won't bother you."

Big Harriet knew how far she could go. It was a game they all played. She could ridicule and tongue-lash the cousins up to a point, but, in the long run, their word was finally law. She scowled, turned and closed the door firmly.

Enrico and Carollo watched as the Rolls pulled up outside the Magnus house. They saw the cousins come running down the steps, and the car pull away again.

They waited for ten minutes before leaving the Mercedes to walk towards the house. Just before they left the car, Enrico switched on the engine, now he moved in front of Carollo, who had shrugged into a loose-fitting raincoat.

When they reached the door, Enrico stood squarely facing it. Carollo stayed behind him, in the shadow. Enrico leaned on the bell.

Eventually a light came on upstairs. There was the sound of a window being opened angrily, and Harriet thrust her head out into the night.

"Shut your row with that bell. What d'you want?"

"We are police officers. We want to talk to Raymond Tobin." Enrico spoke from the back of his throat, lowering the usual pitch of his voice in an attempt to disguise the accent.

"Why?"

"We have to speak with him. It's important."

The window banged down and, a few seconds later, a light came on in the hall. Harriet Magnus opened the door. Behind her, in the hall, was Raymond Tobin. He looked puzzled, a little alarmed.

"What the fuck's this all about?" Harriet's brow was creased with fury at being wakened twice in one night.

Enrico held out his right hand which contained a facsimile of a Metropolitan Police Warrant Card.

"We're looking for Raymond Albert Tobin."

Neither Harriet nor Raymond had a chance to reflect on the accent. Looking past Tobin, Enrico could see two girls standing close together, high on the stairs.

Tobin came forward, gently pushing Harriet back to his right.

"You want me?"

"You are Raymond Albert Tobin?"

"Yes."

Enrico smiled and stepped to one side. Carollo came out of the shadows, a silent ghost in a raincoat. Tobin felt as though he was standing alone in the middle of a large field. There was a split second when Harriet realised what was happening. She could neither comprehend it nor shout a warning.

The Winchester repeating shotgun came out from under Carollo's raincoat in one simple fluid movement which was completed as the barrel levelled at Tobin's chest and blasted twice, as fast as a double sonic boom. The air filled with the reek of powder.

Ray Tobin's eyebrows arched up, his face transformed into a mask of query as the huge rifled slugs chewed into him.

Harriet Magnus screamed, echoed by the girls on the stairs as Tobin was hurled back, as though yanked by an invisible hand, a bubbling red stain soaking the front of his robe before he collapsed in a splay of arms and legs at the foot of the stairs.

Harriet rushed to him, her voice lifting into a high, hysterical screech, a long shocking wail. Above, on the stairs, Valerie and Caroline clung to each other.

Without undue speed, Enrico and Carollo turned and walked briskly back to the Mercedes as Harriet's keening altered, dropping into moans and long, shuddering sobs.

XII

NOBODY BOTHERED TORRY until seven-thirty, and then only to give him the operating address and telephone number of the new premises.

Late on the previous evening, Tickerman had decided that they should not carry out this investigation in strength from Scotland Yard. Since then a lot of people had been busy, not least The Guv'nor, who had provided Tickerman's team with the entire fourth floor of a new empty office building in Kingsway.

Torry arrived just before nine and rode the elevator to the fourth floor in the company of a young detective constable.

The floor was basically open plan, with several private rooms leading from the interior wall, the exterior wall being lined with great double glazed windows which looked down onto the broad stretch of busy Kingsway.

Three rows of desks ran down the centre of the office, each with a telephone, most of them already manned. There were a couple of blackboards at the far end of the room, and, in one corner, a civilian switchboard operator sat at a PX.

Hart was at a desk near the door, sitting with another man whom Torry did not recognise. They were both in shirtsleeves.

"Where's the gaffer?" Torry asked. He noticed that Hart and the other man were working with an Identikit, building a face from the scores of clear plastic sheets of chins, cheeks, mouths, noses, eyebrows, ears, foreheads, hair.

Hart nodded towards a door at the far end of the interior wall. "He's waiting. Morning conference." There was a sting of irritation in the voice, as though he really did not have the time to direct traffic.

Torry crossed the room; pinned to the door was a white

card with a stencilled inscription. DET. CHIEF SUPERINTENDENT TICKERMAN it read. Torry smiled, tapped at the door and went in.

Ticker sat behind a white wood desk equipped with a battery of telephones. There were twelve men in the room with him, and Torry recognised a couple of DIs who were experts in arson and bombs; a pair from C1's Narcotics team, and at least four officers from the Fraud Squad, two of whom had the grey, serious faces of men who spent their lives examining other people's financial affairs. There were also men whom Torry knew by sight from the central pool.

"Congratulations, sir." Torry smiled. Tickerman had waited a long time for the promotion.

"And you." Tickerman removed the pipe from his mouth. "I take it nobody's told you yet?"

"No."

"You've made Detective Chief Inspector. Hart's up to DI. So we've all had a lift."

Before Torry could feel the natural elation at the news of his promotion, there was another knock at the door. It was Hart.

Tickerman raised his eyebrows quizzically.

"Any luck?" he asked.

"Almost got it, but the nose and mouth aren't quite right. We need a little more time."

Torry felt as though he was an intruder: someone from whom information was being withheld.

Tickerman nodded and then raised his voice. "All right, gentlemen. I'd like to get through the formalities. Find yourselves somewhere to sit."

Most of the chairs were already taken, so Torry squatted on the floor, next to Hart and one of the Fraud men, their backs to the wall. He muttered congratulations to Hart.

Tickerman did not waste time, starting to talk straight away.

"You will've realised by now that you're the nucleus of my investigation team for this operation. We've got to work closely and the pooling of knowledge is essential. That's why I've called you—Mr. Harvey—and you—Mr. Wood—from your scene of crime investigations."

Torry knew both of the men to whom Tickerman had spoken:

85

Harvey was from the central pool, and Wood's speciality was explosives and arson. He reflected that a great deal had obviously been happening. It had not been simply a case of setting up the headquarters in Kingsway.

"I'd like to take things in chronological order," Tickerman continued. "Mr. Hart spoke to the Magnuses early last night. You're aware that we've already established links between them and Robert Terrice; also between them and the Dorchester victims."

Tickerman went on, saying the Magnuses had denied knowledge of Terrice but agreed that they knew Denago and Fantonelli, the two men having been introduced to them by a third party, Mallinari, a New York restaurateur and club owner.

"So far, neither of the Magnuses have been questioned regarding their whereabouts at the time of the M2 bombing, or the Denago-Fantonelli shootings. However, there is additional information. Mr. Hart?"

Hart stood up, notebook in hand. He always presented information in a courtroom manner: by the book.

"I interviewed Peter and Paul Magnus at a club known as The Statue of Eros at 20.05 last night. Also present during the interview were three young women: Patricia Anne Gregory, known as Patti Gregory, Valerie Edith Finch and Caroline Proctor. Gregory has three convictions for soliciting, in June and August 1968, and July 1969. Caroline Proctor is the daughter of Robert William Proctor, who, you will know from the Magnus précis file issued to all officers in this investigation, was the one witness in the Drummond disappearance in 1955. Nothing is known on Finch."

He turned the page of his notebook. "Also present during the interview was Arthur Talisman. This man does not show in CRO, but he is a known associate of the Magnuses, and has been for at least three years. I proceeded to check him out further and got lucky with the Ministry of Defence. Four years ago, in June 1968, Arthur Talisman was a captain in the Royal Engineers. He was a bomb disposal and explosives expert and was cashiered after a court-martial in 1969 following the theft of a large quantity of explosives and detonators. He is known," Hart grimaced, "as Boom-Boom Talisman."

There were subdued chuckles.

"These facts seem particularly interesting in the light of the M2 bombing and this morning's first incident."

Hart sat down. He had been bloody busy, thought Torry with a twinge of guilt, mingled with anxiety. Hart was, like himself, a go-getter: smart, fast, using his intelligence with speed and accuracy. To a great extent, Torry had always felt that Hart was a challenge. Now he was conscious that, for the past few weeks, he had not been operating at his usual full stretch. Susan's breach of their engagement had undoubtedly thrown him, and there was a realisation that he had been only doing those things which were necessary, not going out of his way to follow through and use his initiative. Last night, for instance, he could have employed his time by doing a thorough follow-through on Jenny Peterson.

"What first incident this morning?" Torry muttered as Hart sat down.

"The Statue of Eros got done. Burned out."

"Now they tell me." Torry raised his eyebrows. "First incident?"

"There was another. Tobin, the lad who lived with the Magnuses. Couple of heavies posing as the law used a shotgun on him just before six o'clock."

"Where?"

"The Magnus house in Islington."

"Fatally?"

"Very. Terminal."

Tickerman frowned at their muttering, like a schoolmaster scowling across the classroom, summoning silence. "I'd like to hear from Mr. Wood next," he said loudly, the friendly creases around his mouth and eyes notable by their absence.

Monty Wood was a tall man in his late twenties, with a stomach already swelling to a paunch, the natural result of his throat's being a free and regular channel for many pints of Whitbread BB. In spite of this indulgence, which he regarded as a hobby, he knew his job: bombs, mines, explosive devices; arson and the myriad ways you could start a fire out of malice, or from the desire to screw the insurance companies.

He gave his information in a bland, flat voice, not flippantly, but with a tinge of dry humour.

Wood had been called to The Statue of Eros a little after six in the morning. He gave a brief description of the club's layout and the extensive damage resulting from the fire. The station officer was worried when Wood arrived; there was evidence, and distinct signs, that the fire was the result of some kind of incendiary device.

"The team's still working on it," Wood said, "but there's little doubt that the ignition started in what was the main cloakroom."

He went on to tell them that, when he arrived, he found the station officer having trouble restraining a man, later identified as William Charles Shaw, the owner of the club. Shaw was anxious to gain access to his office on the top floor of the building.

"In the end we decided to facilitate Mr. Shaw, and, eventually I accompanied him, together with Sergeant Draper, up the fire escape in the rear of the building. We pointed out that there was a certain amount of structural damage, but this did not seem to deter Shaw."

They reached the office to find that the walls, carpet and furniture were badly scorched and there was a certain amount of damage which could be attributed to the high-pressure hoses. Shaw took a look around and Wood sensed that he was relieved.

"We were in the office for only a couple of minutes before Shaw wanted to leave. I pointed out that if there were any papers, ledgers, documents or books about which he was worried, this was the time to remove them. He became a little agitated. I told him that we could all see the Chubb Record Protection cabinet and suggested that he should clear it. Shaw told me that he did not have the keys with him, so I pointed out that we had the authority to remove anything of value in the building, following a fire under these circumstances, and that duplicate keys could be provided very quickly." Wood looked at Tickerman, his face a mask.

Tickerman raised his eyes to the ceiling. Several of the other officers smirked and there was a subdued chuckle. Wood was a good technical con man.

He described how Shaw suddenly discovered that he had the keys on him after all and proceeded to open the cabinet and remove its contents, packing an assortment of ledgers and documents into a brief case. Among the contents transferred, Wood estimated that there was about 30,000 pounds in cash.

"A lot of loot to leave in the club," he said.

"Yeah, well, we haven't got around to banking this week."

"Bad policy, Mr. Shaw. Temptation for villains."

Sergeant Draper was still out on the fire escape and did not hear the ensuing exchange.

"You planning to verbal me?" grunted Shaw.

"You're joking."

"Look, if you'll forget what you've seen, I'll make it worth your while. Five grand."

"Five grand what? Pianos?"

"Come off it, Mr. Wood. Here and now, five grand."

"I didn't hear you."

"Five and a half. That's as high as I can go."

"I don't hear you, Mr. Shaw, because I don't take. Not even the lot."

Shaw looked flustered. "Only for what you done. For getting me up here."

"I know. But I never take, and if I did, it wouldn't change anything. Like Lord Bacon, if I did it would be from everyone and it wouldn't alter the course of justice. Forget it, Mr. Shaw."

Wood continued to tell them how he advised Shaw that a lot of questions would have to be asked regarding the fire and its circumstances. Shaw reluctantly agreed to accompany him to Scotland Yard.

"He's not too happy about that," Wood grinned. "We've kept him waiting for quite a time and I should imagine he's getting a shade restless."

Now it was Harvey's turn. He gave the facts of the Tobin shooting in precise, clinical detail. Harriet Magnus, even in deep shock, gave them a very clear account of what had happened.

Shortly after eight, while Harvey was still at the Islington house, Peter and Paul Magnus had returned.

"They were unbelievably distraught," Harvey said, looking like a professional mourner. All the officers present knew of the strange mental and emotional attitudes which the majority of villains had towards death, sudden or expected: a splurge of sorrow, after which the main obsession was a good, showy funeral. A couple of weeks later the whole business would be forgotten and the corpse dismissed as though it had never been a person that they had known, loved or hated.

The Magnuses' initial grief appeared to have been more violent than normal. But then neither of the cousins seemed to have even a nodding acquaintance with stability.

"They actually threw things around the hall in rage," Harvey continued. "Peter broke a mirror with his fist, and they both went completely to pieces, weeping and all that. Like a gypsy funeral."

When Harvey finished his graphic description of the Magnuses' freakout, Tickerman sat, silent, for a moment. "It would appear," he said finally, staring at his desk as though it were a crystal ball, "that we have begun this investigation at a time when crisis has struck the Magnus family." He clamped his mouth over the stem of his pipe, sucking in, then nodded in Torry's direction. "I think you all know Mr. Torry. He'll be operating as my liaison officer, spreading himself over all our areas of investigation."

"Like soft margarine," Torry muttered.

"I'd like you all to give him your utmost co-operation." Tickerman glanced again towards Torry, this time with a friendly nod and the familiar avuncular smile. "I've got another piece of info to add"—shuffling through the papers in front of him—"Derek Torry identified one of the Dorchester victims—Fantonelli, as a New York *mafioso*. We've now had confirmation of this from Washington." He held up a thin sheet of paper, the texture of human skin. "Richard (Ricardo) Fantonelli," he read. "Born, New Jersey 1937. Served three terms of imprisonment for grand larceny. There's also a note about him being married to Rosa Fregga, cousin of Giuseppe Vescari, so-called don of the Vescari family."

Torry became alive, alert. It was as though someone had pressed a computer key. "Alberto Vescari's son?"

"So they say. It mean anything?"

"Could be, sir. I'd like to dig a little."

"Shovel away to your heart's content." Tickerman frowned as he said it; then, recovering his usual blandness, "Okay. But there're other things to be done. I think two of our Fraud Squad colleagues should return to the Yard with Monty Wood: friend Shaw will be getting a little restless. Mr. Hart, I'd like you to go back to Islington with Mr. Harvey, especially as you've talked to the Magnuses recently."

Hart pulled a wry face. "Can I just try to finish off that likeness first?"

"If you can knock it off quickly."

"We've almost got it."

"All right. Go to. And the rest of you be about your business. Derek?" He turned towards Torry. "I'd like a word."

When they were alone, Tickerman frowned. Torry noticed that there were lines of strain around his eyes. "This Vescari family, Derek? What d'you make of it?"

"Could be a bit of freelance, but I don't like the smell. You remember there were indications that the old man, Alberto Vescari was behind the Wexton business in '69?"

Tickerman nodded. "The one who got away . . . Tony . . . ?" His brow creased again as he dredged his memory.

"Champion. Tony Champion. Yes, he was one of Vescari's men. But a lot has happened since then. The old man's dead and his son's ambitious." Torry sucked in on his teeth. "It's all nasty. A large quantity of heroin; elimination of a witness together with four coppers; the two Americans at the Dorchester; The Statue of Eros; then Tobin blasted at the Magnus home. It stinks, Tick, and you don't have to be an expert in Anglo-American crime to work out a ground plan."

Tickerman gave a long grunt. "I often think it would be better if our transatlantic friends took over. At least there would be less chance of innocent bystanders being . . ."

Torry whipped around, his face hard. "That's a load of untreated sewage. You've been conned by too many half-baked articles by mafia buffs. What do you think those people are? The same as our bloody villains, except that they're organised on family lines, and the families are slipping. It's not cosy, Tick, and you bloody know it. What about the heroin for a start? A huge injection of shit on the market, obtainable, and how many innocent victims get hooked? Then what about the club owners? The toms? The guys trying to make an honest living out of delicatessens—I should know, my old man ran a delicatessen, my brother runs it now. And the coffee bars? The betting shops? The loans without security? I know some of those people are dubious characters, but some aren't and the rain falls upon the just as well as the unjust. Do you really believe the gentlemen in the silk suits really care whom they hit? Not a chance, Tick. No way."

"How do you read this scene then?" Tickerman did not even try to argue.

"How the hell does anyone read it? I don't have a crystal ball tuned in on the Magnuses or the Vescaris. But I can make educated guesses, like you can, and my instinct tells me we're in for horror, that those two sets of villains are inextricably mixed. I also know that we're at fault, Ticker. The Magnuses should have been nailed long ago."

"We have the facts. How do you link them?"

Torry slumped into a chair, the breath exhaling from his body in a weary sigh. "Oh, Tick, you've been in the job longer than me."

"But your experience of the States . . ."

"I would guess the Magnuses did a deal with the Vescaris. A large supply of heroin as starters. The Magnuses would handle the import facilities and distribution, with a large cut to the Vescaris, probably giving the Vescaris a foothold into the little Magnus empire."

"And it went wrong."

"Very wrong. The M2 thing was more Magnus style than the others. The Sicilians would have been more subtle, they would have cut Terrice off from the herd and then taken him. But it did the trick for Peter and Paul. I've no doubt that Terrice knew exactly who he worked for and had to be hit."

Tickerman clicked his tongue. "Stage two, stop me if I'm adrift. Denago and Fantonelli could be looking after the family interests, the Vescari interests, and they cut up rough. The Magnuses have been relatively big fish in a moderate-sized pond for a long time. Could be they're suffering from criminal *folie de grandeur*. They just didn't know what they were taking on."

"Or didn't want to know." Torry gave a weak grin. "They know now."

"One would have thought so. Their best club wrecked; young Tobin, the apple of their eyes, wiped out, right in the family stronghold. That's classic, almost a ritual. If the cousins don't get the message now, there's little anyone can do with them: unless we untangle it and put them away."

"Leaving the field clear for the brotherhood?"

"If that's what they want." Torry's eyes clouded with worry. "You do realise what we'd be up against if they got a real foot inside the door?"

Tickerman nodded slowly, as though the truth was a lead weight in his head. "I've got a rough idea."

"We'd be up to our necks. They'd do a blanket job, Ticker. Maybe we've got a five per cent count of rotten apples in the Met basket at this moment, but if the family men moved in that percentage would inevitably rise: they offer real payola you know, not the kind of thing the villains here hand out"—he paused, lifting his eyebrows—"or us for that matter. All the borderline coppers out to make a bit on the side would swing overnight. Those people sow corruption like a flu epidemic." He got to his feet. "Can I check out the Vescaris?"

"Of course. You've got your contacts, no doubt—or are you going to work through normal channels?"

"A little of both, I guess."

"Okay, but I'd still like you to sit in while they're talking to Shaw."

"Not the cousins?"

"I'd rather you held off them for a while. Let Hart and Harvey work them over, then we can go in and do the old routine." Tickerman grinned.

"The soft-shoe shuffle."

"The old one-two."

Torry smiled back at his superior: a confident, self-satisfied look. He opened his mouth to reply, but there was a sharp rap at the door and Hart entered. He was carrying an Identikit frame, the plastic sheets held in place with metal clips.

Hart also had a confident look. "Got it, sir." He placed the frame on Tickerman's desk.

Torry looked down at the composite picture in the Identikit frame, his jaw dropping as he took in the face, lean with strong cheekbones, firm jawline and alert eyes under thick brows.

"What's this?"

Hart flicked his eyes away towards Tickerman, then back to

Torry. "I thought I recognised him from somewhere. He was going into The Statue of Eros as I was leaving last night. After I'd seen the cousins."

"You've met him." Torry's voice was hard. "So've I; and I knew of him before then. He used to call himself Tony Champion. We came up against him during the Wexton business. Now do you recall?"

"Christ."

"We had half the coppers in the Met after him and he still got away." He turned back to Tickerman. "That just about clinches it. Champion's definitely one of them."

Tickerman remained silent for half a minute, then picked up the telephone to give orders for discreet checks to be made: airports, port authorities and hotels, starting at the major London places and moving downwards.

Torry made a couple of quick calls and then left for Scotland Yard to watch Monty Wood and the Fraud boys having a go at Shaw.

The hoardings and posters were already out, and the first editions of both evening papers carried stories of the explosion and resulting fire at The Statue, and Tobin's killing in Islington. The two events were making the politics, wars, rebellions, strikes and similar hassles of life take a back seat. GANGLAND VIOLENCE IN LONDON? one editor had presumed to ask in his headline, yet the city went on living as though nothing had happened.

Torry was only too aware of the threat. The activities of the Magnuses, and those like them, were bad enough, but if the cousins had even partially opened the door to one of the families, the result might do untold harm. Worse, Torry suspected that Peter and Paul Magnus had half pulled the door open and then shut it firmly in the faces of the American syndicate . . . if they had done that, then the retribution could be horrifying.

A wave of depression splashed through Torry's mind, and, as if in answer, the first drops of heavy rain splattered onto the car's windshield.

William Shaw, the Statue Man, was also in a deep depression. He was edgy, tired and very conscious that his confidence had

94

spiralled down from a high, safe altitude to almost ground level. Fear was his main motivation: fear of the police officers who had just finished interrogating him, and another, more intrinsic, fear of Peter and Paul Magnus.

They had kept him waiting for an interminable time at Scotland Yard, in a room bland with barren impersonality, as though only the socially dead had passed through it leaving no mark or trace on the clean walls, the unmarked table and the pair of cheap chairs. In spite of this, Shaw was able to keep up the outward appearance of indifference, even when the detective inspector called Wood—the one who had forced him to open the safe in the gutted office—returned with two colleagues whose eyes betrayed the gimlet and grave manner of financial meddlers.

It was the advent of this pair which caused William Shaw the greatest discomfort. He knew the limits and powers of people like the detective inspector, but the other pair was a different thing, when they looked at you it was as though they peered right into the rows of figures, the hidden bundles of cash, the payoffs, assets, totals which people like Shaw had locked safe and secure in his head. The two coppers with Wood knew the way to unlock that kind of information, and the very knowledge of that ability created crawling worms of panic within the Statue Man's mind.

Since his arrival at the Yard, Shaw had had no illusions about the fact that he was being kept incommunicado. His brief case sat on the table in front of him and there was a uniformed constable with him all the time. Another officer came in from time to time, with coffee and, later, breakfast: dry bacon and a fried egg, the yoke of which was hard and rubbery.

The Statue Man did not even bother to ask if he could call his solicitor. There was no point. They had made it plain that there was no question of charges being preferred. They were simply anxious to find out who might have activated the incendiary outrage.

The name of the game was suavity. Everyone was pleasant, even sympathetic about the club. In the midst of even the darkest fears, with his mental safety catch on, the Statue Man found momentary flickers of calm, lulled into false safety by the outward friendliness of the three coppers. After all, his subconscious seemed to argue, he had to call the fire service, knowing that the fuzz would be hard behind. As for the fuzz, they could not hold it against him for calling the cousins; but he could not call them again from the nick, he was in enough trouble already, so that would only be inviting trouble of the greatest magnitude.

Wood played the game well, an expert matched only by the Statue Man's own expertise, going over all the possible permutations—likely enemies, business rivals; larding his questions with remarks like—"Mr. Shaw we're all grown men, if you've been paying protection and got behind, then it's far better to tell us now. After all, we are aware of what goes on in the clubland." A smile which would have seduced a nun.

The Statue Man denied any knowledge of protection or enforcement, bolstering his position with a shrug and—"I have no business rivals who would do that kind of thing. Of course we all have rivals, but it is a friendly business. The Sunday newspapers and television soap operas like to glamorise, and it does help custom. People like to believe they are being very daring, going into places which are thick with thieves, peopled by villains."

"Anybody owe you large sums? Gaming debts?"

"Mr. Wood, we're very careful about credit. We do know our customers. Anyone we don't know: no credit. The law is difficult enough, without making it harder."

The question-and-answer technique went on for the best part of an hour; the interrogation quiet, respectful and circular. Towards the end, another plainclothesman joined them: tall, slim but with broad muscular shoulders and a hard face: a man who dressed with flair; a man with style, even in the way he sat listening to the verbal Ping-Pong.

The two men who had accompanied Wood remained silent throughout the long dialogue. It was only when it became apparent that the Statue Man was going to be as helpful as a cretinous deaf mute that the older of the Fraud Squad officers spoke.

"Mr. Shaw"—the tone was friendly, the speaker cool, unruffled—"we have a problem."

In spite of the situation, the Statue Man stayed loose. "Problems, schmoblems." He grinned.

"A complex of problems, and a problem of some complexity."

Shaw's eyes twitched. "Yes," he said as though he did not believe himself.

The younger Fraud man, who must have been all of twenty-six, nodded towards the brief case. "That's our problem, Mr. Shaw."

Shaw did not reply.

"We have Mr. Wood's statement that you tried to straighten him."

"I don't know what you're talking about."

"Oh, I think you do." The elder, smiling as he carefully filled his pipe. "You offered Mr. Wood some five and a half thousand pounds up in The Statue of Eros."

"Me? Bollocks."

"That's what Mr. Wood will say in court. And there is another witness."

"Rubbish. What'd I want to offer Mr. Wood that kind of bread for?"

"Precisely. That's exactly what's in question."

"But I never . . ."

Wood slowly unwound from his chair. "You're a gifted liar, chum. Who's the judge going to believe? You, or me and my sergeant?"

Shaw paused; enough time to sweep his eyes around the four men. "Bloody law. You've got it fixed, haven't you? You fix the bleeding judges."

"We don't, as it happens," the younger Fraud Squad man said coolly. "But whatever's in that brief case has been recovered from the scene of a crime—the crime being one of arson by explosives. We are therefore within our rights to seize the documents in that case."

"That's my property." The Statue Man made a move as if to clasp the brief case to his bosom like a mother protecting her child.

"That would have to be decided, in or out of court." Wood grinned, it was a kind of leer, distinctly unpleasant.

"We'll give you a receipt." The young Fraud man was taking a pad of forms from his inside pocket.

"But it's mine."

"We think it's really someone else's." It was the first time the late arrival had said anything. They all turned to look at him. Shaw reflected briefly that this one was hard. Hard as stressed concrete. "So's you don't forget, Mr. Shaw, my name's Torry. Detective Chief Inspector Torry. And I don't believe for one moment that the contents of that brief case belong to you. I think they belong to a pair of gentlemen who spend a great deal of time in the club which you own and manage—on paper. I think the gear in there belongs to Peter and Paul Magnus, and you've got two chances: either we take the brief case and its contents and let you go; or we take photostats of the documents inside, and a tally of the cash, and you talk. After you've talked your beautiful head off and signed a nice statement, we let you out of here with the brief case intact."

Shaw was visibly sweating.

"If we keep the stuff," Torry continued, "you will walk out of here into considerable sweat. Doing it the second way, the cousins get their money and the documents. We get evidence, and you have nothing to fear until we tie the whole matter up with pink ribbon and sealing wax. At that time you will be given as much protection as you will need. You will also be expected to stand up in court and tell the truth." He looked calmly at his watch. "The offer is limited. Sixty seconds."

William Shaw's mind rotated in turmoil. It was a moment of truth. A time for decisions, and decisions were not Shaw's strong point at the moment. He was like a boxer, punch drunk, on the ropes, his guard down, open and waiting for the final blow to fall.

The permutations clicked slowly through his head. If he walked out without the brief case he would be dead within hours, and, if not dead at least very badly injured. If he did what the coppers wanted, things could still get sticky. Could he remain cool with the cousins? You never really knew with them. They had people on the inside. They always seemed to know everything. How long before the word got to them? A day? A week? A month? Whichever way you looked at it, talking seemed to give him a little more time. Space to split perhaps?

The Statue Man seemed to move in slow motion, raising his head and nodding. "I ain't got no option have I? I got to do it your way."

"That would appear to be the most sensible decision." The elder Fraud man had lit his pipe and now sucked on it gently.

"How long's it going to take?" The other insects of panic were fluttering in the Statue Man's entrails now. He had already been at the Yard for a long time. If he had any knowledge of the habits and behaviour of the cousins, he was certain that they had some-one in the vicinity, watching, waiting. At least they would know that he had been there for a long time and another three or four hours would decrease his chances.

"It depends what's in that," Wood pointed at the brief case, "and how much you've got to tell us."

In the event it took just over two hours. The police left with smiles and satisfaction. The Statue Man left with the insects, snakes and creeping things operating and squirming fast, deep in his guts, but with the brief case clutched in his hand.

He crossed Broadway, going towards Caxton Street, head flick-ing back and eyes alert, looking for the welcoming sign of an un-occupied cab. He reached Caxton and began to walk hurriedly in the direction of Buckingham Gate. Halfway there he became con-scious of the maroon Hillman. It came sliding up, pacing his step, the window going down and a familiar voice calling to him. "Here, Bill. Peter and Paul want a word."

The Dumper's face was framed in the window, grinning, and Shaw's hand became cold and clammy on the brief-case handle.

Torry left the Yard with the two Fraud men and Monty Wood, pleased with what he had seen and heard. The other three ap-peared to be elated, like young lads who had won a needle match. Yet in spite of his own satisfaction, there was a part of Torry's mind which said that they would never get the Statue Man into court, let alone into a witness box.

But at least they now had more bullets to work with. The pho-tostats, a kind of accounting for the thirty-odd grand, and a state-ment legally signed which gave them a definite tie-in between the Magnuses and The Statue of Eros; firm evidence of big money being filtered off, and one or two names, people upon whom they could eventually lean.

It was almost midday before they got back to the Kingsway offices, and Sergeant Dumphy was ready for Torry with a situation report.

Dumphy would never change; tall, angular, obsessively ordered in his work and manner, an avid reader of the old who-done-it detective fiction, and a compulsive talker.

"They've traced Chassen, sir." He opened up like a light machine gun. "Or Champion, or whatever he calls himself. He's at the Mayfair Hotel but Mr. Tickerman has only ordered surveillance and an application has gone to the Home Office for a tap on his room telephone."

Torry slumped into his chair. "The hotel will love that," he muttered. He had a lot to do: many telephone calls to make, some to the United States. The wheels needed oiling. His whole manner should have suggested that whatever information Dumphy had could really wait. But the prematurely ageing man did not pause.

"They have it all tied up, I understand. There's another message for you as well, Mr. Torry." He looked almost coy. "I'm not sure if it's personal or . . . It was passed on from the Yard." For once Dumphy did not blurt it out, but pushed a message slip across the desk. It was written in the sergeant's round, careful hand.

Message received at 10.27. For Detective Chief Inspector Torry. Miss Peterson telephoned to say that she wishes to talk to Mr. Torry, urgently. Would you call her.

There followed what Torry recognised as her work number where she would be available until five-thirty. After seven she had listed her home number.

Torry thought for a moment. Deliberating on which should take precedence, placing the calls to Washington and New York, beginning the series of local calls, listed carefully in his head, or telephoning Jenny Peterson.

It took a couple of seconds, and with the decision came his old confidence. He lifted the receiver and booked two calls to Washington and one to New York. They would come through at around four in the afternoon. Then, before starting anything else, he dialled Jenny Peterson's work number.

"You've just missed her," the disembodied female voice told him. "She's just this minute gone out to lunch, can I give her a message?"

"Just tell her that Derek Torry called. No, she can't call me back, I'm not at the number she has. I'll call her later in the day, or this evening."

He could not understand the well of disappointment which opened up inside him. It was a strange confusion, an attraction which he was aware of, yet could not comprehend the awareness, his mind filling with a mixture of old habits—the sweet scent of incense, the sacred words over the bread and wine, the file of sins slipping from his guilty lips and into the priest's ear, and the absolution.

Sue, and that telephone call in the night which clutched at his loins and repelled him at one and the same time. It was that call which was the beginning of the end. *Derek, for Christ's sake. We're going to be married. I don't understand you. I just know that I want you. I love you. I want to come over. I want to sleep with you. Darling please understand. I want to feel you in me. Derek, please let me come over, or say that we'll get married tomorrow, or next week.*

Sue, love, you're going to be my bride. I have respect for you.

As he said it, Torry realised that the respect had gone with her words in the wakened silence of the night. It was the beginning of the end, and as illogical and stupid as any human reaction could have been, born out of a clinging to the past, to old ways alive only in guilt and memories; deep-seated superstitions which had their roots in childhood. The old priest telling the group of flushed and embarrassed boys about the ways of men and women and how marriage was a sacred sacrament: all reinforced in a kind of casuistry by his father.

The gentle, predictable Michael Torrini, Torry's Italian father, who, as a young man had come to England from Riccione; leaving the sun-splashed jumbled houses and the hours told by the off-key bell in the stucco campanile, the minutes washed by the Adriatic, into the alien world of rain, cold and thick fogs, to work in his uncle's delicatessen, eventually have his own and marry Florence Tibbits—the Italian and the cockney.

"Derek," his father had said before the boy left for America, an evacuee from Hitler. "Derek" (Florence had insisted on English names for her three sons) "women are there for a man to lose himself in, and that is a sin. But do not sin with your bride, for that only brings contempt. It banishes the respect between man and wife."

On the night after Susan's lonely phone call, Torry had gone out from the Cromwell Road and lost himself in a whore who did not charge him for her special services because he had once nicked her under the Street Offences Act. Only once and never again. She was there whenever he needed that kind of comfort and could not get it elsewhere.

The disturbance in the back of Torry's mind now concerned the lonely Jenny Peterson.

(*But you spent time together. You went steady. We screwed steady.*)

Jenny Peterson. The hand and the long slim fingers clawing through her hair. The Greek puzzle ring. Why should this piece of feminine driftwood disturb Torry now?

He shook his head and got down to the matters in hand. The telephone calls. Exacting, careful, detailed, probing for information: tickling his private sources in London for small facts, anything, about contacts with a man called Chassen, men known as Denago, Fantonelli, Mallinari, Shaw, Peter and Paul Magnus, Talisman. In each conversation Torry inserted the name Vescari, his antennae ready to pick up any change of manner, alteration of tone. One really needed to be face to face to get a full reaction, but time was short. Physical confrontation would have meant three or four days and nights.

After each call, he made notes, meticulous, ready to be typed up for his report, which he would, inevitably have to deliver to Tickerman on the following morning. When the thought of doing the report flashed in and out of his mind, Torry knew that it also entailed writing up this morning's session with Shaw. The details would be in the reports made by Wood and the two Fraud men, but Tickerman would want his version and opinion.

Just after three, Tickerman, Wood and Hart came in, heading towards Torry's desk.

"They've picked up Talisman," announced Ticker.

Torry smiled; a bitter, pleased humour. "You'll be expecting a report then."

Wood groaned, creasing his brow.

"He's at the Yard. You want to come along?"

102

Ticker was obviously playing it very close. No suspects were being brought to the Kingsway building. Torry briefly reflected that even with those precautions the Magnuses would almost certainly know about Kingsway and the special operation within a matter of days.

"Sure." Torry pushed back his chair. Faced with the alternatives of action or paperwork, he would always choose action. Routine was the bulk of the job, but it always remained a drag. "Can you give me a couple of minutes?"

Tickerman nodded assent and shepherded the others towards the duty desk at the far end of the room, tactful in all things.

Torry tried Jenny Peterson's number again and was passed along from switchboard to office and, finally, to the girl.

"I had a message," he said, after telling her who he was, though he was sure she recognised his voice.

"Oh, thank you for ringing. I've remembered something, just a small thing, but you said . . . anything."

"Yes?"

"Well, I can't really. . . ." An uneasy pause.

"You can't talk?"

"Difficult."

"When can I see you then?"

"I thought you'd never ask."

He did not imagine the breathlessness. "You free tonight?"

"I'm free any night."

"Okay. I don't know what time I'll be through, but I'll call you as soon as I can."

"Where will you take me?"

"Too proud for fish and chips, eh?"

"Let me put it another way. How do you like your women to dress?"

"I don't have any women, and in my experience they dress to please themselves, and I thought this was business."

"Don't you ever combine business with pleasure, Inspector Torry?"

"Detective Chief Inspector. I got promoted."

"Then there's something to celebrate. Can I call you Chief Inspector or do you prefer Derek?"

"Mmm." A noncommittal grunt.

"I see. You don't trade first names on duty."

"Derek . . . Jenny." He felt the unfamiliar nervous tweak in his stomach. An intimation? "Wear something sleek and sexy." Almost regretting it, then shrugging it off with a grin which she could not see in her smart office among the literary marvels.

"That's what I like to hear. Call me when you've finished, I have to dash."

He cradled the receiver, picked up his notebook and pen, walked over to the switchboard and gave instructions for the American calls to be transferred to the Yard. He would give them an extension number as soon as he arrived.

Peter Magnus was thinking about the black girl they called April. He was vaguely conscious of his brother's voice, but his mind was full of the girl, black and supple, undulating, moving like an animal, panting and filmed with sweat. He could even hear her, the gasps of orgasmic pleasure as she arched her back.

"Isn't that right Pete? PETE! Isn't that right?"

Paul Magnus was shouting at his cousin across the room, his face set and the eyes hard and bright as rocks.

They were in the manager's office on the second floor of The Graven Image which was, now The Statue of Eros had been gutted, the cousins' best property.

The Graven Image was slightly smaller than The Statue of Eros, but it was situated in the Mayfair area, and while it did not have the same kind of casual, large, flowing membership, its clientele tended to be wealthier and more constant.

What The Graven Image lacked in size it certainly made up in amenities: a considerably plush line in gaming rooms on the ground floor, and a large restaurant, bar and grill on the first floor, where the diners were titillated, thrice nightly, with a floor show of unrelieved eroticism.

It was the floor show which had set Peter off into his randy reverie, Paul having given instructions for the four black strippers to be provided with a new set of parallel bars (their own had been destroyed at The Statue of Eros) and the act moved into The Graven Image that night. "I'm not having them sitting around airing their drawers and collecting salary for nothing." Paul knew that the quartet was just about the hottest strip act in town, and he was not a man who liked to see money hanging around doing nothing for him.

Peter Magnus pulled his mind back to matters in hand, though he was still conscious of the pulsing in his loins.

The room appeared to be full of people: Paul behind the desk with Rube Rubenstein, the "owner-manager" of The Graven Image on his right. On the other side of the desk, the Statue Man was on a straight-backed chair, his posture controlled, spine like a ramrod, but his face the grey texture of a dead codfish. There was a brief case on the desk and the Statue Man constantly kept looking at it, sly little flicks of the eyes, as though it were a dangerous animal.

On the far side of the room, Dumper Doffman lounged against the wall, a thick-set man of around forty, who looked as though the bulk of his life had been spent in gymnasiums—successfully, because his clothes had the mark of taste and style, the patina of a senior executive; well groomed and set up. It was only when one looked hard at the Dumper that you could detect something not quite right, something that put him in a different category, something indefinable which showed around the man's eyes and at the corners of his mouth; in the way he gestured and moved. It had a great deal to do with the deep and dark things that were the root basis for his motive forces. A skilled psychiatrist attuned to personality vibrations might have put his finger on it; most people reacted with a sense of fear, of evil, a foreboding in the presence of the man.

At the moment that Peter Magnus looked up, the Dumper was smiling, as though he held some secret amusement which could not be shared by others. As he smiled, his eyes never left the Statue Man.

With the Dumper were three other men, all large, heavily built, all loungers, propping themselves against the wall after the manner of street-corner louts.

"Isn't that right?" Paul Magnus thumped the desk.

"Isn't what right, Paul?"

"Jesus, you been asleep or something?"

Peter Magnus grinned sheepishly. "Or something, Yeah."

"Bloody daydreaming about birds again. You'll go sodding blind, Pete, blind as a stone angel."

One of the men leaning against the wall laughed loudly.

"Or get hairs on your palm." Paul liked receptive audiences. "What I said was that the responsibility for what happened at the Statue lies with the Statue Man here."

"Of course. Stands to reason."

Bill Shaw the Statue Man, opened his mouth, then closed it again, then went through the process for a second time. "Paul, I can't have my eyes everywhere. And at least I got all the books, and the loot, out."

"Still your responsibility, son." Paul knew the right amount of fear he could engender with a look or the casual manner in which he spoke. "We know some bastard left a parcel in the cloakroom and didn't take it away when he left the club."

"Well, the girl should have brought it to my attention, shouldn't she?" The Statue Man was desperately attempting to defend himself without drawing undue attention to the edgy guilt, which scratched at his mind. Every second he spent in the Magnuses' company took another protective layer off his conscience and, by this time, he had begun to think the cousins could see into the very corners of his brain.

"Then why didn't she?" Peter Magnus was entering into the spirit of things now. "Why didn't she bloody come to you?"

"Only one of two answers there." It was the first time the Dumper had spoken, his voice quiet with soft menace. "She didn't report it to you because either she was too afraid of you or not frightened enough. I reckon you run a bloody soft outfit, Bill. Too bloody kind and nice with them girls."

"You got to be reasonable to the girls to keep 'em there." The Statue Man spread his hands. "Doesn't do to push them around. Not these days."

"You've been proved wrong, haven't you, Bill?" Paul again, leaning over the desk. "It's a standing rule in all the clubs, bloody elementary security. Anything left in the cloakroom when the club closes has to be brought to the attention of the manager. This girl didn't bother, which means she's got careless, which, in turn means she doesn't worry about her job or her boss. You haven't been jumping hard enough, Bill."

"Okay, then I'll give her the push."

"You should be so lucky. Discipline is what the birds need, and by Christ that one's going to get some discipline. Old-fashioned bloody discipline. But it still goes down to you, Bill. The whole catastrophe. And while we're at it, you spent one hell of a time with the law."

"That wasn't my fault." As he said it, William Shaw knew his voice was wrong. It signalled concern, guilt.

"Nobody said it was your fault, Bill. I just said that you spent a bloody long time with them." Paul's smile was that of a rapist. "Why, Bill? Why?"

"Because they kept me hangin' about, didn't they?"

"You tell me."

"Well, I told you they didn't want me to go up to the office in the first place. They said the fire had caused structural faults. Then after I come down they said they had to ask questions. Naturally I told them to ask away, but they said they had to ask down the nick."

"But it wasn't the bleedin' nick was it? It was down the Yard."

"I didn't know that until they got me in their motor. Then the poncy one who had me . . ."

"His name?"

"Wood. A DI. Monty one of them called him. Monty Wood."

Paul looked across at the Dumper. "I want his form today."

The Dumper nodded, squinting down and making a note on a cigarette packet. It was a habit, a reflex through the years. Once the Dumper had written a name, an address, or a number, he could destroy the paper, or, more usual, a cigarette packet, the writing indelible on his memory.

"Wood's all right." Shaw was too quick with the character reference, and he knew it.

"You mean he's been straightened?" Peter asked softly.

"No need." Again too fast. "He was just doing his job. Even apologised for keeping me waiting so long. Got called away to some conference when they got me to the Yard. They even give me breakfast."

"V. bloody I.P.," hissed the Dumper.

"You're bloody stupid, Dumper." Shaw sounded angry, the irritation laced with fear. "He only asked the obvious. What any copper would ask. If I had enemies in the trade, stuff like that. He asked about the staff. Anyone with a grudge."

"A grudge?" Paul spat out. "Fucking heavy grudge, planting a bomb and burning the place out. So what you tell him, Statue?"

"The obvious, Paul. Christ, what d'you think I'd tell him? That Pete and Paul Magnus have got some Yank heavy mob up their tails?"

"I wouldn't know, Statue. I do know that you were there a bloody long time and I don't know what you was talking about. I'm pretty bloody certain you wasn't talking about the weather, or who was going to win the pools, or how little Cinderella lost the glass slipper. The law knows that Cinders really lost her knickers as well. They don't need those kind of stories."

Another loud laugh from one of the heavies against the wall.

Paul leaned back and lit another cigarette. "I want to know what he asked about the stuff in that brief case."

"Nothing. Nobody asked nothing about that. They were interested in the bomb and the Statue being done over."

"They mention us?"

"Not a peep."

"There wasn't a bit of kid law there called Hart, by any chance?" Peter's lips were wet, unpleasant.

"What, the one who come up to see you last night?"

"Hart. The one who was there."

"There was this DI called Wood and a couple of other coppers. No names, but Hart wasn't there."

"And they didn't look inside the case?"

"The case wasn't mentioned. You weren't mentioned."

"Well, we'll see." Paul reached out and touched the brief case. "Once Felix has gone over the stuff in there."

Felix was the cousins' accountant. A young, sharp man, with shoulder-length hair, trendy suits and a brain which worked like a computer. His style was not that of most of the men who worked for the Magnuses, but both Peter and Paul trusted him with good reason. He hid assets like a squirrel hoarding nuts, and had an ability to cover up sources of income in a way that would have filled a camouflage expert with covetousness.

The Statue Man was gripped with an even more profound terror when Paul mentioned Felix, because the accountant, he knew, had the same skills as the pair of coppers who had been with Wood at the interview. For all William Shaw could tell, Felix might even be able to ascertain that the documents, now snug in the brief case, had been run through a photocopying machine.

"You look dead unhappy, Bill." Peter spoke, but the Statue Man knew that they were all giving him the hard eye.

"'Course I'm bloody unhappy. I been pissed around by Old Bill, the club's been wrecked, and I've been hanging onto bloody books, papers and loot which could get us all landed in the nick, send us to the island, no doubt."

"Not if you didn't go copper, or let them have a look at it." Dumper still had the smile on his face.

"Come on, Dumper," Paul Magnus grinned, an obvious note of sarcasm in his voice. "You wouldn't suspect our old mate the Statue Man to go copper on us, would you?"

"I'd suspect me own grandmother of talking to the law if she was in the nick as long as the Statue Man here. I never underestimate the law, Paul, they've got their ways. If the law wanted to, it'd get juice out of a bleedin' brick."

"Maybe. Anyhow, Felix'll tell us. In the meantime, let's have the name of this girl that was on duty in the cloakroom last night, Bill."

The Statue Man told them about Marylin Hughes. He also gave her description, though he did not have her address. He had not bothered to remove the employees' files from the office at The Statue of Eros.

Paul looked across at the Dumper who, in turn, nodded to one of the heavy young men. The man detached himself from the wall and went out without a word.

He had been gone for only a minute or so when there was a knock at the door, heralding the arrival of Crippled Eric. Crippled Eric acted as a part-time manager, a locum when other managers were on holiday, or ill, or in trouble. He was also a kind of liaison officer for the cousins, and he was not really a cripple, though he walked with a pronounced limp inherited from a run-in with muscle imported from Newcastle three or four years before, when a gang from the other side of the river had got a touch of folie de grandeur and made an abortive attempt to pressurise the cousins' manor.

Crippled Eric was short and looked insignificant. He also usually looked happy. Apart from his work for the cousins, his main preoccupation was pulling birds, which, in his kind of business, was relatively simple, hence the normally happy expression. Today he looked far from happy. Like the Statue Man, and most of those who knew the cousins well, Crippled Eric was aware that bringing bad news to Peter and Paul was about as healthy as sleeping with a typhoid carrier.

Crippled Eric came with the news that Boom-Boom Talisman had got himself nicked in humiliating circumstances. At the moment when the law had walked into the hotel bedroom in which Boom-Boom was staying, the unfortunate Talisman had been performing unusual, if most satisfying, sexual offices upon the person of Patti Gregory. Both of them had been taken off to the Notting Hill nick where they now awaited the arrival of officers from C1.

Tickerman, Torry and Hart had discussed strategy in the car on the way over to Notting Hill. It was strange, Tickerman said, that they should be bringing Talisman into the particular area where Terrice had lived.

It was agreed that Hart should open the interrogation, linking it to his meeting with the cousins and Talisman at The Statue of Eros on the previous evening, and making it appear that they were interested in Talisman because of the explosion and fire at the club.

Torry was to talk to the girl, a task which he did not altogether relish, but Tickerman had agreed to his being in on at least the first part of the Talisman interrogation to start with.

Sitting in the small interrogation room, with a uniformed constable standing by the door, Boom-Boom Talisman looked as happy as a man who has just lost his pension. He put on a bold front when he recognised Hart.

"I might get some sense now," he said, rising. "Sergeant, we met last night I think. I demand to know why my fiancée and I have been brought . . ."

"I've come up in the world since last night." Hart walked coolly over to the table and sat down opposite Talisman, indicating with a brisk wave that he should be seated again. "You're now talking to Detective Inspector Hart. These other gentlemen are Detective Chief Superintendent Tickerman and Detective Chief Inspector Torry, and if Patricia Anne Gregory, known as Patti Gregory, is your fiancée, then I'm sorry for you, she's a tom."

Talisman raised his eyebrows as if to indicate that he did not understand. Tickerman sighed, loudly.

"A tom, Mr. Talisman," rumbled Tickerman. "A brass, a whore, a common prostitute. She's on the game, lad. Or she was anyway."

"I resent the implic——"

"Resent away." It was Torry's turn. "Maybe she doesn't advertise in newsagents' windows anymore, but she's still at it, for friends of the Magnuses, no doubt. Miss Gregory is the original lady who only does it for friends and has very few enemies."

Hart looked across slyly. "I'd always thought that particular method was just talk. I didn't think it was possible until the sergeant who copped you gave me a vivid description."

Talisman looked furious. "I was told we were needed to help you in your enquiries. Nobody has yet bothered to tell me the nature of those enquiries." He was still wearing the dark blue business suit which Hart had seen him in on the previous evening. It had been a heavy night for Talisman, Hart reflected, the man looked a lot older now. Booze with the Magnuses at The Statue of Eros and then back to the hotel with Patti Gregory in the small hours. It was early afternoon when they had been located, still in bed. Beddie-bye with Miss Gregory could obviously take its toll.

"You are Arthur Talisman?" Hart became very official.

"I am."

"In February 1969 you were court-martialled at Aldershot on a charge of illegally disposing of explosives and explosive mechanisms in your care?"

"I pleaded not guilty."

"At that time you held the commissioned rank of captain in the Royal Engineers?"

"The army was my career, yes. I was a captain at that time."

"You were found guilty and cashiered."

"I did not dispose of the items listed against me, but the court martial found me guilty. Yes, I was cashiered."

"You are a known associate of Peter Magnus and Paul Magnus?"

"I was with them last night at the club, yes. But I wouldn't say I was an associate."

"What would you say then?"

"Well, I knew them, I know them."

"How well?"

"I see them once in a while."

"Once in a while? What does that mean? Once a year? Once a week?"

"From time to time."

"You know them well enough to be invited to The Statue of Eros for a booze up, some nosh and a bit of grumble laid on for you, eh?"

"They asked me out last night. Me and Miss Gregory."

"Your affianced," Torry muttered loudly enough for Talisman to hear.

"I would suggest to you," Hart continued, still in a steady, official flow, "that you know Peter and Paul Magnus very well indeed. I would even suggest that you see them more than regularly. I would suggest that you spend a great deal of time with them. Over the past four years you have spent many happy hours with them."

"All right, I see them quite a bit."

"You are an explosives expert, Mr. Talisman."

"I was trained to handle explosives in the army, yes."

"Mr. Talisman"—From Tickerman—"Mr. Hart was making a statement. He said that you are an explosives expert. True or false?"

"I was trained to handle explosives in the army." Talisman's voice reflected the stubborn expression on his face.

"Do yourself a favour," Hart leaned back. "We've looked at your army record. You were a trained and skilled demolition officer. You know about explosives and explosive devices; you can make bombs of all kinds, you can render explosive devices harmless; you can demolish anything from a stray, unstable grenade to a large building. We know. You were very good. It says so on your record."

Talisman nodded slowly. "Okay, so I used to be good with explosives. Four years is a long time to be away from it, I don't know if I'm any good now."

"You ever get a yen to practise?" asked Tickerman.

"In the civilian world you don't practise with explosives."

"Somebody did." Torry, terse and clipped.

"The bombing of that police car? Yes, Mr. Hart mentioned that last night." Talisman seemed remarkably steady.

"I wasn't thinking of that specifically. You seen a newspaper or heard the radio today?"

"We slept late."

"Oh yes, I'd forgotten. You were in the company of Peter Magnus, Paul Magnus, Patricia Anne Gregory, Valerie Finch and Caroline Proctor until what time last night, or I should say, this morning?"

"About midnight, a little later, perhaps. Twelve-thirty."

"And you were in The Statue of Eros the whole time?"

"Until we left, yes. Can you tell me why you're . . . ?"

"Just answer the questions. We know the Magnuses left with Finch and Proctor in their Rolls. They give you a lift?"

"We took a cab."

"And you went straight to the hotel where the officers found you this morning?"

"I've been . . . I should say *we've* been living there for the past couple of months. No secret about that."

"Miss Gregory was with you all the time?"

"She didn't actually come into the bathroom with me, but, yes, she was with me until your people broke in this morning."

"You leave anything at The Statue of Eros last night?" Torry looked up casually.

"I don't think so. What kind of thing?"

"Some magnesium, powdered aluminium, iron oxide and some black powder, I shouldn't wonder. Possibly an electric detonator."

"What're you on about?"

"If you were in possession of the items I've just listed what would you be likely to use them for?"

"I haven't handled items like that for years."

113

"I said, if you had them, what would you be likely to use them for?"

"I wouldn't use them for anything."

Hart was patient. "Let me put it another way. If you were a policeman and you picked up someone with those items in his possession, what would you reckon he was going to use them for?"

"Some kind of incendiary device."

"At last."

Torry had been through this sort of thing so many times in his career. It was what the job was about: careful, painstaking probing, questions and answers, the ears always open, then the writing, the reports, the notebooks, the eyes always on the lookout, the nose always sniffing. After a time you developed a special sense, a smell for people and things. Whatever else Mr. Boom-Boom Talisman had done, Torry knew he had nothing to do with the bombing of The Statue of Eros. The deaths of Terrice, Mann, Robins, the police driver and the constable on the M2 was another matter altogether.

Hart was still at it. "At 5 A.M. today there was an explosion at The Statue of Eros. The explosion caused a fire and there has been extensive damage. It has been established that the initial explosion took place in the cloakroom. Almost certainly someone left a case, or a parcel there. Was it you, Mr. Talisman?"

"Why should I do that? Peter and Paul Magnus are my mates." It slid out and Hart sunk his claws into it.

"But you just said that you simply knew them. You weren't their associate. Now they're your mates."

Talisman had recovered. "They're mates of a kind."

"It's odd you should mention them in connection with damaging The Statue of Eros, Mr. Talisman." Tickerman had risen and walked over to the table, leaning on it with his palms on the wooden surface. "Our information is that The Statue of Eros is owned and managed by a Mr. William Shaw. Why doing something to Peter and Paul Magnus?"

There was a second's pause. "I thought they had an interest in the place. I don't know, but it's what I gathered. I'm probably wrong."

"What's your job, Mr. Talisman?"

"My job?"

"What do you do for a living? For money?"

"I'm self-employed."

"What kind of business? It must pay well. Living in hotels like that one can come expensive."

"I do all right."

"What do you do all right?"

"I don't really have to do much. It's done for me."

"Self-employed and it's done for you?"

"A couple of years before I left the Army I came into money."

"Big money?"

"Enough. It's invested. I had a wealthy aunt who lived in Brazil."

"Where the nuts come from," Torry muttered.

"Her late husband left her money. Stocks, shares and all that. I came into it. Check it at my bank."

"Oh, don't think we won't," Tickerman said with his avuncular smile.

"It brings in a steady income."

"A steady fixed income. What with inflation and rising prices, I hope it remains steady."

"I told you. It's enough."

"And you do nothing else?" asked Hart.

"I dabble."

"Like a duck? Dabble in what?"

"I've been thinking of going into the catering trade. A restaurant."

"*Specialité de la maison,* Bombe Surprise," grinned Torry.

"That's why I spent time with Peter and Paul Magnus. You must know that they have interests in the trade."

"They've got interests in a lot of trades. And you must know that." Hart sounded heavier than at any other time during the interview.

Any minute, Torry thought, Ticker will step in.

"I only know about their connection with the catering trade."

"It covers a lot of ground. Catering for many needs."

"Restaurants and clubs."

Tickerman straightened up and took over, nodding at Hart to vacate the chair.

"In all the time you knew the Magnus cousins can you say, in truth, that you never worked for them?"

"They were friends. They were advising me."

"Over four years they were advising you?"

"On and off."

Nobody was going to get anywhere with Mr. Boom-Boom Talisman this time around, thought Torry. Except perhaps in an oblique sense, to put the explosives expert in trouble with the cousins. The longer Tickerman and Hart kept him at Notting Hill, the more uncertain the cousins would become. They had a pathological mistrust of people who had been interrogated by the police. It was time for him to have words with Patti Gregory. He rose, Tickerman turning his head a fraction to nod his assent.

Patricia Anne Gregory was not a beauty, but she made the most of what she had. Around five-ten, in her late twenties, she had a body, if you could believe what you saw when she was dressed, which undulated and curved in all the right places. She used the body with a careful control perfected over the years so that every movement spoke of erotic pleasures to be had.

Torry could not deny that she looked better, after the rigours of the past twenty-four hours, than Boom-Boom Talisman. True, she had darkening shadows under her eyes which would disappear with the careful application of make-up. Yet, considering the relatively short time she had been given to dress and prepare herself for the trip to Notting Hill, Patti Gregory had done a good job.

Her hair fell around her shoulders, a grey-blond cascade, neat and clean, but a confusion of anxiety, incomprehension and disbelief could be detected deep in her large grey eyes.

She wore well-tailored, faded flared jeans and a Biba top. Torry noted that a claret suede coat was thrown casually over one of the other chairs in the interview room which differed little from the one he had just left.

There was a policewoman in attendance, a cup on the table, the remains of black coffee, cold. Patti Gregory's hands were in constant motion, the fingers playing in turn with what seemed to be an overabundance of rings.

Torry smiled at her, walked slowly over to the table and sat down, his eyes never leaving her face. Did he imagine the flutter of desire, the sexual snake rising in his mind?

"The name's Torry, Detective Chief Inspector. How've they been treating you, Patti?"

"I know your name. I know who you are." She spoke low, the policewoman would not have been able to make out the sense. "I'm a mate of Rita's."

In the first seconds they had touched a danger area. Rita was the girl to whom Torry had gone on the night after Susan Crompton's telephone call which had been the beginning of the end for the planned marriage. It was always a dread, to every CID officer in the Met—coming up against a friend of someone who enjoyed the particular protection which a ranking copper could give—and they all gave special protection for one reason or another: for information, to shield a relative, for sex, in some cases booze; a variety of motives existed, yet there was always the danger that pressure would be brought to bear.

Torry nodded, his mouth turned down, creases around his eyes.

"Out." He turned towards the policewoman who remained by the door. She paused as though to argue. It was a breach of rules. But she had seen rules broken before. She shrugged.

"I'll be just outside the door, sir."

"I'll call you. It's my responsibility. I'm pulling the rank."

When she had gone, Torry pulled out a battered packet of Benson & Hedges and offered one across the table.

Gregory lit up and pulled the smoke back into her lungs, leaning forward so that her breasts became firmly outlined against the shirt top, the nipples showing clearly. She wore nothing under the top.

"We can have the same arrangement you have with Rita," she said calmly.

"Your friend, Mr. Talisman says that you're engaged to him."

"Silly bugger. There's one who doesn't know the score."

"What's the score, Patti?"

"Oh Christ, Sir bloody Launcelot. You know, Mr. Torry. It's a tough world for a girl."

"Working for Peter and Paul makes it tougher."

"Maybe, but at least it's more steady than being a strict disciplinarian or a fluffy French kitten for sale and never really knowing who the next client's going to be. Takes a lot out of a girl, not being sure if you've got the filth or a nutter in your room."

"I'd have thought it was less dangerous than working for the cousins."

She drew on her cigarette again, making no comment.

"You ever heard of a girl called Anna Paulik?"

"I know about that. I know what I'm in, which is more than Talisman. He thinks it's a big deal."

"Look, love. I believe you. You know what you're into. You can walk out of here without a thing being written down. No hidden mikes, no home movies." He spread his hands wide. "Nothing up my sleeves."

"All you want is a few words and maybe a promise, and perhaps a favour some night when you're feeling old and unloved."

"Something like that."

"You know girls." She gave a smile, a hint of cynicism. "We all give it away once in a while—to coppers and to people like Peter and Paul. It's necessary. Like air, we need it to stay alive."

"Come on Patti, I don't need your body . . ."

"No, you've got Rita when you want her."

"Twice in two years. It's not my normal scene. I don't need it."

"I need my health. I need to go on living."

"You'll go on living."

"You want words?"

"Some."

"Ask and I'll see."

"You're still on the game?"

"In a private capacity."

"How private?"

"I work as a hostess. At The Statue of Eros."

"You mean worked."

She frowned, not understanding.

"I forgot, you won't have heard the news. The Statue got done over this morning. A bomb. Bonfire night. Nobody's going to work there for a long time."

Patti Gregory crushed the cigarette into the tin lid which served as an ashtray. "Then I'll be at one of the other places."

"You're just a hostess? You chat up the marks?"

She chuckled. "Not quite. We use the kids for that. Me, I'm special."

"Particular clients? Friends of the cousins?"

"Something like that. Visiting firemen."

"And people on the payroll?"

"I've been with both the cousins before now."

"The big time."

"Not really. I think they were giving me a test run. I must have passed the exam. They're good to me, Mr. Torry. I don't go short."

"I'd put money on that. But you're an intelligent girl, Patti. There's no future in it."

"You said you had questions. Keep asking."

"You come across anyone called Terrice?"

"Come across for him, or met him?"

"Both if you like."

"Never heard of him." She spoke flatly, and Torry's experience was that she was giving him an affirmative answer.

"More names. Fantonelli, Denago, Chassen, Millinari."

"The first two. But I never said it."

He nodded. "If I give you a telephone number, will you call me if you're in trouble, or want to tell me anything?"

She gave a tight little nod. Torry took out his notebook.

"Just tell me, I'll remember. I don't like going around with bits of paper in my handbag."

He gave her the Yard extension number which would pass on any messages to him. She reached forward and pulled the notebook towards her. "You got a pen?"

She wrote a number on the empty page—round, schoolgirl figures. "If you ring there and say that you're Chuck, I'll know who it is."

Torry rose and went to the door, before opening it he turned to face the girl.

"Vescari?"

"You what?"

"Another name. Vescari."

"Sounds like a pasta, or a sports car."

"Maybe it is, but do you recognise it?"

She shook her head.

"Keep your eyes and ears open then, and, Patti?"

"Yes."

"Try to be a good girl."

"I'm very good. The best."

"I bet." He opened the door and called to the policewoman. "Miss Gregory is free to go now."

Tickerman and Hart were still at it with Talisman. The ex-captain looked worse, haggard. Torry stood just inside the interview room, trying to attract Tickerman's attention. At last the Chief Super padded over and they closed the door behind them.

"Any joy?"

"No through road in any direction." Tickerman still had his pipe on the go. "We'll keep him as long as possible. War of nerves." He chuckled. "Works both ways. The Magnuses'll give him a hard time, and they'll all be shit scared. What about the girl?"

"She might be co-operative when the time comes. I've let her go."

"Going soft."

"Quite the opposite."

Tickerman allowed himself a thin smile.

"I've got more work to do. You still need me here?"

"I think we'll manage without you. Only just."

"You want me to leave a number?"

"If we get desperate, we'll keep trying you at home. Okay?"

Torry left the police station with dozens of threads weaving in his head. It was five-thirty and the traffic was starting to build up, but he managed to catch a cruising cab and was back in his Cromwell Road flat before six. It was too late to get Jenny Peterson at work, so he settled for a hot bath, a shave and a change of clothes. He would call her just after seven.

Marylin Hughes had not seen a newspaper, looked at a TV screen or listened to the radio. She had stayed on with her new-found lover, Stephen, until quite late in the day. Neither of them were due to be on duty until five-thirty, so they lazed away the hours—dozing and giving each other the pleasure of their bodies.

In the end she did not get away from Stephen's apartment until just after four, dashing back to her flat to bathe and change before going down to The Statue of Eros; and it was only when she was in the taxi on the way to the club that she realised how tired she felt.

She rarely took a cab right to the club, preferring to be put down near the Columbia cinema and walking the rest of the way. There was logic in her actions. If Bill Shaw, or any of the other management people, saw her consistently arriving by taxi she argued that they might question what they were paying her.

It was not until she was almost on top of The Statue of Eros that she realised there was something wrong. A group of staff crowded the pavement, talking volubly. The façade was blackened and scarred; above, some of the windows were missing, and what you could see of the foyer was alarming: a wrecked, burned shell.

She was about to move over and join the other staff when a voice behind her asked, "Miss Hughes?"

She turned. The man was in his early thirties, tall, not particularly attractive, strong-looking and heavily built.

"Yes?" The query in her voice contained no hint of fear, only the mixture of surprise and anxiety stemming from seeing her place of employment gutted and shattered.

The man grinned, relaxed. "Mr. Shaw would like to see you. There was a fire here last night, but you probably know about that . . ."

"No, I only just . . ."

"Well, we're having to lay quite a lot of people off. There are jobs for a few, but we want to get them away quietly. You know how it is."

"Mr. Shaw's got another job for me?"

"If you want it."

"Well, of course . . ."

"He'll talk to you anyway. The motor's over there." He pointed to the maroon Hillman across the road. "Just walk over there and get in the back. Or in the front with me if you like. It's open."

"Where're we going?" Marylin asked as the Hillman pulled away.

As she said it, she realised that she did not even know the man's name, had no idea who he was. She had been completely trusting, gullible. As far as she knew, she had never seen him before.

"Over to The Graven Image. You're Marylin, aren't you?"

He had only addressed her as Miss Hughes, it was reasonable enough.

"Yes. I've never been inside The Graven Image. You work there?"

"Yep"—his manner was easy—"between there and Winner Takes All. The name's Charlie, Charlie Fenner. You been at The Statue for long?"

" 'Bout a year. Year and a couple of months."

"The old Statue Man seems to think a lot of you."

"Don't know why. I never had much to do with him."

"Well, you're one of the chosen few, girl."

There was silence between them as Charlie negotiated a difficult one way stretch, easing the car, quite fast between those parked on either side.

"Do they know how the fire started?" Marylin asked.

"They've got a rough idea. I don't know much about it myself. Been a busy day down at The Image."

They had to walk about a hundred yards, from the place Charlie finally parked the car to the front of The Graven Image. Marylin thought the atmosphere was nice, friendly, as they walked through the foyer. Charlie led her up the stairs, right to the top, to the heavy oak door with the gold painted sign on it which said MANAGER.

Mr. Shaw was not in the room as Charlie ushered her in. There were three men, one, youngish, in a blue suit, long hair; the other two she knew from The Statue of Eros. She did not know them well, but, like everyone else at The Statue she was aware, and much in awe, of their reputations. They were Peter and Paul Magnus.

"Marylin Hughes," Charlie announced. His voice seemed to have changed, become flat and less friendly.

The younger man ignored her. "I'll be on my way then. Unless there's anything else . . . ?"

"No, Felix, you've done us proud. Great. It'll all be taken care of. Look after yourself."

The young man called Felix nodded with a stiff smile and left without even looking at Marylin.

She knew the man who had spoken was Paul Magnus. "Sit down, Marylin." He gestured towards a big leather chair, then looked over at Charlie Fenner. "There's work for you. Down-stairs."

Marylin was nervous now. Charlie said nothing, simply left the room.

"I was told Mr. Shaw wanted to see me." Her voice trembled a little, she could hear it as she spoke.

"Well, Mr. Shaw isn't available at the moment, Marylin. But we can talk to you, or at least my cousin can. Do you know my cousin, Peter?"

"I've seen you both at The Statue of Eros, yes."

Paul stood up and set off towards the door. "I'm sure Peter'll be able to fix you up," he said before he left.

Peter Magnus was lounging in a chair which matched the one that Marylin was sitting in. He had an odd look in his eyes and was smiling, only you couldn't really call it a smile, it was a kind of smirk, the right side of his lower lip twisted up and between his teeth.

"You were on duty in the cloakroom at The Statue last night, weren't you, darling?"

She did not like the way he looked at her, the eyes steady, as though they were boring into her brain.

"Well, were you, or weren't you?"

A silence. In her head a confusion of images. The club. Stephen. The man sitting there: his reputation.

"You lost your tongue, gel?"

Her mind swam, a blur, floating as though hypnotised.

"Yes. Yes, I was in the cloakroom last night, Mr. Magnus."

"No need to be formal, darlin'." The way he spoke was soft, but there was a hard, unpleasant undertone. "You seen The Statue today?"

"Yes. It's terrible. All that damage."

"Nasty. Lot of money tied up in that property. Very nasty." He leaned back, lips smirking and the voice coming out even more soft than before. "Tell me about last night, Marylin."

"What do you mean?" The edge of a precipice coming near and her unable to stop the headlong dash towards it.

"Just what I say." The softness gone. Steel replacing it. "Tell me about the parcel that got left in the cloakroom. Or was it a case?"

"The parcel?"

"Come on, a customer left something in the cloakroom, didn't he, sweetheart?"

"But how . . . ? Yes, but . . ."

"Just tell me about it."

She told him about the raincoat and the parcel. "It often happens," she said.

"And what are you supposed to do when some mark leaves his gear in the cloakroom?"

The apprehension became worse, her stomach developing butterflies and lizards. Unbidden, a memory tripping in the brain. A time at school, when she was quite small, about seven or eight. She had been caught, with two other girls, smoking in the lavatories and they had been sent up to the headmistress. There was this same thing in her stomach then, when waiting to see old Miss Brumage.

"We're supposed to report it to the manager. To Mr. Shaw."

"Then why didn't you report it to Mr. Shaw, darlin'?"

"Well, I couldn't see him anywhere . . . and . . . and, well, I wanted to get off."

"You wanted to get off. Quickly. Why?"

"I had to see . . ." She changed her mind, searching in the vacuum for an excuse which had nothing to do with last night.

"You had to see someone? Right?"

"Right."

"You had a date?"

Something was terribly wrong and she did not know why.

"You had a date? Right?" Hard, as though hitting her.

"Yes."

"So you didn't report the raincoat or the parcel to Mr. Shaw?"

"No."

"And you've seen the damage?"

"Yes."

"Have the coppers talked to you?"

"The police? No. Why . . . ?"

"If they do talk to you, you were nowhere near The Statue of Eros last night. You were not on duty at the cloakroom. You never saw no parcel, no raincoat. Nothing. Right?"

"But . . . why . . . ?" Just pieces of jigsaw in her brain, none of them fitting.

"Because, my dolly little cloakroom attendant, that bloody parcel caused the damage. You not reporting it caused the damage. You're responsible for that lovely club bein' how it is now. Just 'cos you had a date."

"But . . . ?"

"How do you feel about that, Marylin? How do you feel about causing all that damage? Just 'cos you wanted to get away and into some little ponce's bed . . ."

"He's not a . . ."

"But you were randy for him, darlin', it shows. You wanted to get away to screw, didn't you?"

Revulsion but no words.

"So, Marylin, how do you think you're going to pay for all that damage?"

"I don't . . . Christ, Mr. Magnus . . ."

"Peter, darlin'. I told you to call me Peter." He seemed to pause and gather some particular strength. "You want to go on working, Marylin?" You could not tell if it was a threat or a question.

"Mr. Shaw'll never have me back . . ."

"We're not talking about Mr. Shaw, gel. I said, do you want to go on working?"

"Nobody'll trust me in a cloakroom after . . ."

"No, not in a cloakroom. There's plenty of jobs around for randy little birds like you."

"I don't know . . ."

"You don't know what I'm talking about? Course you bloody know, don't come the frigid innocent with me. You've caused a lot of sweat, darling. On account of dashing off to practise for the Olympic screwing team you've caused a lot of sweat, and that might just mean you got real talent down there. In turn that might mean I can get you a job where you can make enough bread to pay off some of the sweat you chalked up last night. A job which don't

125

have no responsibilities like reporting parcels and raincoats what get left behind . . ."

"I don't think I . . ." Marylin felt sick.

"It's not up to what you think is it? It's what we think now."

She felt weak, her legs and stomach.

"See, gel, there're a lot of people who might want to be unkind to you about last night. People who'd see to it that you never worked again. Blokes who'd carve up that pretty little face, or do horrible things with bottles or acid or whatever. My cousin might feel like that, Marylin. You don't really have no choice."

"What would I . . . ?"

"Got to see what talent you got . . . that is, if you want to go on working. Go on working anywhere."

"I could go away. Get a job out of the clubs. There's plenty of jobs."

"No, darlin', you don't follow me. Last night was different. You did something last night that won't be forgotten. You wouldn't be allowed to take a job out of the clubs, and if you tried to run away you wouldn't get as far as Waterloo Station. Now, if my cousin had his way, you'd already be treadin' water ten feet down, but with my protection we just might. . . . Anyhow, let's see what kind of talent you got."

He rose and walked towards a door which, until now, she had not really noticed. As he opened it, she glimpsed a bed and a couple of chairs, a mirror on the far wall and a washbasin.

XIII

SHE WORE A crimson pantsuit and a navy shirt with small white polkadots. She looked desirable by any standards. The drawn sunkenness of her cheeks was gone and there was no trace of redness about the eyes.

"Hallo," she said with a smile to match.

"Hallo yourself." Torry had called her at five after seven and said he could come right over.

"Super." There was the same breathlessness, a husky quality, over the telephone. "Come straight up. I'll be waiting."

Now, as she stood in the doorway of her flat, Torry had some inkling of why she had turned somersaults in his mind all afternoon. There was a spark closing the circuit between them. Jenny Peterson, he thought, might not simply be able to take Sue Crompton's place in his mind and body but also erase the ache and guilt.

"Come in," she said, and he crossed the threshold.

"You look better than when I last saw you. In fact you look pretty fabulous."

"Never trust a copper. Isn't that what they say?"

"It's what they say, but I'm off duty and I still think you look fabulous."

"Thank you, sir. But I thought we had a tryst with truth," she giggled. "Or what do you call it. Info?"

"You said we should mix business with pleasure. I like your place." Torry had taken in the room with a quick glance. Not quite what he had expected, though he did not know why: neat, tidy, white walls, a three-piece suite in a dusty brown colour, a modern table in steel and glass, a couple of lamps, a large bookcase which held a stereo unit as well as books. No pictures, he

127

noted, thinking there was something odd about that. One closed door. The bedroom? Another, open, revealing a small kitchen, shining white.

"Sit down." The hand with the puzzle ring waved casually. "Drink?"

"What've you got?"

"Vodka, gin, whisky, and—yuck—sherry."

Jenny was very much her own woman, here in her natural environment. Torry reflected that some of her words, the image projected at their first meeting, could have been a distorted mirror of the real person—the character warped by shock. He remembered being surprised by her comment on the relationship with Terrice (*We screwed steady*). It had jarred, seemed incongruous, then; now he wondered if it was really so strange. The elusive emotion of love could well have existed between Jenny and Robert Terrice, but this self-confident young woman would never have admitted it. She was one of the new particular breed who refused to think or act in conservative terms. To them, love was a trap (at least until the mid-thirties when their looks were on the blink). It was a snare which tied you down, made you dependent on your partner and him on you. It was inhibiting and the free, natural, spirit demanded more than the steel shutters of total commitment. If the spirit was really free, the shutters became soft, warming cushions full of trust and truth, devoid of the bondage demanded by the married state.

"What're *you* having?" he asked, realising that he was staring at her.

"My besetting sin is vodka." Hanging her lower lip for a second, running it between her teeth like a knowledgeable, naughty schoolgirl.

He smiled. "It can be mine at times. And tonic?"

"Coming up. Funny, I'd have put you down as a scotch man."

"Wrong. I can't stand whisky."

She smiled, and started to set up the drinks, moving with minimum effort, a compact manner which did not give way to flamboyant gesture or posing. She handed the drink to Torry and sat, firmly, without flopping, into the other chair.

"Cheers." Raising her glass.

"To the stars." Torry did not know why he said it. It was a salute he had never even heard, let alone used before.

"My—a romantic policeman."

"You'd rather have a laughing one?"

"Romantic'll suit me fine, my intentions being what they are, highly dishonourable. I'm really trying to get you stoned before you start interrogating me."

"Hang about, I've got the bright lights and the rubber hoses down in the car." He smiled again, then felt his face go into repose. "You've really pulled yourself together."

Her eyes lost some of their brightness. "It doesn't do to let it all show. It's a hard lesson, but I learned it a long time ago. Your private life's *your* private life. Yours and nobody else's—unless there's someone special you have to share it with. I'm not a great believer in flooding other people with what's really going on in my head, or my heart, or my guts. Sorry if that's an unladylike word, but I'm not a ladylike person."

"It's the best word." He paused, trying to time his encroachment into her private world. "You said you had something to tell me."

"Ah. The unromantic policeman."

"I'd like to take you out to dinner," he said easily. "And I'd like that to be . . . memorable. It won't be if there's still work to do. So let's do the work now and then forget about it."

She gave a small nod. "I like you, Derek Torry. You're . . . Direct? I think that's the word."

He waited for about fifteen seconds. "Well? What is it?"

The slight pause was punctuated only by an inbound jet on finals for Heathrow. "A telephone conversation. That is, one side of a telephone conversation. I can't promise to get it all right. Verbatim. But there are a couple of things. Can I ask you something first?"

Torry inclined his head.

"Derek, what's a stoppo driver?"

"Was that part of the conversation?"

"Yes. A part I didn't understand."

"Put it in context."

"I'd like to know. Bob evaded it."

"I'm evading it now. Put it in context."

"If I'm honest, it was bloody frustrating. It was in the flat . . . his flat. We were making love. The telephone rang. And that was odd, it hardly ever rang when I was there, and if it did, he'd never answer it." She gave a sad little smirk. "He used to make a face at it and say, 'I don't want to talk to you. I've got my bird here, and I don't want to talk to you.' But this time . . . he was on edge, nervy, and he leaped off me as soon as it rang."

"When was this?"

"A Saturday afternoon."

"No. When? How long ago?"

"About a month before he went off to France. Probably less, two weeks maybe." Her eyes clouded again.

"And?"

"I don't usually listen to other people's telephone conversations but I was furious." She gave a snort. "I thought it was another bird. But it was a man."

"You're sure?"

"Yes."

"How did you know?"

"Just the way Bob spoke. I thought it was a woman, because he said, 'No, I've got someone here.' It was sort of furtive. Then his tone changed. I don't think he'd have spoken to a woman like that. He said, 'No mate, not at all.' Then the fellow at the other end must have said something to annoy him, because he was quite sharp. Heavy. 'I want to know what's in it,' he said. Then, 'No, not what's in it for me, what's going to be in it when I get back. I can't work in the dark.' The other person talked for a long while and Bob was trying to cut in on him all the time. Finally he managed it and said, 'You can tell them what you like. Peter and Paul know I'm good. . . .'"

"You're sure of that?"

"What?"

"You're sure it was Peter and Paul?"

"Certain. I remembered it all last night, and I thought about it for a long time. He said, 'Peter and Paul know I'm good. I've done the lot for them and never let them down: stoppo driver, bloody chauffeur, the whole bit. If I do this then they've got to trust me. I have to know what I'm carrying.' What's a stoppo driver, Derek?"

"Is that all the conversation?"

"All I can remember. What's a stoppo driver?"

"Do you really want to know?"

"Yes."

"You won't like it."

"I didn't like Bob getting killed like he did."

"Okay. A stoppo driver's a getaway driver, the kind they use on bank heists, jobs like that. A good stoppo driver's a highly paid, and very specialised, villain."

She looked defeated. "That's nice. So Bob was a getaway driver."

"Among other things. I know how you feel, it's like suddenly finding out that your best friend is . . . what? . . . a bigamist?"

"I'd have forgiven that."

"It won't be any consolation, but we didn't know about him either; and the Met prides itself on knowing all the good villains. You're sure that's all you can tell me?"

"Just about."

"Would you be prepared to make a statement? You'd have to repeat it all again, and we'd write it down, then you'd have to sign it."

"Anything. When he came off the phone I asked him what a stoppo driver was. He laughed and said it was a motor racing term. I didn't think much about it at the time." She gave a nervous laugh. "He was at it again pretty fast." Her laugh was not meant to be amusing.

Torry smiled in sympathy.

"Well," she went on as though making an excuse, "he was very good, and I think I loved him." The tears were there, very strong, brimming in her eyes. Torry felt helpless.

"Yes, I know," was all he could muster.

"You don't bloody know. Nobody knows. I don't even know myself. I certainly don't love his memory now. Does that sound terrible?"

"It's natural."

"But, at the time. Oh, all the bloody times, and whenever I went out with him, I think I loved him. I never told him, or anyone else until now. I never once told the bastard, not even when I was . . . oh, you know . . . when I was coming. Does that shock

131

you? I didn't even tell myself. And he was a bloody criminal. At least he could have told me that. For Christ's sake, take me out to dinner, Derek." She was on her feet. "Hang on, I've got to go to the bathroom."

The bathroom obviously lay on the far side of the bedroom. Jenny's economy of movement was gone, and she plunged across the room, through the door, a hand to her mouth, body out of control.

It was ten minutes before she returned: smiling, the composure restored.

"I'm ravenous, Derek. Not fish and chips again tonight, please."

"Well," he picked up the mood and put on a studied, worried look, "a copper's pay being what it is . . . oh, hell, this is a special occasion. I can rise to bangers and chips."

He held her coat for her and they went out laughing, down the stairs to the car which he had borrowed from the motor pool.

It was not as humiliating as she first feared. Peter Magnus ordered her to strip, leaving little doubt that things would only get rough if she did not do exactly as she was told.

"Take 'em off slowly, darlin'. I want to see you move. You got to pretend you don't know who I am. All birds can be good actresses when they try. It don't take any special training. But if you don't try, maybe you'll lose a few teeth—advance payment on the Statue getting burned. And when we make it, I want to hear you, so if you can't then you'll have to come the songbird, right?"

Marylin felt sick and her hands trembled as she began to unbutton her dress.

Peter Magnus noticed straight away. "Look, sweetheart. Listen to me. You got yourself in a jam leavin' those things in the cloakroom, all I'm trying to do is help. I'm fixing you up with a job that'll pay off a fucking sight more loot than you've ever seen in the whole of your tiny life. Do it well, and you'll be in clover. Do it bad and you'll have no job, no teeth, and probably no tits to speak of."

Oddly, his threats, while still making her nervous, seemed to release sensuality in her. She became aware of her body and its potential. Marylin had known for a few years now, that, given half a chance, she could look as good, and as sexy, as any of the toffee-nosed tarts she saw around The Statue of Eros. Her hands steadied as she climbed out of her dress and slip.

"I got to feel that you want to screw me and nobody else." Peter ordered. "For Christ's sake, look at me, you can't do it all with your tits."

She unslung her bra and began to take down her panties without letting her eyes leave his face, except for quick glances lower down. She was wet, turned on, even though the previous hours had been full of sex with Stephen.

Peter Magnus stood up and began to undress rapidly. "Come on then, doll. Don't just stand there. I got a roaring jack on for you . . . Help me."

Afterwards, conscious of the raw soreness of her body, Marylin had a strange mixture of power and erotic sensuality within her. She had read in a magazine that the most rewarding thing any woman could feel was the sense of achievement in bringing a man to climax. Peter Magnus had climaxed massively.

"You'll do. With a bit of training, you'll do, gel." He looked at her with a certain amount of pride in his expression. "You stay here, now. Have a bit of a rest. I'll get one of the boys to bring some nosh up for you."

As he got to the door, Magnus turned, asking casually, "We've got your address haven't we?"

"Yes."

"Okay. Someone'll go over and fetch your gear. You'll be working from a new address from now on. Right?"

She nodded placidly. There was no option.

"Oh, and, doll?"

"Yes?"

"The geezer you were with last night? The Olympic screwing trainer. Who's he?"

"Stephen?"

"Yeah, Stephen. Stephen who?"

"Stephen Derollo."

"Works where?"

"A waiter at The Statue of Eros."

"Okay."

"Why do you want to . . . ?"

"Just make sure he's okay. Nothing to worry your pretty little head about, sweetheart, nothing at all." He smiled so pleasantly that Marylin Hughes believed him.

Half an hour later, Charlie Fenner came in with a tray—smoked salmon, a rare steak, potato croquettes, peas, lemon sherbet and a bottle of Pommard. By the time she had finished the meal, Marylin Hughes was actually wanting Peter Magnus to return and do it all over again.

Stephen Derollo was depressed. For the time being he had no job, though they had told him that there would probably be something for him in a few days at one of the other clubs, or perhaps at one of the restaurants. His apartment was redolent with the recent memories and scents of Marylin, and he felt flat and stale, tired.

He had only been back at the apartment for a couple of hours, lying on the bed, trying to read a sci-fi paperback, when the bell rang. Perhaps, he thought with a thrill, that Marylin had come over to talk about the recent turn of events at The Statue. He had not seen her outside the club, among the employees who had gathered in front of the blackened hulk.

There were a couple of men at the door. He knew their faces but not their names, and thought that he might even have waited on them at The Statue.

"Steve Derollo?" One of them asked. He was big, broad shoulders and a heavy face.

"Yes."

"Bill Shaw wants to see you."

"Mr. Shaw?"

"That's what I said. You know Mr. Shaw, don't you?"

"Yes. Yes, of course. I work, worked, for him . . ."

"Well, that's why he wants to see you. You and a few of the others. He's trying to fix people up—the people from The Statue."

"A job?"

"Well, he doesn't want to see you just to tell you that you're good with a tray full of french fries."

"No. No, of course."

"Get your gear then."

"Okay, give me a minute."

They took him down to a maroon Hillman waiting outside.

Nobody saw Stephen Derollo again. He was listed on the Metropolitan Police Missing Persons list a couple of weeks later, and his description circulated to all other forces. No body was ever recovered. There were one or two pieces of circumstantial evidence, but nothing that could ever be used by the police.

The home office clearance for a tap on Suite 780 at the Mayfair Hotel, occupied by the man known as Anthony Chassen, was received at nine o'clock that evening.

The hotel management had no idea that the three extension telephones in the suite had been tapped, and, while the whole operation was not activated until the clearance was received, the arrangements had been made during the afternoon by officers on the team which had Chassen under surveillance.

Shortly after two o'clock, Chassen was seen to leave the hotel. He took a cab to Harrods and was assiduously followed by two plainclothesmen.

At two-fifteen a smartly dressed young couple entered the hotel and took the lift up to the seventh floor. The girl wore a fashionable black coat trimmed with fur, the hemline of which came well down to mid-calf.

There were no hotel employees near suite 780 when the couple reached the door. The female officer, Bridget Thompson, slipped out of her coat, revealing a maid's uniform underneath. Her companion draped the coat over his arm and began to fiddle with his watch as the girl quickly unlocked the door of 780 and stepped inside.

She took less than four minutes to insert the miniature radio microphones into the three telephones—one by the bed, the second extension in the main room, and the last in the bathroom.

Within seven minutes the couple were walking out of the hotel.

Nearby, in Mayfair Place, a small Post Office van, yellow and easily recognisable, was parked next to an STD junction box. The license number on the van would have meant nothing to members of the general public. Only the elite of the Serious Crime Squad, some of C1, and certain Post Office officials, would know that the letters in the number indicated that the vehicle was one used by police officers with Home Office permission. In the cramped rear of the van, two men sat with a conglomeration of electronic equipment, including a high-frequency radio tuned to an allocated frequency and a sophisticated tape recorder linked to the radio.

These men did not switch on any of the equipment until the Home Office clearance arrived shortly after nine o'clock.

TRANSCRIPT OF TELEPHONE COMMUNICATIONS TO AND FROM SUITE 780, THE MAYFAIR HOTEL, LONDON W1. DATE CODE: EF/21/C. HOME OFFICE PERMIT NUMBER PO/GH/COM CRIM/ 36782A. OCCUPANT: ANTHONY CHASSEN (ALSO KNOWN AS ANTHONY CHAMPION AND ANTONIO CAMPELLI).

Timed at 21.7 hrs.

HOTEL EMPLOYEE: Room Service.

OCCUPANT: This is 780 . . .

HOTEL EMPLOYEE: Seven-eighty. Okay.

OCCUPANT: I want a half of scotch.

HOTEL EMPLOYEE: Yes. One small scotch. Brand?

OCCUPANT: No, half of scotch.

HOTEL EMPLOYEE: What you mean, a half of scotch?

OCCUPANT: I mean a half of scotch. A half bottle of scotch.

HOTEL EMPLOYEE: Ah. A half bottle of scotch?

OCCUPANT: Yes . . . one syphon soda. . . .

HOTEL EMPLOYEE: Only bottles. You want large bottle?

OCCUPANT: One large soda.

HOTEL EMPLOYEE: Okay.

OCCUPANT: Hold it . . .

HOTEL EMPLOYEE: One moment . . .

(Pause of thirty-two seconds)

HOTEL EMPLOYEE: What number is that?

OCCUPANT: Seven-eighty . . . one smoked salmon, one beef sandwich.

HOTEL EMPLOYEE: One round smoked salmon sandwiches, one

beef. Right. Seven-eighty, right?
OCCUPANT: Right.

Timed at 22.14 hrs.

HOTEL SWITCHBOARD OPERATOR: Your call to New York, Mr. Chassen.

OCCUPANT: Thank you.

NEW YORK CALLER: Antonio?

OCCUPANT: Here.

NEW YORK CALLER: You did well.

OCCUPANT: Thank you. Tonight we do the next one.

NEW YORK CALLER: The club?

OCCUPANT: If you agree. I been waiting on this call.

NEW YORK CALLER: Of course I agree. They gotta be fixed good.

OCCUPANT: They are being fixed.

NEW YORK CALLER: Tony, I'm coming over.

OCCUPANT: Over where?

NEW YORK CALLER: I'm coming over to you.

OCCUPANT: Over here?

NEW YORK CALLER: Where else?

OCCUPANT: I can manage it. It's okay.

NEW YORK CALLER: I know you can manage it. I've got plenty of confidence in you. I just want to come over.

OCCUPANT: You think that's wise?

NEW YORK CALLER: Look, Tony. I know you're doing good. It's just that we had a deal with those guys. They've reneged. But we still have a deal. We're gonna take over, Tony. This town's not open any more. We all need a change.

OCCUPANT: You can get in?

NEW YORK CALLER: No sweat. I can get in any time. Me and as many people as I want. I'll be in touch.

OCCUPANT: You'll be in touch?

NEW YORK CALLER: Look at the calendar of religious events in London. That'll give you some idea.

OCCUPANT: Okay, I'll do that. And tonight's okay?

NEW YORK CALLER: Fight fire with fire, Tony.

OCCUPANT: We'll get on with it.

NEW YORK CALLER: Good boy, Tony. I'll be seeing you soon.

OCCUPANT: That'll be good.

NEW YORK CALLER: *Ciao* Tony.

OCCUPANT: *Ciao*.

Timed at 22.16 hrs. Outgoing call to London Number

OCCUPANT: Enrico?

LONDON NUMBER: Yes.

OCCUPANT: It's Tony.

LONDON NUMBER: Tony the wop, eh? (*Laughs*)

OCCUPANT: (*Laughs*) Tonight's on.

LONDON NUMBER: Good. You hear from him?

OCCUPANT: I heard, and it's on.

LONDON NUMBER: Okay. We got it together. You want we should come over?

OCCUPANT: No. I'll meet you. You and Carollo.

LONDON NUMBER: Okay. Where you want to meet?

OCCUPANT: Somewhere nobody would expect.

LONDON NUMBER: Nobody knows.

OCCUPANT: Those Magnus guys have got to know now, after last night. They can't be that dumb.

LONDON NUMBER: (*Laughs*)

OCCUPANT: There's a swell hotel next to Kensington Gardens. The Royal Garden Hotel. On the ground floor, off the lobby, they got a restaurant called the Garden Room. I'll make a reservation, now, for ten forty-five. Okay?

LONDON NUMBER: Okay. Where do we park the heap?

OCCUPANT: There's a car park under the hotel.

LONDON NUMBER: We'll be there, Tony.

OCCUPANT: You betcha life you'll be there.

LONDON NUMBER: (*Laughs*)

Timed at 22.20 hrs.

ROYAL GARDEN HOTEL SWITCHBOARD: Royal Garden Hotel, can I help you?

OCCUPANT: Garden Room.

SWITCHBOARD: One moment.

GARDEN ROOM EMPLOYEE: Garden Room, can I help you?

OCCUPANT: I'd like to reserve a table for three in, say, half an hour.

GARDEN ROOM EMPLOYEE: In half an hour, sir. One moment . . .
That will be fine, sir. Can I have your name?
OCCUPANT: Chassen. Anthony Chassen.
GARDEN ROOM EMPLOYEE: Table for three in half an hour, Mr.
Chassen. Thank you.
OCCUPANT: Thank you.

Jenny Peterson talked about her work and how she liked being involved with creative people. On their first meeting, in Notting Hill, she had said that being an editorial secretary was like being anybody else's secretary; now, calmer, it came out with more reasoning. She actively enjoyed being part of a creative machine, watching literary projects grow from the initial conception, through the editing, PR work and the interesting side problems like jacket design, blurb, posters and other point-of-sale material.

She talked easily, and neither she nor Torry made any reference to Terrice, their conversation back at her apartment, or the violent causes which had brought them together.

Torry had splurged, driven her into the West End and taken her to that most stylish of French restaurants, Chez Solange, where Mme. Rochon, an old friend of Torry's, greeted them like long-lost friends. Jenny followed Torry's lead, and they both ate the same choices: salad Niçoise, coq au vin, meringues Chantilly. They shared a bottle of Pouilly-Fuissé.

"Publishing's an incestuous business," she laughed, "but it's a way of life."

"Always the same with incest, they tell me." Torry smiled. "Keeps all your skeletons in the family closet."

"You could say that."

"And what does your friend do? What's her name? Mary?"

"Yes."

"What does she do in publishing?"

Jenny looked away for a second, like a small child caught off guard. Then a tiny sigh.

"Yes, that was naughty of me. I know . . . I did give you the impression that Mary was in publishing."

"She isn't?"

"No. I told you I had friends at the office, and then, when you were being so sweet and concerned about me, I mentioned Mary."

"No sweat, Jenny. What does she do?"

Again the look, a hint of worry in the eyes.

"I think you're going to be very cross."

Torry felt his nerves contract. Instinct? The copper's friend you did not talk about.

"Tell me and see." He sounded relaxed. Inside his gut felt like it was forged out of iron.

"What I said about Mary was true. We were . . . we are . . . mates. We used to go out for jaunts in her car at weekends. I met Bob with her in Esher." She paused. "Derek, I wasn't going to tell you this because I didn't think it was anyone else's business, but when you told me about the stoppo driving thing . . ."

"Go on."

"I think Mary had known Bob for a long time when I met him. She was always calling me with messages for him."

"What sort of messages?"

"They seemed harmless enough . . ."

"How harmless, Jenny?"

"She'd ring me at the office and chat, then she'd ask me when I was going to see Bob. I'd tell her and she'd say, tell him his cousins say it's okay for Thursday, or Friday, or whatever . . ."

"His cousins?"

"Yes. Is it important?"

"You might just say that. It links with the telephone conversation you heard. What's her full name?"

"Mary's? Mary Chester. That's what I know her as, but . . ."

"But what was her job, Jenny?"

"I don't know." The voice rising to an edge.

"What do you think?"

"I might be wrong. I don't know, but I get the impression that she's a kind of high-class tart."

"Superwhore."

"Something like that. I know a lot of girls who lay it around . . ."

"All part of the great promiscuous scene."

". . . But Mary wasn't at it like that. Superwhore's probably a good word."

Torry gave a sigh of weariness. "How come you get mixed up with someone on the game?"

"What's a nice girl like me doing in a place like this? I met her, Derek. Just like you meet any other girl. I don't even think of her as being on the game. She's not one of your Pretty Pussy for Sale, or Stern Disciplinarian, or Young Model Seeks Interesting New Position."

"No, but you're disturbed by what you think she's at. Concerned that she might be on the game. Shame on you, a liberated girl like you."

Jenny clamped her lips together: a look of petulance. "I'm not worried or disturbed, or concerned about Mary selling it. That's her business. But I do know something about life. I know the kind of people she would have to mix with if she's doing the high-class tarting. The money's big, so the people have to be bent, don't they? People like . . ."

"People like Bob Terrice?" He did not mean it unkindly, regretting saying it the moment it was out of his mouth.

It seemed like a whole minute, frozen: Jenny sitting there, white-faced, fork poised between plate and mouth.

Then, she spoke quietly: "They say all coppers are bastards." It was not hatred or bitterness. Disillusion, maybe.

"I'm sorry . . . I didn't mean . . ."

"Oh yes you did, and you're quite right. Mary has to mix with people like Bob, and worse. My trouble is that I like her. I don't want to see her splattered over some road, or carved up."

"You say you think she's a tom. What kind of tom? What do you really mean?"

"It's a feeling, no, more than a feeling. It's things I've heard from her, and seen. I think she's under somebody's influence, like Bob was. I think somebody's controlling her, that she does free-lance jobs when she's told to. Selective jobs. I think she screws people for money when she's told; there are times when she does it because she's afraid. Look, Derek, I know two people I'm pretty certain she's had under orders. Important people, influential. She talked as if they were just men she's met and had casually. But, since you told me about Bob, not just the drugs thing, but the stoppo driver bit, well, a lot of other things fit into place."

"You can name names, as our glorious press say?"

"I can tell you two names she's mentioned. It may mean nothing."

"Name away."

Her voice dropped. "Basil Crest and Lord Mervyn."

Torry's mind did a silent whistle. Basil Crest was a Member of Parliament who had played a prominent part in the last Royal Commission on Crime. Lord Mervyn was a man of great financial power in the City.

"You got a picture of Mary Chester?"

"I think I have a snapshot."

"Can I see it?"

"It'll be somewhere in the flat. You want to come back and let me find it?"

"I think it would be sensible." He looked worried. "Jenny, I don't think Mary should know that you've seen me."

"She knows I saw you the other day—at Bob's flat, and after."

"That doesn't count. Just don't let her know about tonight, unless you've already told her."

"She doesn't know."

"Good." He nodded. "Keep it that way."

"You sound very hard. Like a tough TV cop."

"I have to be. Sometimes, the TV soap operas play it down. We're often harder than they like to show." He sipped his coffee. "I ought to take a look at that picture. I hate to say it, love, but you may already be guilty by association with Bob Terrice. I'd hate to see you in the same boat with this girl, Mary. I've also got to tell you that you just might be in danger from Bob and Mary's little playmates. I'm not being melodramatic, but it could get rough."

Peter Magnus came back for Marylin at five minutes to eleven.

"Come on then, gel," he grinned. "You've got a brand-new life ahead of you now."

"Where're we going?"

"To your brand-new life."

"But where?"

"To the diamonds and minks and silk-knicker land. To your new flat. Money, clothes, everything you dreamed about when you were still in your gym slip." He gave her an odd leer. "You used to wear a gym slip didn't you, gel?"

She giggled, the hard knot which had been skulking in the pit of her stomach began to dissolve. She smiled. It was strange, she thought, on the way down to the car, how one's life could change so drastically in such a short space of time. Yesterday all she wanted was the fifty quid a week she pulled in from tips and salary at The Statue of Eros, and the firm, hard and effectual body of Stephen Derollo riding her. Now she hardly thought of all that.

TRANSCRIPT OF CONVERSATION BETWEEN ANTHONY CHASSEN (ALSO KNOWN AS ANTHONY CHAMPION AND ANTONIO CAMPELLI) AND TWO MEN REFERRED TO, THROUGHOUT, AS ENRICO AND CAROLLO. CONVERSATION TOOK PLACE IN THE GARDEN ROOM RESTAURANT, ROYAL GARDEN HOTEL, KENSINGTON HIGH STREET. OBTAINED BY RPT PRINT-OUT IN COPY OF THE EVENING STANDARD PLACED ON SPARE CHAIR AT THEIR TABLE.* DATE CODE EF/21/C. HOME OFFICE PERMIT NUMBER PO/GH/COM CRIM/ 36782A.

Timed at 23.20 hrs.

CHASSEN: Nice place, huh?
ENRICO: Swell.
CAROLLO: Got style. Hope the food's good, I'm real hungry.
CHASSEN: You have everything with you?
ENRICO: Downstairs. In the basement. In the car.
CHASSEN: We'll need it tonight.
CAROLLO: Don Peppe says it's on?
CHASSEN: All the way.
CAROLLO: Same as the last time?

* The RPT Print-Out is a recent development in electronic surveillance devices imported from the United States. It incorporates ink similar to the electronic conducting paint which has been in use for some time. RPT stands for Receiver-Processor-Transmitter, and the necessary printed circuits are combined into a single sheet of newsprint. In this case the page was inserted into a copy of the *Evening Standard* and placed by DWC Thompson within minutes of the trio's arrival at the Royal Garden Hotel.

CHASSEN: No, we gotta have variations. They'll be wising up by now.

CAROLLO: Nah, they're dumb, those guys.

ENRICO: What kinda variations?

> (Here the conversation was interrupted by
> the waiter taking their orders.)

CHASSEN: We were talking about how we do it. I tell ya. No intrigue, no pussyfooting around this time. We do it the good old-fashioned way—straight in from the car.

CAROLLO: It'll remind me of the old days, pitching pineapples through club windows.

ENRICO: Ah, you never did that, baby, you were too young ever to have done that. You? You were the kid they sent over to the beauty parlours and the hairdressing salons.

CAROLLO: Yeah, I did that too. With the hives of bees and the mice. I did all that.

CHASSEN: You two sound like a couple of Moustache Petes.

ENRICO: We did last night. I tell ya, Tony.

CAROLLO: Jesus, that was some hit.

ENRICO: Point-blank, Tony. The kid just disintegrated.

CHASSEN: You guys getting soft. Put it out of your heads.

ENRICO: I like a woman after I make a hit.

CHASSEN: You like to score after you've scored.

General laughter

CHASSEN: You watch it with the women. These Magnus guys got a lot of real estate tied up in cunt.

CAROLLO: Okay, Tony, we're not stupid. When we pull this stunt?

CHASSEN: Sometime tonight, you know, in the wee smalls. When we're set.

ENRICO: You going to be with us?

CHASSEN: I'll drive round the block with you, on the dry run. I won't be in the car when you hit.

CAROLLO: Thou shalt not make thyself any graven image . . .

Laughter

ENRICO: Yeah, we'll be the wrath of God.

CHASSEN: I got other news for you guys.

BOTH: Yeah?

144

CHASSEN: Peppe's coming over.

ENRICO: Over here?

CHASSEN: Where else but here, where d'ya think?

CAROLLO: What for? What for's he coming over?

CHASSEN: Because he misses the sweet smell of your ass, Carollo.

ENRICO: Ha.

CHASSEN: Because he's had enough of these Magnus runts. They've pulled too many strokes. He's bringing more guys with him, more soldiers and he's going to annihilate them.

ENRICO: When?

CHASSEN: I don't know when. Soon . . .

(At this point waiters arrived near the table
prior to serving the meal.)

TRANSCRIPTION CONTINUES . . .

The snapshot showed a tall girl, in her mid-twenties, Torry judged; dark, good figure, dressed well in an oyster-coloured suit, expensive, but not flashy. The face was clear, good bones, big eyes. There would be no trouble getting an ID if she was known.

"Can I take it with me?" he asked.

Jenny had made some more coffee and was in the act of pouring it. "Of course." She looked up. A smile which went back to the dawn of time. "Take anything you fancy."

"I fancy you," he said, surprised at the steadiness of his voice.

Her face lit like a neon tube, a bonfire, a sparkler held by a small child, a frenzy of floods—lit by every image you could conjure. "I've fancied you since the other day when you were so good after . . . after I found out Bob was dead. . . . I thought it was terrible . . . the guilt . . . A lover dead and some other man making mincemeat of my . . . Well, my . . . You know what I mean."

She stood up and came towards him, but the first kiss was not the expected explosion, the thing you read about in books or watched on the movies. It certainly was not the Hemingway special (*Did the earth move?*), yet her lips trembled, pulsing, and Torry felt himself quiver.

He held her very close, rocking her gently.

Afterwards there was little memory of the moments in which he propelled her through to the bedroom, undressing her and then himself, spreading both their bodies onto the white cover of the bed. Other things would stay with him: her body, naked, the curve of flesh and the lilting movements, the points of contact enlarged in his mind, as though by some memory-operated movie camera.

They remained on the bed, wrapped in the quiet of each other, and the knowledge, eternal and obvious, that human emotions were not simply the extensions of fulfilled animal desires. They said little; there was little to say apart from the fact that they both sensed that this had been different. In those tender minutes, they stroked each other, with wonder, and murmured the old, common-place words, smoked cigarettes, watching the small grey blossoms dribble upwards to expand over the ceiling, spreading as if trying to clothe their abstract thoughts.

Half an hour later, Torry looked at his watch. "Christ, it's nearly one o'clock."

"Stay, boy."

He barked and smiled. "Of course. But I have to ring in."

"The policeman's lot?"

"You said it the other day. Like doctors and priests."

She gave a nervous smile and indicated the telephone.

Torry dialled.

"Mr. Torry." The Duty Officer sounded relieved. "Good, we've been trying to get you. Mr. Tickerman wants you, fast."

"Where? Do I phone him?"

"No, you've got to get over to Kingsway as quickly as you can."

He replaced the receiver and told Jenny.

"Please come back." Her eyes showed concern. "You can have a key."

Torry thought for a second. "No," he said calmly. "I've got a spare for my place. But I'm not going to live with you, Jenny. That's not the way, and it's all too fast."

"I know it's fast. But . . . ?"

"But nothing, little darling. I want to talk again. Tomorrow. It's all emotion now."

"You feel though."

"I feel emotions. I feel with my body. I want you. I think . . ."

"Okay, tomorrow we'll talk. Call me."

"You can depend on it."

Torry pulled the car away from the kerb, heading back into London and Kingsway, the instinct of concern hard in his head. Tickerman had obviously been trying to get him for some time. A panic? More action? He glanced at his watch. The time showed ten minutes past one.

At one o'clock Harriet Magnus turned restlessly in her bed and moaned. For the first time in years she felt the full weight of her age and there was no deep sleep to push away the horrible vision: Raymond's body, hurtling backwards, the terrible explosion in the hall, blood splattering the walls and the mirror; little Raymond all but cut in two. Her conscious and subconscious minds merged into a long, louder, moaning, which finally escaped in a scream.

At one o'clock The Graven Image was still doing good business. Valerie Finch was not in evidence, though Caroline Proctor was at the Magnuses' table in the restaurant. Rube Rubenstein was also present with Paul Magnus. Paul ate a steak slowly, with enjoyment. His cousin was in the upstairs bar where the floor show was still in progress.

Paul was worried about a hundred things: his mother, The Statue of Eros, the way things were shaping up generally, Paul, and, most of all, Boom-Boom. Boom-Boom Talisman was still in the nick and none of them knew his real strength. Boom-Boom was a good bloke, but he didn't have the background like he had, or Peter, or people like the Dumper. The coppers were getting tricky, too bloody clever by half and Boom-Boom could grass without even knowing it.

Caroline Proctor reached out and ran her fingers lightly over the back of Paul Magnus's hand. She was a good kid, he thought, but he could do without her tonight. He wished to Christ the Dumper was back from Essex.

147

At one o'clock Dumper Doffman was sitting in the back of the motor. Bernie, Frank and Charlie were there, Bernie at the wheel. They were all silent. It had been a long day and an even longer night. There was sweat and hassle on, and the Dumper did not like the way things were going. For one thing Peter and Paul were not telling him everything, for the other, Bill the Statue Man had been a mate for a long time. He did not like to think of the things he had been forced to do to his old mate, yet, he supposed, he should be thankful for small mercies. If either of the cousins had been there they would have required more. They would have wanted him to do even nastier things, like the suggestion Peter had put to him: "Ram a bottle up his fat arse and then smash it with your boot." True, he had done things like that before now, when the cousins had insisted, and been present, but he would not have liked doing it to an old mate like Bill Shaw.

For the Statue Man it was reasonably quick. Humane. They had kept him happy on the way down to the farm—if you could call it a farm: one clapped-out cottage, three outhouses and four acres of scrub. It had been Magnus property for three years, and they were always talking about having it done up: putting someone in and running it as a real farm. But nothing ever got done and it was used occasionally as a retreat, a hiding place, for people wanted by the filth—or for dealings like this.

When they arrived, Bill Shaw seemed relaxed. He had been down to the farm before, and was perfectly happy at the idea of staying down there until the heat was off.

Halfway between the car and the cottage, Charlie blagged him hard on the base of the skull with a piece of heavy rubber hose he carried for that purpose. The Statue Man did not even grunt, going down like a pole-axed cow, Bernie and Frank catching him under the arms and lifting him, carrying him, like a small child, into the largest of the three outhouses: the one which had once been a barn.

They placed him in the solid wooden packing case, pushing him in like a rolled carpet so that he automatically assumed the embryo position. After that, Dumper Doffman shot him twice in the back of the head, pointing the pistol downwards so that the bullets would remain in the body.

Then they weighted the packing case with stones and nailed down the lid, using big six-inch nails. Finally they marked a chalk cross on the lid. Later, somebody else would come with a truck; the packing case would end up at the bottom of a river, or a lake, even the sea, maybe. The Dumper did not want to know where.

By this time, Frank had attached a long plastic hose to the outside water tap, near the cottage door. There was a green plastic sprinkler rose on one end, and, moving carefully, Frank obliterated all traces of footprints—from the car to the cottage, and then back to the barn.

Seven miles away, on the return journey, they stopped the car by a bridge and the Dumper stripped down the automatic pistol, a 1935 Canadian-made 9mm Browning. It came apart into eight separate sections. Each section was disposed of, from different river banks, into varying streams during the journey home.

Finally, an hour out of London, they pulled into a secluded layby and changed all four tyres. The ones they had used on the way down, and at the farm, were dumped in the boot and ended up on various rubbish tips in and around London, each one being transferred first to other waiting cars or vans. The Dumper was not a man who liked to run high risks.

At one o'clock Marylin Hughes could not believe her luck. The apartment was large and beautifully furnished. It was like something out of the colour supplements, or the fifties movies she liked watching on television: one main room with white leather furniture, a bedroom with luxurious king-sized bed, side tables built into the velvet-buttoned headboard, and a long white dressing table with an oblong mirror lit by neon tubes. There was cupboard space everywhere; a stereo unit which could be channelled through any of the other five rooms, including the blue-tiled bathroom and the small white kitchen.

Marylin had been happily surprised to find that the clothes, which filled one wardrobe appeared to be her size, as were the shoes, and the underclothes, neatly folded in one of the dressing table drawers.

"You'll be okay here, gel," Peter Magnus told her. "I'm leaving Charlie Fenner to look after you, so you won't be frightened, or alone, tonight. In the morning one of the other gels'll be over to tell you about the work."

Charlie was attentive, going out to get vodka, gin and tonic, a dozen eggs, bacon, tea, coffee, bread, milk, sugar and other immediate necessities. It was only when Marylin yawned and said she was going to bed, that she realised the young man was not there simply for the pleasure of making certain that she was not frightened.

He followed her into the bedroom, taking off his jacket.

"Which side do you prefer then, Marylin?" he asked, indicating the bed.

She summoned the calm centre from the midst of her gutty fear. "Look, Charlie," resting a hand gently on his arm, "I've had a rough day. Maybe some other time . . ."

"Peter won't like it," he shrugged, and she knew it was impossible. They were breaking her in the hard way. It had been Peter Magnus, now it was Charlie Fenner. Tomorrow there would be others. As many men as possible in a short space of time. Marylin Hughes sighed and began to unzip her dress.

Fenner smiled happily. "That's more like it. It's the sensible way."

Now, at one o'clock in the morning, she began to feel that maybe it was the sensible way. After all, what did a few minutes loan of her body really mean? Certainly very little to give in return for an apartment like this, the clothes, and, maybe, a lot of other nice things besides.

At one o'clock Arthur (Boom-Boom) Talisman was still awake, lying on the narrow bed in the room which might just as well have served as a cell, in the bowels of New Scotland Yard. He was a frightened man. He had admitted to nothing, but they had put it plainly to him: he could go, leave the Yard, and take his chances at his hotel or on the streets; but their arguments had been convincing. If he left, they would expect him back first thing in the morning when they would be asking more questions. The older copper even named a dozen men, close friends of the Magnuses, who had suffered injury following police interrogation. It would be safer, they thought, for him to stay the night.

Boom-Boom Talisman had been privy to many conversations between Peter and Paul Magnus. He knew what they were like; knew the psychotic state both of them could get into if they imagined someone, anyone, had crossed them up.

There were certain areas in Talisman's memory which he would rather forget, but he had neither the power, nor the ability to erase the images from his imprinted brain.

At one o'clock a tall, dark and quite lovely girl called Mary Chester lounged in an armchair. She wore a silk robe. Opposite her sat an alert, heavy built man, square-faced, with what might be described as rugged good looks. He had thick blond hair, cut unfashionably short. On the table between them, a tape recorder was playing.

"Please come back. You can have a key," said a girl's voice from the tape.

"No. I've got a spare for my place. But I'm not going to live with you, Jenny. That's not the way, and it's all too fast," a man's voice said.

The girl: "I know it's fast. But . . . ?"

The man: "But nothing, little darling. I want to talk again. Tomorrow. It's all emotion now."

The girl: "You feel though."

The man: "I feel emotions. I feel with my body. I want you. I think . . ."

A rustle of clothing from the tape.

"Blimey, love's young dream," laughed the man opposite Mary Chester.

The voices on the tape were fading.

"I wish we'd put one in all the rooms." Mary Chester's forefinger was poised over the OFF button. "It was always a long shot anyway."

"I'm looking forward to the movies."

Mary chuckled. "Well, you'll have to wait until tomorrow. I can't get in there until she's gone to work." She moved her shoulders. It was a movement of great sensuality. "Though I must say, for a copper, he sounded worth the sweat."

"A bloody sight better than Bob Terrice."

"Do you mind?" Mary pouted. "I knew exactly how good Bob Terrice was, poor bastard." A pause. "And how bad."

"Made me quite randy, that."

"You're a rotten bugger." She paused again, indecisive. "All right, Bennie. Have one on the house. It's got me going as well." She stood up and slipped the silk robe from her shoulders. Underneath she wore only a minute pair of lace black briefs.

Bennie, face flushed, followed her into the bedroom.

At one o'clock Detective Inspector Eric Hart, Detective Chief Superintendent Tickerman, Detective Inspector Monty Wood, Detective Inspector Harvey, one of the Fraud Squad officers and a couple of detective sergeants, together with half a dozen detectives and a pair of DWCs, including Bridget Thompson, who had been involved in the bugging of Chassen's hotel suite, were ranged about the large outer office of Tickerman's Special Operations Headquarters in Kingsway.

They were all getting on with work in hand, but the atmosphere had a taut intensity about it.

Tickerman looked at his watch for the twentieth time in as many minutes. "If we don't raise him within ten minutes or so we'll have to get through tonight's epic without the benefit of his brilliant advice." His manner was one of extreme sarcasm.

Somewhere, at the far end of the room, a radio crackled into life —a voice, nasal and static-backed.

At one o'clock Peter Magnus watched the four black girls going through their strip routine on the parallel bars. The move from The Statue to The Graven Image, which had slightly less floor space, did not seem to have fazed them in any way: they went through the acrobatics with their usual fluid grace, stripping whilst performing fast and accurate exercises. To Peter Magnus, the eroticism was almost a visible thing, flowing from the girls in a great clawing cloud, kneading at his genitals, surrounding his brain, seeping into the unwashed corners of his mind.

He centred concentration on April as she flipped the length of the bars, her skirt and top dropping from her as she landed on the mat at the far end. Peter knew that if he did not have her soon, he would be plunged into that pitch-black desert which he had experienced only a couple of times before.

As the performance came to a roaring finish and the black bodies glistened in their stimulating nubility, the girls' smiles imparting a sense of joyous sexuality, Peter Magnus crooked his finger at Dempster, the minder on duty in the bar.

"Go back and tell Miss April that Peter Magnus would like to buy her a drink," he said. Dempster nodded and walked, without comment, towards the artists' entrance.

At one o'clock Anthony Chassen, together with Enrico and Carollo, sat in The Pink Mink, a night club off Berkeley Square, sipping whisky sours. Their car, a Hertz-rented Mercedes, was parked across the street.

A couple of hundred yards further down a black Jaguar was stationary at the kerb. Two men sat in front, both detective sergeants from Tickerman's Serious Crime Special Operations Squad.

At one thirty-two, Torry walked into the Kingsway headquarters.

"Where the bloody hell have you been?" It was unlike Tickerman. He rarely got angry, and even when he did it was not characteristic of him to berate a colleague in front of a mixed bag of brother officers. "We've been looking for you half the night. I only hope to God you've got something worth while, because we've got a gutful here. Incidentally, you've had three calls from the States and nobody could find you."

Jesus, Torry swore at himself. Idiot, fool, cretin. So hung up on Jenny Peterson that he had even forgotten about the calls he had booked to Washington and New York.

"I've got something, all right, sir." His face a mask. It was not often that he called Tickerman "sir." "What's up here?"

Tickerman did not soften, he simply inclined his head towards his office. Torry followed, closing the door behind him.

"Look, sir . . ." he began.

"Sorry, Derek . . ." Tickerman raised a hand. "Wrong. Very wrong, but I've had a bellyful. Let's not argue. I want you to hear these." His finger was on the PLAY button of a big Philips tape recorder.

In silence, Torry listened to the taped conversations—between Chassen and the man in New York; then to Enrico; and, lastly, the three-way table talk in the Garden Room.

The facts added up. The Vescaris and the Magnus cousins were on a collision course, just as Torry and Tickerman had suspected. Torry's calls to New York and Washington were now superfluous, and they now faced a number of classic decisions.

"The transatlantic call is Peppe Vescari, I'd stake my warrant card and driving licence on it."

"You're lucky to have a driving licence the way you handle a car." Tickerman's anger appeared to have abated. "But I think you're right. The tape's been played to Washington for a voice-print ID. It'll be Vescari. I've done my homework as well, Derek."

"And those bright lads of his are going to hit The Graven Image tonight."

"Don't worry about that. It's being taken care of."

"You're not pulling them in? Not at this stage."

Tickerman gave a snort. "I should. By the bloody book I should." He looked up at Torry from half-closed eyelids: the glance of a man who might be carrying a sack of guilt. "Talked to your friend in the FBI. Your Washington call."

Torry understood and smiled. "What? Hank Hankerwitz?"

"Is that his real handle or a code name?"

"Real."

"He seemed to think that we'd do ourselves a good turn by letting Vescari into the country."

"Of course."

Tickerman bridled. "No of course about it, Derek. Like it would be madness to let those three villains hit The Graven Image tonight. It'd be lunacy to let Vescari into the country."

"It's lunacy to let Peter and Paul Magnus still operate in this city."

"And criminal insanity to let the Vescaris and Magnuses loose in the same city."

154

"You're going to do it though, aren't you?"

The atmosphere softened.

"Of course." Tickerman gave a conspiratorial wink. "But God help us if it doesn't pay off."

"Amen to that."

Tickerman drummed his desk top, fingers moving with impatient precision. "What succulent pieces of info have you got, then?" he asked.

Torry's face went into repose and then tensed. "I can get a statement linking Terrice with the Magnuses. It'll give you facts to work on, and we might even get an identification of Terrice as a heist driver—a stoppo man."

"We can't put Terrice in the box or the dock."

"He's already in his box. A lever, Ticker, just one lever to jemmy the lid off the whole stinking box of shit. I'll have a cast-iron statement. The lady concerned will go into the box."

Tickerman raised his grey eyebrows. "The girl? Terrice's girl?"

"Yep. There's another link I've got to check out. I use your phone?"

The DCS nodded. "You want me out?"

"Just don't watch me dialling. I know the dubious ways of you old coppers."

Torry stabbed out Patti Gregory's number with his forefinger. At this time of night he was pushing it. The number rang eight or nine times. Then Patti Gregory answered.

Crippled Eric approached the table in The Graven Image's restaurant where Paul Magnus sat with the girl and Rubenstein. He advanced with some caution, not making a direct line towards the table, but crabbing in obliquely, attempting to let Paul Magnus see him and be prepared for his arrival.

Crippled Eric was acting in his capacity of messenger. The cousins had a sick joke about that; they often called him their runner.

Rube Rubenstein saw him coming and leaned over to whisper across the table. Paul Magnus did not look up. He spoke a few words to Caroline Proctor, who reached out, touched his arm, then rose and left, walking slowly towards the exit.

Magnus turned to face Crippled Eric, Rubenstein waving a hand towards Caroline's empty chair into which Eric slumped gratefully.

"What can we do for you, then?" asked Paul Magnus, the lift of his head, his attitude, the manner in which he sat, the tone of voice all suggesting and conveying an arrogant, imperious euphoria.

"Slater's come in with the word you wanted on a piece of filth."

"Yes?" Noncommittal.

"You wanted to know about Monty Wood: a DI with C1."

Slater was one of the Dumper's people, a good nose. A case, but reliable for sniffing out facts.

"Let's hear it."

"Wood's just an ordinary bloke. Plenty of experience, special knowledge of explosives. We've got nothing on him. Straight as a bloody needle."

Magnus grunted.

"There's more."

Magnus grunted again, like a rutting pig.

Rubenstein said, "Let's have it then, shorty."

"That kid saw what was up at The Statue the other night."

"What? Hart?"

"Hart. Been upped to DI. He's an untouchable as well."

"Fucking Elliot Ness."

Rubenstein chuckled. Paul Magnus gave him a hard look and the manager shrank back into his chair.

"Bleedin' law's getting too much telly publicity. Getting to think they're all white bloody knights."

"What about Hart?" Rubenstein asked quietly.

Crippled Eric hunched his shoulders in a shrugging gesture. "Seems he's working with Wood and a lot of other filth. Fraud Squad, Drugs, people from all over. Something special. Wood and Hart're both C1, but they don't seem to be operating out of the Yard."

Magnus slid the tip of his tongue across his lips. "Tintagel House?"

"No."

156

"Wembley?"

"No."

"Then where?"

"We don't know yet."

"Why the hell do we push dropsy at the bloody law if we don't get results then?"

"Situation's not clear. But there's something up. You know a DI called Torry?"

Magnus nodded again: a weary gesture.

"Torry's in on it. Upped to DCI. Torry's a bastard."

"I don't have to be told the obvious. I know about Torry, they turned over a stone and there he was. Nobody screwed to produce Torry."

A waiter weaved among the tables, bending low to whisper in Rubenstein's ear.

"Seems we might have something on him," Rube Rubenstein smiled.

"Torry?"

"Who else? I got a call from Sid."

Magnus's eyebrows lifted a fraction. "What's he at?"

"You know what he's at."

"Whore minding."

"As always. But he's always had initiative."

Magnus appeared to be caught up in thought, as though in a private world into which no other living soul could enter.

"Yes," he murmured at last. "Sid was keeping an eye on young Terrice's women."

"I'll go and talk to him." Rubenstein left the table.

He returned five minutes later, a smile of satisfaction creasing the broad, blue-jowled face. He looked like a man who owned precious secrets. "Sid's paid off," he said softly, the voice edging on a laugh.

Paul Magnus said nothing. He just looked at Rubenstein, no query on his face: a hard indifference.

Rubenstein smirked. "He's got some goodies on friend Torry."

"Real goodies?"

"Substantial. Similar to the ones we've got on Mr. Crest and Lord Mervyn. Torry's been, shall we say, indiscreet."

"Speak."

"Sid got all that stuff from Terrice's apartment, remember?"

"With the bird, Jenny?"

"Her and others. But Sid doesn't leave things to chance. He had Jenny's place monitored—the bedroom, just in case."

"Bedrooms are good places to monitor. Pillow talk's the in thing."

"Torry's on the Terrice investigation and Jenny Peterson's a material witness: Terrice's steady lay. Investigating officer screwing a witness with a possible 'guilty by association' charge. Bloody hell, Paul, it's like doctors and their women patients. Seems Sid's got an earful and probably more in the morning."

Magnus's mouth speared out in a wide gash, a kind of smile, like a pike about to gobble a small fish. Then his lips clamped together. "So, now we'll see if Mr. Torry can be straightened."

"Sid tells me that with the stuff he's got you could straighten the Battersea Helter-Skelter."

"Dumper'll be back soon. He'll handle it. He's very good at taking the kinks out of pigs' tails."

"You want me to have a go at our Yard people?" Eric had been patient.

"I want to know what these C1 filth are about: where they're working from and why." Magnus did not sound too concerned. In the back of his mind he was leaning on the facts that Old Bill worked out of Tintagel House and another Crime Squad in Wembley when it came to what they called Serious Crime. It seemed unlikely that these three members of C1 were on attachment to either subsidiary. Yet a slight itch remained. Hart had visited The Statue on the night of the bombing; Wood had been there afterwards; and, from what he could understand, Torry was nosing about everywhere.

"Just get on to our bloke." He locked eyes with Crippled Eric. "Tell him there's a monkey in it for him if he comes up quick."

Crippled Eric rose, nodded, and hobbled out. He was happy enough. Five hundred quid. The way it worked out he would pick up a ton; Slater, a century and a half, and the grass at the Yard would take two and a half ton. It was fair.

At two forty-five there was not much traffic heading out towards Richmond. There was a detective constable at the wheel of the Triumph 3500PI. Torry sat beside him, and another DC lounged in the back, eyes alert out of habit, missing little as they shifted up Kensington High Street. Next to the DC a dark, tough little DWC sat as though to attention. The car whipped past Olympia. It would not take long to reach the Richmond address.

At two-fifty, Chassen, Enrico and Carollo left The Pink Mink, climbed into their rented Merc and took off slowly, heading for Soho.

The two detective sergeants in the Jag watched them go. Their names were Morris and Wright, and their experience with cars was vast. Both were drivers of great skill, and their knowledge of London's traffic systems, back doubles and short cuts, would have baffled even the most assiduous cab driver.

The Jag took off fast, Morris at the wheel, Wright talking quickly into the radio unit. They had the advantage over the Merc, in that they knew where it was heading, also that it would make one dry run past The Graven Image.

With their familiarity, Morris and Wright did not have to spend much time thinking about which route the Merc would take, nor the way it would approach the club. They were sure that they would be in position at least five minutes before the Merc made its first run.

April was even more luscious at close quarters. Sitting beside her at his secluded table in the bar of The Graven Image, Peter Magnus felt an increased need for her. The burning need within him was fast becoming a physical fire risk.

"You want a night out, April?"

She smiled, but it did not reflect any happiness, her eyes full of knowledge, and, though Peter Magnus could not detect it, a touch of scorn.

"What do you mean, a night out?"

"Well . . ." His mind was ablaze with pictures of her body naked, as he had seen it so many times when she performed. There was a confusion as the pictures crossed with those of the girl half-clothed: the black nurse, schoolgirl, nun.

"You mean"—she drew on her cigarette—"that some evening you would take me out to dinner, show me a good time and expect me to go to bed with you."

"April"—the soft voice—"I've watched you for a long time. I have feelings for you, deep feelings." His face hardened. "On the other hand, I can put you out of business any time I want. I can see to it that none of you work again: not in any of our clubs; not in any club; not in this city anyhow."

She sipped her drink. "I know it."

"So?"

"So I have to do what you tell me. For the time being."

He relaxed. "Right. Clever girl."

"When?" She did not look at him.

"Tonight. Now."

April faced him this time, the dark eyes reflecting a loathing which Peter Magnus could never, in a million years, either fathom or understand.

"You want me to come with you tonight? You want me to have you tonight?" It was more a hiss of escaping breath than a sentence.

"I fancy you, April. You don't know what I could do for you, how I could . . . You fancy me a bit, don't you?"

"You fancy me. Okay, Mr. Magnus."

"Peter."

"Okay, Peter. Where do we go?"

"Back to my place."

"You must be joking. Your place? Islington with your cousin and his Mama? Where Raymond Tobin got killed last night? I'll come with you, but I'm not sleeping in that house."

Peter thought for a moment. "Okay, where do you want?"

"Somewhere with real class. Say . . . The Inn on the Park."

"At this time of night? We'd never get a room."

"I thought the Magnus cousins could get anything they wanted." Even the tilt of her breasts against the mauve satin top she wore had a sense of violent taunt about them.

"I'll get a room." No emotion. "For you, the best suite they've got." His manner became more gentle. "You know, April, I don't even know your surname."

She made a face, wrinkling her nose. "Would you believe April May?"

Morris and Wright were in position. Seatbelts tight. The Jag's engine turned over quietly, a soft pulsing underlining the coiled spring of tension straining within the two men.

Their orders were explicit. Chassen and the pair of hit men were not to be roused into suspicion or action. This was purely a holding operation. As soon as the radio crackled out the code word, "Beam"—relayed by the DC, slumped and disguised as a derelict on the corner—they would pull out: two half-drunk businessmen on the toot in their flash motor. It would take only a fractional swerve and the Jag's bumper would lock with the Merc. With luck, and some acting, the three Americans would be quickly convinced they had been accidentally involved in a minor shunt.

A uniformed man would be there within seconds, doing the "Hallo, hallo, hallo, what's goin' on here?" routine, pointing an accusing finger at Morris and Wright. There would be profuse apologies to the Americans. No questions. Only argument between the Jag's occupants and the beat man.

Straightforward. Yet, both Morris and Wright knew of the slight danger of panic which could spark catastrophe. It was for that reason that they carried revolvers, loaded but holstered under their jackets.

Peter Magnus returned to the table. April smoked a cigarette and stared at her drink.

"Told you, gel. The best suite in the whole damned place."

"Big deal." She refused to be drawn until she was ready. If she had to save the future of the act—in which she was partnered by her two sisters and a close friend—then she would do it this way. It would not be difficult to simulate pleasure with Peter Magnus (she knew enough about men to realise that it was no good for her to merely lie there and accept the inevitable). The price was really so small that it hardly mattered.

For the first time since she had joined Magnus, she looked at him and allowed herself to smile with her whole body, turning on the sensuality which was always there to be tapped, a trick learned in her teens behind cycle sheds, in parks and at the back of dance halls.

She shifted slightly, knowing that the small motion of her body would send erotic messages crackling into Peter Magnus's nervous system. She saw his eyes soften, the nostrils flare a fraction. Magnus's desire for her was almost tangible, but with it April sensed something else, her well-developed instincts telling her that, immature though he might be, this big, bullying man loved her—whatever that meant to a man with such warped emotions.

"Let's go then." She forced a laugh in her eyes and from deep in her throat.

Peter Magnus nodded soberly. "Have to drop in and tell my cousin I won't be coming home tonight."

April arched her eyebrows. "You're like fags, you and Paul." She meant it in a teasing way. "Like twin sisters. One of you can't do anything without the other."

The silence was like a cut from an open razor. "You say anything like that again, April, and you'll be the sorriest lady alive." He leaned forward, his face almost touching hers. "I'm in business with my cousin. All our lives we've been like comrades in arms; and anyone—I mean anyone—who tries it on between us can watch out. One more crack like that, even though I think you're special, I'll twist you round your own neck. Right?"

"Let's go and see your cousin, Peter. It'll be all right," she soothed.

Paul Magnus was still at his table in the restaurant. Rube Rubenstein was there and Caroline Proctor had returned. Magnus was making mental notes; calculations; permutations. Everything was going well: there were five long firms operating at this very moment, two of which were about to fold and make money. Felix had told him that the profit from those two alone would be somewhere in the region of fifteen grand. The profit from protection stayed around a steady seven grand a week, and the toms brought in another straight eight.

162

The four clubs had been paying off between forty and forty-five grand a week—the profit made mainly from the fact that the booze was obtained either through long firms or loose loading (the practise of arranging that drivers of long-distance lorries left their vehicles vulnerable to theft).

In fact things could not have been better—except for the bloody Vescaris. Paul Magnus was just beginning to see that they might have bitten off more than they could chew with the Vescaris. Things were good, apart from the Vescaris and The Statue getting blown. That was going to take a lot of bread—bleeding great loaves of bread.

Peter was heading across the room. He looked happy. Smiling. When Peter looked happy, Paul tended to be concerned.

"Wotcher, Pete." He waved his hand towards an empty chair.

"Not stayin' mate, won't sit down. Got to be off."

"Yeah, well hang about. I'll come back as well." Paul turned, about to ask Rube to get Chung Yin round with the Rolls, but Peter chipped in quickly.

"I won't be back to Islington tonight."

"No?"

"No. I got a date."

"Something classy?" The sarcasm was barely hidden. Both cousins knew what was unsaid, the intimation being that the bit of class thought Islington beneath her.

"It's not like that." Peter kept himself very much under control.

"Glad to hear it, Pete. Who is the lady?"

"None of your business."

"You must be bleedin' joking, none of my business. What you think I do all day, Pete boy? Play canasta with the Queen Mum and help feed the royal corgis? I run our business, mate."

"And I don't?"

"You do some things, but when it comes to the hard, dodgy graft . . ."

"What you think I was up to with that little scrubber Bill Shaw had in the cloakroom at The Statue, then?"

"I would say, Pete"—Paul like solid ice now—"you was fixing it to keep her quiet like you said. In common language you was screwing her sideways and indulging in unnatural practices with her, before popping her into one of those fancy cages we keep for birds of her talent."

"Screw you." Peter Magnus turned on his heel and began to walk out of the restaurant. Paul glimpsed April loitering on the other side of the glass doors and it all fell into place.

"Make sure they get away okay," Paul mouthed to Rubenstein. "See they get a cab and that." Rubenstein left the table and went fast after the disappearing Peter Magnus.

As April and Peter Magnus, followed by Rubenstein, began to descend the main stairway of The Graven Image, the Merc turned into the street and slowly cruised towards the club.

"Not going to be easy," muttered Chassen. Cars were parked on either side of the street, leaving only a narrow clear passage in the centre. They could see the neon sign and the chrome and glass doors of The Graven Image. The street appeared to be deserted of pedestrians, but it was obvious that the hit would mean stopping in front of the club. Either Enrico or Carollo—almost certainly Carollo, as Enrico was driving—would have to leave the car for about fifteen seconds to hurl the plastic bomb into the foyer.

They were about twenty yards away from the club entrance, on their left now.

"Christ," spat Enrico.

A big man with a striking young black girl on his arm was coming out of the club. They were quickly followed by another man wearing a dinner suit.

"That's Peter Magnus." Chassen's voice was clipped. "Out, Enrico. Move. We don't want to be spotted."

It all happened in a fast, tangled blur. The Merc's engine surged, but before they could gather any speed, a Jaguar swept into the street from the turning to their left, some twenty yards past the club, its headlights full on, the vehicle weaving violently.

"*Non corra tanto.*" From Carollo.

"Jesus, drunken bum." Enrico slapped his brakes hard.

"Careful . . . easy . . ." Chassen clinging to the dash.

Enrico swung the wheel, an automatic reaction, as the Jaguar slewed across the road. There was one slight bump as the Merc hit the door of one of the cars parked to their right, and then a more solid crunch as Merc and Jag locked bumpers.

The silence seemed infinite, like a moment prolonged in a vivid dream. Then, in the headlights of the cars, a figure staggered, shouting obscenities in a voice thick with alcohol.

Chassen took only a second to sum up what might happen. This might just be a stupid accident caused by a drunk, but intuition told him that the arrival of a single policeman could lift the situation into high danger. He shifted quickly in his seat, turning to glance back down the street. Sure enough, a uniformed policeman was running towards the car. The driver of the Jaguar appeared to be leaning over the Merc's bonnet, giggling.

It was all too dangerous and Chassen took the only action open to him: pushing open his door, flinging himself out and sprinting up the road as fast as he could go.

As he passed the Jaguar he knew that he had done the right thing. The car had another passenger, and he locked eyes with the man for a fragment of a second. The man in the Jag was no drunken joyrider.

Enrico had his seatbelt off. Tony Chassen's departure was so fast and unexpected that it only served as the instrument of panic. Enrico saw the Jag's driver leaning over the bonnet. He caught a glimpse of the two men and the black girl on the pavement a few feet away. Then, as he turned, he saw the uniformed policeman coming at them, moving at a determined trot.

The panic fused, a crescendo of flickering possibilities and ideas rioting in his mind, filtering through his senses, bringing him to one, unconscious, conclusion and triggering his brain into automatic reflex action. Enrico's hand reached down onto the ledge below the dash and came up again in one fast movement.

The beat man, a tall Yorkshire boy by the name of Geoff Parker aged twenty-six, had been given explicit instructions. They had told him all that he needed to know, and he was intelligent enough to understand that there were minor risks involved. He saw the driver of the Merc turn but did not even have time to recognise that the hand held anything, certainly not the big Browning Hi-Power automatic. He heard nothing and felt little, only the immense push in the chest, lifting him, throwing him,

165

skidding, back down the street. He could not understand how the front of his uniform had become so suddenly wet, nor the blackness which was enveloping him. His last thought was whether his young wife, Marjorie, had remembered that he wanted kidneys for breakfast.

Both Detective Sergeant Wright, in the Jaguar, and Morris, leaning over the Merc's bonnet, reacted as one man. They saw the Merc's driver turn, heard the two explosions and saw the beat copper go spinning down, spouting blood like some human lawn sprinkler.

Enrico did not even have time to turn back before Morris put two bullets through the windshield. Enrico arched and slid into the street.

Wright was out of the Jaguar, his .38 Smith & Wesson up, grasped with both hands, his legs apart in the classic stance. The man in the rear of the Merc fired once, the bullet boring into the Jag's bonnet.

Wright squeezed twice.

A month later ballistic and forensic specialists could still only guess at the cause. It seemed likely, they thought, that Wright's second shot had smashed into the firing mechanism and detonator which was plugged into the plastic explosive, probably packed into a large tin and held by Carollo Postaro.

At the moment of the incident nobody had time to think about causes.

There was a deep crimson fireball, blooming outwards from the Merc, hurling glass, metal and human fragments outwards like bullets; a tremor and roar followed—pressure smashing at the eardrums—as the fireball leaped upwards, edged with dark black smoke.

A section of the Merc's engine crushed Wright's chest. Part of the cylinder block severed Morris's head, tearing it from his neck.

On the pavement, outside The Graven Image, April May caught a large jagged piece of the Merc's rear door in her stomach. Another portion of the same door severed Rubenstein almost in two.

As the explosion reverberated and died into silence, the only person left alive in the street was Peter Magnus. He looked down at the broken and bloody mess which had been the black girl and did not understand. His clothes were splattered with her blood, it was even on his face, warm.

There were other sounds now. Feet running, shouts and a buzzing. Peter Magnus hesitated for one moment, his foot touching the black girl's body. Then, with a series of little animal noises, grunts of fear, he began to run wildly up the street towards the blackness. There was a shrieking within him and it seemed as though his eyes kept filling with a red mist. Then came the thumping in his head.

He kept thinking of Marylin Hughes. If it had not been for her The Statue would still be in one piece and he would have been nowhere near The Graven Image. April would not have been here either. She would still be alive if it was not for Marylin Hughes . . . And he wanted to hurt someone . . . something . . . perhaps smash up a church, like when they were evacuated and they told him about his Mum and Dad . . .

XIV

MARY CHESTER'S APARTMENT was on the second floor. Torry insisted that they pull in to the kerb around the corner from the old Victorian house. The idea of police cars screaming up to buildings in the middle of the night was strictly for television and the movies.

They locked the doors of the Triumph. Torry lit a cigarette and all four—Torry, the pair of DCs and the WDC—walked casually to the front door. It was open, and Torry made some remark about bad security as they went in and climbed the stairs.

The door to Mary Chester's apartment was exactly the same as that of Jenny's apartment on the next floor up. It even had the same kind of bell push and a white card with the name MARY CHESTER neatly typed.

One of the DCs, together with the WDC, took up positions near the wall to the left of the door. The other DC stood behind Torry, slightly to his right.

Torry gave a lopsided grin and leaned on the bell push. They could hear it buzzing inside, a long, continuous whirr which seemed to go on for five minutes.

There were noises from within. Torry could have sworn that he heard two voices: a man and a woman. Then it went quiet and only the woman's voice could be heard calling out, "All right, I'm coming. Who the hell is it? Paul?" This last from the other side of the door. Close, as though she had her lips an inch or two away from the wood.

"Not Paul, darling," called Torry. "The police. Open up, there's a good girl; and I mean open up now, or we'll be through your door like the galloping woodworm."

The pause was one of only minor hesitation, then the chain was unclipped and the door opened. She was easily recognisable from her photograph, perhaps even more attractive with her hair ruffled and the glaze of sleep still in her eyes; naked but for a loosely wrapped towelling robe, the right hip slung out and her left foot forward—a provocative pose.

Torry flashed his card. "Torry. Detective Chief Inspector."

The girl looked startled for a second, then her manner changed: a subtle clearing of the eyes, and her mouth, which had been set hard, softened into what was almost an inviting smile. Torry felt uneasy, the smile was that of a female spider inviting a doomed male into her lair.

"Come in, Mr. Torry," the door opened wide as she gestured with mock elegance. "I'm Mary Chester."

"Can I bring my friends?"

"Any friend of yours . . ."

All four of them trooped into the apartment, which, Torry noted, was laid out on the same principle as the one owned by Jenny Peterson.

Mary Chester went over to a small, modern sideboard and poured herself a drink. "What can I do for you, Mr. Torry?" She tossed her head back to look at them. "In fact what can I do for all of you?"

"Sit down and answer some questions."

"How boring. There's much more I could do for three of you, and, at a pinch, I've got a speciality that I could provide for the lady."

The WDC did not flinch. "Sit down," she said. "Few people ever call me a lady."

"I can imagine."

One of the DCs took a step forward, as though to restrain the WDC. He need not have bothered, the WDC merely walked over to Mary Chester and suggested that she should sit down. The invitation was backed up, not with threats or menace, but a calmness which implied that if Miss Chester did not comply, the WDC would see to it that not only did she sit, but also that it would be a painful process.

Miss Chester gave the WDC a look which would have destroyed lesser people. Nevertheless she walked to the long leather settee and sat, clutching her glass.

169

Torry dropped into a chair. The others remained standing.

"Want to talk to you about a Robert Eric Terrice," said Torry. His eyes did not leave her face, but he became aware of something else—the big Philips tape machine on the table between them; also a 720 tuner amplifier on one of the bookcase shelves near the old white-painted fireplace. A lead ran from the 720 to the tape machine. The tiny concern hit Torry again. He was more conscious of these two pieces of equipment than Miss Chester's face, which registered indifference.

"Robert Eric Terrice," he repeated. "Robert Eric Terrice, deceased."

"Yes?"

"How well did you know him, Miss Chester?"

"I knew him."

"Yes, but how well?"

"How well does any girl know a man?"

Torry stood up. "Okay, get your clothes on."

"What for?" She leaned back, the confident smile consolidated.

"Because I'm not playing games."

"Games? Who's playing games, for Christ's sake?"

"Word games . . . How well does any girl know a man?" He did a bad imitation of her voice. ". . . For Christ's sake . . ."

"*He* asked his judge 'What is Truth?' You should know that, a good Catholic boy like you."

"Get dressed."

"Won't do you any good."

"Get." From the WDC who leaned forward and slapped the glass from Mary Chester's hand.

"Why?" Chester did not move. The glass on the carpet, unbroken, a wet stain spreading from it and a sprinkle of droplets running over the table, barely missing the tape machine.

"We would like you to come down to New Scotland Yard and identify Robert Eric Terrice . . ."

Her face drained. She looked sick. "Bob's dead . . ."

"There are such things as photographs."

For a second or two she had revealed fear. Now she leaned back, relaxed again, the colour returning to her face.

"Can you force me to come with you?" Her voice was under control.

"We can ask you. If you refuse, then we can force you. It'll take one telephone call."

Silence. Two animals facing each other. Torry leaned over to his right where a telephone sat on the carpet, a long lead coiled, like some thin, obscenely stretched worm.

His fingers curled round the receiver.

"All right. I'll talk to you."

"Good. At the nick."

"You said . . ."

"That was then and now is now, baby. I'm a one-chance copper. You had your chance."

"Bastard."

"Where?" smiled Torry looking around. "I make the call or you get dressed. Pronto you get dressed."

"Okay, but you should do yourself a favour."

"I've given them up for Lent. Like a good Catholic boy."

"Come on, Miss Chester, move." The WDC was longing to get rough.

Mary Chester spread her hands wide. "It's your funeral." She smiled nastily.

The WDC walked firmly to the bedroom door, opening it. As Mary Chester rose, the larger of the DCs closed in on her like a sheep dog.

"My, my, Mr. Torry," said the WDC from the door, "we seem to have company."

Torry walked over to join her. In the big bed with the black satin sheets and white headboard, a thick-set man lay, his head propped up with black pillows, a copy of a girlie magazine drooping from one hand, a cigarette between the fingers of the other.

"Sidney Pringle," said Torry, "what's a nasty boy like you doing in a place like this?"

"Very comical, Mr. Torry." Sidney Pringle took a drag on his cigarette.

"Bloody hysterical," muttered one of the DCs. He knew Sidney Pringle.

"I think," Torry smiled, "that we'll have a double act down at the nick. You want to come along, Sid, or do I have to call Mr. Tickerman and get a warrant?"

"What you going to nick me for, then, Mr. Torry? Kipping with a bird who isn't my old lady?"

"I'll think of something, Sid. I promise you I'll think of something, even if it's only melting an igloo with felonious intent."

"Quite the joker tonight." Sidney Pringle leaned back against the pillows. He was really much more unpleasant than Torry remembered.

"Sidney Pringle, I'm telling you to get out of that Uncle Ned, slide into your threads, and come down the nick with us. If you're not on the way by the time I've counted five, I'm going to do you for assaulting a police officer in the course of his duty."

"I'm not going to assault anyone."

"I know that, but it'll look like you did."

"I want to call my solicitor."

"From the nick, lad. Ready? . . . One . . . Two . . ."

"You'll be sorry."

". . . Three . . . Four . . ."

"You've got a policewoman in here. I'm not going to get dressed in front of a . . ."

"I've seen it all before," said the WDC.

"I'm surprised," chipped in Mary Chester, who, oblivious of the three men standing in the doorway, had taken off her robe and was climbing into her underwear. "Turn you on, do I, Mr. Torry?"

". . . Five . . ."

Sidney Pringle was out of bed and fussing with his clothes.

"Do I turn you on?" Mary Chester asked again in a husky voice, giving him a full frontal in her bra and pants. "Turn you on like Jenny Peterson?"

"Shut up, you stupid brass," Pringle shouted.

The jigsaw fitted in Torry's mind.

"Keep an eye on them," he told the WDC and one of the DCs. Then, looking at the other DC and inclining his head towards the living room he said, "You come with me."

He closed the bedroom door behind him. "Hang on," curtly to the DC as he went to the 720 tuner amplifier and flicked its switch, turning it to RADIO. The setting, he noted, was on short wave.

Torry turned up the volume, walked back to his chair and picked up the telephone, dialling Jenny's number. As he heard the ringing tone in the earpiece, the clamour of a telephone bell rasped from the large twin speakers mounted on each side of the fireplace.

Torry, still with the telephone in his hand, switched off the 720.

"Hallo," said Jenny at the other end of the line.

"Hi, sweetheart, it's Derek."

"Where are you?"

"Can't tell you, but I'm going to leave a nice tall, dark and handsome Detective Constable outside your door . . ."

"What for?"

"Because he's prettier than me, and younger, and I want to make sure you're properly looked after. You're alone?"

"Of course I'm alone. But Derek, what . . . ?"

"Trust me. I think you're cosmic, or whatever the phrase is nowadays."

"But . . ."

"Trust me." He replaced the receiver and turned on the tape machine, running the spool through FAST REWIND.

When the rewind was completed, Torry turned down the volume and pressed the PLAY button.

There was some distortion, then came a series of noises: sighs, grunts and the rustle of clothing.

Jenny's voice groaned, then said, "Oh darling . . . that way . . . that way . . . yes . . . yes."

Then his voice, unmistakable, said, "Jenny . . . Jenny darling . . . Christ . . . Jenny . . . Jenny . . ."

It was enough. He grinned at the DC, who looked puzzled.

"I want you to go and stand outside the apartment on the next floor up," Torry said. "It's occupied by a Miss Jenny Peterson, who's a material witness in the Terrice–M2 car bombing. You'll stay there until I can have you relieved. I'll make it as soon as possible. She must not leave and nobody can go in unless they have my written authority. You carrying?"

The DC nodded and patted his hip.

"Any questions?" Torry asked as he depressed the FAST REWIND again.

"No, sir."

The DC moved on out.

The spool rewound and Torry depressed the PLAY and RECORD buttons, making certain that the controls were all turned down. Then he walked into the bedroom.

Mary Chester sat at her dressing table doing things to her face and hair. The dressing table was loaded with bottles containing cosmetics made by Estée Lauder, Mary Quant and Revlon. Miss Chester was an expensive and elaborate lady, Torry reflected.

Sidney Pringle sat on the bed. He was dressed and looked surprisingly happy. "You'll be sorry," he said, looking at Torry.

"Everything okay?" asked Torry.

"Splendid," said the WDC with an impish grin. "I didn't know that villains like Sidney Pringle wore crimson knickers."

Torry winked. "Come to that, some DCIs do as well."

The WDC batted her eyelids and turned to Mary Chester. "You putting on a rainmaking slap, or is it just anti-pig paint?"

Chester paused, a brush poised. "It's a special. Once it's on I can do a dance that'll rid the Met of one very troublesome Detective Chief Inspector."

"Faster," said the WDC in a low voice.

Torry held up a hand. "Give her all the time she needs. We've got nothing else to do." He thought of the spool of tape being quietly cleaned of any recorded evidence in the next room. He also thought of the number of spools which must be around with other things on them—including matters concerning Mary Chester and her clients.

He went back into the living room and dialled the Kingsway Headquarters. Tickerman was not there, so he left a message advising a search warrant on Mary Chester's apartment. Then he went back to the bedroom and waited. Just before Chester was ready to leave he walked back into the living room. The spool was running out so he stood and watched it, pressing the STOP button as the bedroom door opened.

As he expected, Sidney Pringle's eyes flicked quickly towards the tape machine as he came through the door. As they went down the stairs, Torry was happy to note that Pringle retained his broad and secret smile. There was no point in disillusioning him yet.

TRANSCRIPT OF TELEPHONE COMMUNICATIONS TO AND FROM SUITE 780, THE MAYFAIR HOTEL, LONDON W1. DATE CODE: EF/22/C. HOME OFFICE PERMIT NUMBER PO/GH/COM CRIM/ 36782A. OC-CUPANT: ANTHONY CHASSEN (ALSO KNOWN AS ANTHONY CHAMPION AND ANTONIO CAMPELLI).

Timed at 3.36 A.M.

HOTEL SWITCHBOARD: Your call to New York.

OCCUPANT: Put them through, please.

NEW YORK LINE: Hello, who is that?

OCCUPANT: Is the Managing Director there?

NEW YORK LINE: Who is that?

OCCUPANT: This is urgent. It's Tony. Is . . . ?

NEW YORK LINE: Tony, what the hell're you calling . . . ?

OCCUPANT: Is he there?

NEW YORK LINE: He left, Tony. He left a couple of hours ago.

OCCUPANT: When're you expecting him back?

NEW YORK LINE: He's on his way . . . you know . . .

OCCUPANT: Not the trip he was planning?

NEW YORK LINE: Jesus, yes. Hey, Tony, what's the matter?

OCCUPANT: Can you get him?

NEW YORK LINE: Nobody can get to him. He's making contact when he arrives.

OCCUPANT: He's already on his way? You can't get him at JFK?

NEW YORK LINE: No way, Tony. What's up?

OCCUPANT: Jesus . . .

NEW YORK LINE: Tell me . . .

OCCUPANT: You know I can't. Not on this line.

NEW YORK LINE: No.

CONNECTION BROKEN BY NEW YORK LINE.

He had skulked in doorways, hidden in the dark pools away from the streetlights, and walked the best part of three miles. The thumping was still in his head, and April's blood had now dried on his face and clothes.

Across the street, the apartment block looked like a cardboard cutout against the early morning lightening sky. He could not hide any longer. People and vehicles were beginning to move in the streets. Soon someone would see him. It had not been his fault, but they would want to know about the blood.

Peter Magnus glanced quickly from side to side and ran, with a crabbing lope, across the road. The foyer was empty, the lift down. He leaped inside and jabbed the button for the seventh floor, his muscles tight and a tic going in his right cheek. His fists were bunched and he stood with one foot forward, ready to meet anything or anyone who might be on the other side of the doors once they slid open.

All through his journey, from the scene of the sudden ripping violence, the fear had been of things rather than people. People did not worry him any more, only the strange shapes and lashing demons which haunted his mind. They were there, he had seen them lurking behind the darkness, glimpsed them as they shuttled and shuffled after him.

They were not new to Peter Magnus. He had seen them before, on other nights, though never as clearly as this. He had also known, for a long time, how they could be appeased and erased from his mind and body. He had never had to do it before, but this time it would be necessary because they demanded it, and he was certain that, once it was done, the things would stop their visitations. Had they not told him? More than once, in a sweat, deep in the night with one of the young birds lying close to him, they had spoken as clearly as now. It was the only way.

The lift came to a halt, the little circular light, imprinted with a seven, blinking green. The doors opened and there was nothing in his way. He counted the paces down the hall: a trick from childhood when there was nothing else to occupy his mind. Fifteen . . . sixteen. An even number was always lucky, and it brought him in front of the door.

Peter Magnus pressed the bell, and went on pressing in a series of quick bleeps.

"Jesus." A voice from inside. Charlie Fenner casing him through the peephole.

The door swung back. "Jesus, Pete, what happened?" Charlie had a towel wrapped round him and Peter did not strike until he was inside and the door closed.

He chopped Charlie Fenner hard on the back of the neck. Fenner went down heavily, hitting his head against the door. Peter knew that it was not necessary to finish him off—not necessary to the things. But the other plane on which his mind worked told him that he must leave nobody to tell tales.

There were no weapons except his bare hands, and when he had finished using them on the man's windpipe, Charlie Fenner was very dead.

Slowly, Peter Magnus got to his feet, turned and walked towards the bedroom from where Marylin Hughes was already calling out: "Charlie, who is it? Who is it, Charlie?"

Paul Magnus took the Dumper back to the Islington house. Chung Yin drove, Caroline Proctor was with them, and the Dumper brought Frank and Bernie with him. They left word at The Graven Image so that Crippled Eric could get hold of them once he had checked out their inside man at the Yard. Paul Magnus was still not desperately worried about the activities of the filth, though he knew, somewhere in the back of his head that he should be. He did need to have strong information; he was dead worried about his cousin. The carnage in the street outside The Image was enough to worry anyone; what with the spade dolly dead, and his mate Rube Rubenstein, and a large percentage of plate glass removed, by blast from the club's windows. Glass was getting to be an expensive item. Even though he was trying to remain calm, Paul could not escape the facts. The filth and the Vescaris were getting very active.

After the explosion the whole area had been crawling with rozzers, which was not really surprising. It was all alarming, though again and again he realised that the major cause of his anxiety was his cousin. Peter was missing. One of the coppers even hinted that he could be dead. Shredded into little pieces, though that did not seem to be on. Peter had split. He was on his own, and that was something Paul did not like. It kept coming back to him like a terrible nagging nightmare that, until the Vescaris had arrived on the scene, things were relatively easy. Certainly the filth had always been a thorn in their flesh, but over the long term, the filth could always be handled—either straightened or given some small sacrifice, like a couple of the lads going down for a stretch or two.

The filth had asked a lot of questions after the shooting and explosion, like an episode from "Z Cars" written by someone with an overactive imagination.

Paul reflected on what had happened since the Vescaris had become involved: the score. At least four of the Americans were down. The Dumper had seen to the pair at The Dorchester, and there were the two who had gone up with the Merc outside The Graven Image. Two of the Magnuses' people were dead: young Terrice, that had saddened him because the boy had great talent with the motors; it worried him as well, the coppers being killed. Paul, like anyone else born to this particular line, knew that the filth did not rest when one of their own kind got done. He was also unhappy about the Statue Man, but that had been inevitable, just as it was inevitable that something should be done about Boom-Boom Talisman. Rubenstein was a tragic accident. Then he remembered Raymond Tobin. Ray was not really one of them, Christ knew they had kept him clean and away from it all. But the Vescaris had brought him in. The Vescaris were bastards. Whichever way he thought of it, Peter was the worry now. Peter away and on his own just had to be dangerous to them all.

The Dumper had some of the boys out looking for Peter, so he could do no more. Here, back at the Islington house, it was time for the grand strategy, time to find the way for cutting loose from the Vescaris.

Paul packed Caroline upstairs and told her to get some sleep.

"You'll need it, gel," he grinned. "When I've finished here, I'm going to be up to you and you won't know which way to turn."

Dumper, Frank and Bernie laughed raucously. You always did when one of the Magnus cousins came on joky.

Caroline could easily be banished, but not Big Harriet. She heard the men arrive, and after a decent interval of some fifteen minutes, she appeared in the doorway, the famed golden hair falling to her shoulders, face prepared as though by some professional make-up artist, a brocade housecoat over her nightdress.

"What the sod's going on?" she snapped.

"Council of war, Ma." Paul smiled.

"Shit," was her first comment. Then—"You made enough bleedin' noise, comin' in." She looked, in turn, at their faces. "Where's young Peter?"

They all shuffled uncomfortably and looked at their feet.

Paul spread his hands. "We don't know, Ma."

"What d'you mean, you don't know? What the hell's up now?"

Paul quietly told her about the shootout and the Merc going up in front of the club, and how Rube Rubenstein and the spade dolly were dead, together with a pair of the American heavy mob and a trio of filth.

Big Harriet, usually a woman of immense buoyancy and determination, sat for some time looking like an old woman. It may have been the anxiety coupled with a trick of the light, but the whole thing was eerie: the face and body appearing to age in a matter of seconds. The vital and vibrant woman turning into a hunched and beaten shell. Paul's concern heightened. This was his Ma; the woman who had conquered so much in her life and who had been a goading influence on both the cousins. He had never, at any time in his life, thought of her as an old woman. She was his Ma, a gutsy, highly sensual woman with a strident, sometimes violent, tongue, and occasionally a glut of sound advice based on her considerable knowledge and experience among the organised villains of London. Big Harriet Magnus had known them all: the good, bad and sad men and women who, by accident of birth, or choice, lived in the harsh world of sudden violence, cheap kicks, easy money, hard money earned at risk with shooters and chivs, deals, setups, constant worry, life spent on the brink of mistrust, values not shared by those in the other world. Big Harriet had learned a great deal in her time, and, like the now outdated villains, she felt strongly about certain areas of villainy.

Slowly the old bloom returned to her face, her back straightened and she sat up in the chair. "You're a bloody fool, Paul. I always said it and always will. What you want to get mixed up with the fucking Americans for?"

"It was a good deal."

"Yes, it *was* a good deal. You're a greedy bugger, Paul Magnus.

When I was a nipper and a little clever-arsed teen-ager, I thought the Yanks were a big deal. They had it really away in all those gangster pictures. But that's not life, Paul, it's only a dream. You're as bad as the half-hard screwsmen we all know who spend their lives dreamin' up the greatest tickle ever and always end up inside. You want to grow up, boy. I told you at the time you shouldn't get mixed up with them."

"Well I did . . . we did. We got mixed up with them and now we're stuck." Paul bridled.

"And what for?"

"For a bigger slice of the cake. Christ, Ma, you've said it your-self, hundreds of times. The bloody politicians and the coppers have it all their own way and there's never anything left for the likes of us."

"I hadn't noticed you starving."

"No, and I won't neither, because I've always looked after meself and me own kind. Anyone who's been loyal to the Mag-nuses has nothing to be afraid of. God help them who haven't been loyal."

"And God help you, because of the innocent who've died." She spat. Paul knew what it was all about. Young Raymond was what it was about. "You should have learned by now, Paul, to stick to your own line."

Paul smiled. "Just trying to open up the game in our favour."

"And?"

"And what?"

"And how did you go about it?"

"You know how." Paul hunched forward, his best chat-up posi-tion, as though taking his mother into some great confidence. "Look, Ma, we had it all sewn tight up West—the clubs, the brasses, spielers, and every little caff, strip joint and con club payin' us their whack, not to mention the side deals. But what were we missing, Ma? What's the biggest percentage today?"

"You don't have to hear that from me. I know that drugs is the big money. You don't have to make that point any more."

"Well then, what cut are we getting there? Sweet Fanny, Ma. It's all kid stuff, run by kids for kids. We took a cut, yes, but where was the percentage in that? What sort of cut is there in dexies, or hash or even acid?"

"You know how I feel about it, and I know the only big percentage is in something really hard."

"So?"

"So, to make a percentage you've got to sell it and to sell it you've got to hook people."

"That's business, Ma, just business. With the Americans providing the pure grade A hard stuff we could have upped our take all along the line. Do you realise we could have made almost twice as much in a week from that as we do now from the brasses and the minding alone?"

"And you kill people into the bargain. We've been into all this before, Paul."

"Yes, we've been into it, Ma, and you don't want to talk about it because you know I'm right . . ."

"Grow up, my boy. How the hell can you be right? When you pick up your first load the law jumps it. So what do your bloody maniacs do? You kill—coppers an' all. Then you kill again and you wonder why they burn The Statue, murder your foster brother and try to blow up The Image, and they kill Rube and this coon tart. It's bloody mad, Paul, and young Pete's out there alone and doing God knows what, while you're here ready to talk killing and setting them bang to rights. You're fucking maniacs, all of you." She stood up. "I ought to have seen you was put away years ago . . ."

"Don't come it, Ma." Paul was on his feet, blazing mad.

"Steady, Paul," from the Dumper.

"Keep out of it, Dumper. Look Ma, Pete and I, we done very well and you've never refused anything we gave you . . ."

"Straight villainy's different . . ."

". . . Never refused a penny, so I don't see as how you've any right to . . ."

"You don't have to give me nothing, Paul. Not a bloody thing. No more. I've finished since all the killing and maniac behaviour. I lost your dad and then I lost young Raymond. They was the two people who meant most to me in the whole world, and if it hadn't have been for you and Pete being tearaways, your dad and I wouldn't have been in that soddin' pub that night and he wouldn't be dead now; and if it hadn't been for you and Pete getting mixed up with the Americans, young Ray wouldn't be dead now. So I've had it up to me ears. They were the only people I regret losing. Losing you and Pete'll be nothing."

She meant it. She really meant it. Paul could see and tell, even by the way she walked towards the door.

The telephone started to ring.

"Get the blower, Dumper," he said, sounding tired and feeling as though he was falling off a cliff. Fuck the sodding Vescaris. His ma was right really, they should never have had anything to do with the Americans.

The Dumper answered the telephone. It was Crippled Eric and he had good news and bad news.

A lot of questions were going to be asked. Torry did not have to be told that. When they got back to the Yard he rang Tickerman at the Kingsway office and the DCS sounded reasonably happy.

"What've they got to look for at this tom's place, Derek?"

"Tape recordings. Photographs. The usual kind of stuff for putting on a little black."

"Thy will be done."

Torry told him about leaving the DC outside Jenny Peterson's apartment and Tickerman said he would take over that chore.

"Can you get over here fast, Derek?"

"Do I have to? We've got Talisman, this tom, Mary Chester, and our old and valued friend Sidney Pringle. Lots of questions and answers."

"I've also got Monty Wood and Harvey there with some of their playmates. All probably in the canteen having breakfast. Go and tell them what it's all about and then get over here, Derek. I need your help."

Torry used a short, sharp expletive and said he would be at the Kingsway office as soon as possible.

Crippled Eric and Slater called the Magnuses' contact at Scotland Yard. They called him at home and he was none too happy about that, him having been on late turn and only getting four hours' sleep. But they persuaded him that it would be all worth while and he should drive down to the first Fortes service station on the M4. He agreed and met them there an hour later.

He was an old and embittered DI who had been passed over so many times he felt like the Red Sea. Peter and Paul had been on to him, and into him, for a long while, and the inside man always gave them value for money, just as the cousins did to him.

They explained what they wanted.

"I was going to give you the wink anyhow." The old DI was known as Burnsides, not that it was his name, but because he had once told a bloke that he liked his burnsides, meaning sideburns, a twist anyone could make, especially when they had a quart of Guinness in them. Anyway, the name stuck, as names do.

"I thought you ought to know," he said, "it's all dead schtum, but it's a special op to check out Peter and Paul. I didn't get to hear about it till last night and that was only by accident."

"Jesus," mouthed Crippled Eric. "What's the full strength?"

"Don't ask me, lad. I only got that much. DCS Tickerman's the Guv'nor and he's got people from everywhere working for him."

"Bloke called Wood?" asked Slater.

Burnsides nodded. "Wood, Hart, Harvey and Torry from C1, and others. He's got Fraud Squad and Drugs and Christ knows who else. If you want my advice . . ."

"We don't."

"You may do. If you want my advice you'll persuade the cousins to go easy. Go off for a rest. Go somewhere in the sun . . ."

"Like Scunthorpe?" Slater had always carried a facetious streak.

"If you like," sighed Burnsides. "I was planning on getting the full strength today anyway. They've got some kind of a setup in Kingsway and I'm going to get myself sent down there for a couple of hours."

"We'll keep in touch then."

"Do that, but it'd be best if I called you. There's a lot of people asking awkward questions."

"Call me at my gaff," Crippled Eric told him. "Then I'll meet you straight off. All right?"

"As long as you bring the dropsy."

"You won't go short."

They went back to Crippled Eric's gaff in Camden Town where

there was a message waiting to say that Mary Chester and her minder, Sid Pringle, had been nicked. Someone had to get over to one of the other minders to pick up the key and fetch the tape which was on the machine in Chester's living room. It then had to be taken to Sid's solicitor, who knew what to do with it. Slater volunteered and Eric rang the Magnus house in Islington. The news was not greeted with unanimous joy.

Tickerman handed Torry the latest transcript taken from Chassen's telephone. Torry read it.

"He's on the way then."

"Fast today, Derek. You catch on like gin at a whore's funeral. Strategy's the thing. I want to get one jump ahead of them. I've got something bugging me and I can't put my finger on it."

"Comes from mixing with rubbish like the Magnuses. DDT used to be the thing."

Tickerman allowed himself a small smile. "Vescari's entry, I'd like to have that tied up so we can keep an eye on him."

"The transcripts any help?"

"I've read them a dozen times, but I've got a feeling that you're the boyo who can put them together."

"Let's have a look."

Torry read the transcripts three times.

"It's here," he smiled. "The first conversation with New York. Have we had a voice-print on that yet?"

"Still waiting."

"I'll assume it's Vescari. Listen. Chassen says, 'You can get in?' Vescari talks big and says that it's no sweat and he can bring as many of his people as he wants. Then Chassen asks, 'You'll be in touch?' And Vescari says, 'Look at the calendar of religious events in London . . .' That it?"

Tickerman nodded. "Cracked it. Presumably Vescari's a good Catholic. You know the form. We know roughly when he left New York. Can you check it out?"

"Anyone can check it out."

"I'd rather you than any DC."

"Okay."

Torry went down to his car. He was nervous, a strange kind of nervousness, like he used to feel before making his confession when he was a kid.

He had not seen Father Conrad in a long time.

Peter Magnus stretched out in the bath. There was no fear any more because the things had been appeased. Marylin Hughes, or what was left of her, was in the bedroom, and Charlie Fenner was still by the front door. Fenner was nothing, it had been Marylin Hughes who had appeased them. She had been so frightened. It had made him feel good, the power when he knew she was frightened.

He soaped his whole body, his face as well, getting rid of the blood—not just April's blood now. His clothes were in a terrible mess, but he would phone Islington in a minute and get them to bring some clean gear: Paul would fix that, but he'd have to drag Charlie Fenner into one of the other rooms. Not the bedroom because he did not really want to look in there again even though it had all made him feel so good at the time. Much better than all those games about nuns and schoolgirls and nurses. The games were only a kind of preparation for the real thing. There had always been a certain amount of brutality in his attitude to sex, but this was the great thing.

She had not screamed, even though she had been so frightened. She trusted him, of course, and that had made a difference. Now that he'd done it once it would not be so hard again. Not that he would have to do it often. Only when the things wanted it. Now they would stay away . . . for a while . . . until next time . . . he had . . . he was getting hard again at the thought.

Peter Magnus got out of the bath, towelled himself dry and went through into the living room to dial Islington.

Slater felt something was up as soon as he unlocked the door. The other minder had given him the spare key to Mary Chester's place and he had come straight over.

He pushed the door open and saw them standing there. Two big bits of filth. They smelled of it. Slater turned and began to run, but they collared him and pulled him back into the apartment. The tape machine was on the table with the tape still on it. There was also a pile of tapes, neat on their spools, lying beside the machine, and the room looked as though it had been turned over by a team of professional screwsmen. The filth knew their trade well, Slater reflected; after all, they had plenty of opportunity to learn the business.

Slater let his eyes drift to the table again. As well as the tapes, there were a few reels of film and a pile of photographs. Judging by the one visible on top of the stack, they were not the kind of pictures you would want in your family album.

"What've we got here, then?" asked one of the filth. He did not expect an answer.

"I know the face, but . . ."

"Seen it in the Monkey House at Regent's Park, I expect," chanted the other.

"No, it's got a name, I know. Name of Arnold Slater. Right?" Looking at Slater.

Slater gave a quick nod. He was unhappy about all this.

"So what're you doing here, Arnie?"

"Just passing." It did not sound convincing.

"Your apartment is it, Arnie?"

"No, but I come here sometimes. Do a bit of cleaning and that."

"The only cleaning you've ever done is cleaning out drunks. Do yourself a favour, Arnie. Where d'you get the key?"

"I keep one. I got the tenant's permission. Straight up. Ask her."

"Oh, we will. Who's the tenant, Arnie?"

"You should know." Then, an afterthought. "Where is she anyway?"

"Her name, Arnie."

"Mary. Mary Chester."

"A gold watch for the winner. Nice girl, is she, Arnie? Only does it for friends, has no enemies?"

"She's all right."

"What were you going to clean, sweetheart? The tapes?"

"The usual. Do the washing up. Bit of dusting and that."

Both of the CID laughed.

"Washing up," said one.

"Cleaning and dusting," the other chuckled, then he pointed at the tape recorder. "Mark the one on the machine, Jack, then we'll all go down the nick."

"What you nicking me for?" Slater's face a framed picture of innocence.

"Just to talk. Nicer down there. We can all have a cup of tea. They do a good cup of tea at Central."

"You're fitting me, aren't you?"

"Come on, Arnie, nobody's going to fit you. We just want to know why you're here."

"I told you."

"And we won't wear it." The one who was talking waited until the spool on the tape machine rewound. He put a gummed label on the spool, grinned and placed it on the pile. "Confession's good for the soul, Arnie. Let's go down and have a chat, eh?"

The church was empty. Out of habit, Torry genuflected to the Blessed Sacrament and went over to the Sacred Heart statue, slipping fifty pence into the box and lighting a candle before he knelt on the faldstool. He told himself it was a reflex, and these were not prayers, just moments of fond remembrance, and where better to do it than here in the church of his boyhood. He remembered his childhood friends, brothers, sister-in-law, his mother, the people he had known in America—at school, and later, at Albany when he was studying law. He remembered Joey Donalta. Joey was a constant memory because, when Torry had quit law school and joined the New York City Police Department—before he had anglicised his name from Torrini to Torry, come home and returned to British citizenship—Joey had been his partner: the partner gunned down because Torry had, for a second, lost his concentration. He remembered his father who had died in London soon after, and his comrades in the Special Air Service, and those who he had known throughout his time with the Met.

He rose and walked slowly from the church, across the small, cobbled, courtyard to the presbytery and rang the bell.

Father Conrad did not seem to have changed. He never altered; another link with the past, forged by the years: a tall, thin man, the aquiline face perhaps a shade more wrinkled, topped by a little less hair which, in turn, was slightly more grizzled.

"Derek." Tinged with surprise and delight.

"Sorry I didn't give you any warning, Father."

"My dear boy, come in, come in."

He followed the priest through the hall, again the highly polished tiles. The picture of St. Theresa of Lisieux, the Little Flower; the small statue in the tiny niche beside the study door, Our Lady of Lourdes. Then the study itself, unchanged as everything else: austere with the big roll-topped desk, the prie-dieu under the simple crucifix, and the walls lined with books.

The old man motioned Torry into a chair, then went back to the desk. "Next Sunday's sermon," he said apologetically, a smile crossing his face like the autumn sun flitting through a gap in the clouds. "It's probably only a variation on some theme you've heard many times before. But what brings you here, Derek? It's been so long."

Torry was silent for a moment, knowing what the priest wanted to ask him and feeling the shred of guilt in his own conscience.

"Yes, quite a long time, Father. I'm sorry. I seem to be very much a fair-weather friend. I could just as easily have telephoned you," aware, at that moment, why he had not telephoned.

"Well, I'm glad you didn't."

"Like all the coppers who come to priests, I'm here to ask about a client."

"You're not just a copper to me you know. And, about your client, I might not be able to help, but you know that."

"I don't suppose you've ever heard of him, Father. Anyway, I'm not naming names."

"All right."

"Is there any special religious meeting, or function, taking place in London within the next few days that would bring people in from abroad—particularly America? I'm thinking of something that would be fully organised, like the Lourdes pilgrimages are organised: charter flights and that kind of thing."

"The World Council on Catholic Communication." The old man nodded. It came out pat, fast and without a second thought, as though he had prepared the answer. "You haven't been reading your *Catholic Herald?*"

"I'm afraid not, Father. I don't . . ."

Father Conrad held up a hand. "No, Derek. The World Council is probably what you would call another Catholic dodge. It's an attempt to bring Catholics of all races together in England for a few days. They're coming from all over: yes, most of them on charter flights booked through the organising committee; from all over Europe, from Africa, India, America." He looked at his watch. "They start arriving tonight and will be shepherded by stewards who'll be meeting them at Gatwick and Heathrow. At eleven o'clock tomorrow morning there'll be a High Mass in Westminster Cathedral. The following days will be taken up with lectures, discussion groups, sightseeing tours."

"Where would I get information on the flights?"

The priest told him where the central organising office was located, and gave him the telephone number. "Perhaps we might even see you at the Mass in the Cathedral tomorrow."

"You'll be there?"

"I'm one of the stewards. Old parish priests like me are fair game for this kind of thing. It would be nice to see you at Mass, Derek."

"Yes, Father."

You could count the seconds of silence. Twenty-four.

"I still pray for you."

"And I still need it, Father."

Eighteen seconds' silence.

"I know. In God's good time you'll come back."

Torry wondered at the certainty in Father Conrad's voice. "I see Roberto and your Mother regularly."

"Yes, they tell me."

They talked for a few minutes, Torry feeling the discomfort building between them; the things unsaid; the things he thought he wanted to say, about the whole idea of the Church and God, and the things which the priest wanted to say; things Torry had heard many times before. He could almost see the words forming in the air between them—"When you've done questioning the Faith, Derek. When you've gone through the decisions and indecisions, it all amounts to a personal leap, a jump into the dark. Once you've made that jump and fallen through the blackness, you suddenly find yourself in the arms of Christ, and you never have to question anything again."

The priest had said those lines to him on more than one occasion, and would doubtless say them again.

Big Harriet Magnus jumped slightly as the telephone shrieked through the house. The boys were still downstairs, but her hand hovered, automatically, over the handset. Paul answered, and it was Peter on the line.

"Where the hell you been, Pete? We've all been worried off our loaves. Ma's going spare, and there's a lot on."

"I had things to do, Paul."

"We thought you'd got caught in the blast."

"No. Rube caught it. And April."

"Where the hell are you?"

"Over at Cedar Mansions."

Harriet Magnus knew what that meant. He was with one of their poxy whores. They had a flat at Cedar Mansions. Flat Seven. She had to admit it was one of their class joints.

"Who've you got there?"

"It's where I stashed the cloakroom girl from The Statue."

"Bit flash for her, isn't it?"

"I expect it was."

Paul picked it up quicker than Harriet. "What you mean, was?"

"Paul, I want something dumped. I need the Dumper."

"What you mean, Pete?" Anxiety in the back of the voice.

"I need some clothes."

"Oh." Relief.

"I need some clothes bringing over. And there's a couple of things have to be taken out."

"What sort of things, Pete?" The anxiety back again.

Harriet knew, just as Paul must know by now. Had they not both dreaded it for a long time? Peter Magnus was a nutter.

"What sort of things, Pete?" Paul repeated, his voice soft, coaxing.

"I had to do it, Paul. They were in my head. I had to do it.

190

Charlie Fenner was nothing, but I had to do the girl. They needed it."

"Jesus Christ, Pete."

"Don't forget the clothes, Paul."

"You stay right there. Don't open up to anybody but the Dumper. Don't answer the telephone. Just stay there. They'll be over within the half-hour."

He was shouting for the Dumper before the handset was even recradled.

Slowly Harriet Magnus dialled 999. She had suffered enough. Her husband. Raymond Tobin. Her whole life. It was time to put it all away.

Crippled Eric's telephone rang. It was one of the minders telling him that Slater had got himself nicked trying to pick up the tape at Mary Chester's apartment.

He tried the Islington number, but it was engaged, so he rang straight through to Sidney Pringle's solicitor and left a message. The brief would know what to do.

Crippled Eric wished that Burnsides would call him.

When Torry got back to Kingsway there was a lot of sweat on. Tickerman had a pair of uniformed DIs with him and explained that they had come over for liaison work. They were from the Yard's Operations Room.

"You got what we want?" Tickerman asked.

"I think so." Torry explained the possibilities, giving the DCS the address and number of the central organising office for the World Council on Catholic Communication.

"Should be able to pick up the flights easily enough. We've got photographs of Vescari. You think he'll stick with the bunch for a while?"

"I can arrange it." Torry thought that Father Conrad would make a good watchdog over a bundle of mafiosi. The thought amused him.

"Right, I'll handle it for now. When we've placed Vescari's flight we can arrange the rest. Derek, I want you to get over to

Richmond and bring in Terrice's girl. We're going to need her statement on paper. Everyone else is sitting tight and mum. That statement and a bit of heavy stuff should open the game."

"We going to do the old double act?"

"I said we would, didn't I?"

The pair of uniformed DIs chuckled as if it was an old joke they knew well.

Tickerman raised his eyes and looked at them like a sad spaniel. "You two can give me a hand with those charter flights. Get on the blowers and chat up the organizing. . . ." He was cut short by his red phone.

Tickerman listened intently for a few seconds. Then he said, "Jesus Christ," twice. Then, "Where?" Some more listening, followed by, "Okay, take him to Central. We've only got Slater there. No press. No comment. I'll be in touch. This has got him bang to rights. Pull his bloody cousin in as well. It's the end." He put down the phone, his face bloodless.

"What . . . ?" Torry started.

"Twenty minutes ago, Central got a tip, from a woman. The area car whizzed it to Cedar Mansions, Flat Seven. They found Peter Magnus there, nude, with two corpses. Charlie Fenner, a Magnus minder, and a girl. The girl had been screwed all ways and strangled with a stocking . . ."

"It was always . . ." Torry tried.

"Then she'd been cut about with bits of broken glass and pottery. It's a mess. They're getting Magnus over to Central."

One of the uniformed DIs looked worried. He had a nickname in the job. People called him Burnsides.

The Dumper was in the front passenger seat of the Jaguar with Bernie driving. They saw the police car as soon as they turned into the road. Probably the area car, pulled right up close to the big glass doors of Cedar Mansions. There was the hee-haw sound of another car, or an ambulance maybe, coming fast from the other direction.

"Shit," said the Dumper, even though he had not relished the thought of doing Peter Magnus and leaving him there. "Get out,

Bernie. Not fast enough to cause attention, but don't hang about."

It was an ambulance, going as though Jackie Stewart was in the saddle. As the Jag passed Cedar Mansions, they saw the observer and one of the uniforms from the area car bringing someone out. They had him in a raincoat—a woman's, it looked like—but he was easily recognisable.

"Christ, it's Peter, they've taken Pete."

"Nearest public blower—stoppo fast." The Dumper hunched down in his seat. He owed it to Paul. He had to get Paul out and it was no good hanging about.

Torry did not leave Tickerman's office with the uniformed DIs, but stayed for a brief moment to check on a couple of points with the DCS while the DIs went off to start the phoning which should bring in the information concerning flights from New York. Neither Vescari nor his soldiers would be travelling under their own names, but with the information to hand they should narrow the field to at least three or four flights. After that, matters should be relatively easy.

None of the other DIs from C1 were in the main Kingsway office. Hart, Wood and Hadley would be over at the Yard working out Talisman, Pringle, Chester and company. Torry looked casually around the main office as he went through. Something jarred.

He did not figure out what until he got into the street and saw the figure of one of the uniformed DIs in a public telephone box across the wide road. He could just be calling his wife, but . . .

Torry dodged the traffic and came up to the box at an angle, away from the DI's line of vision. Very gently he pulled back on the door.

It was pure luck that Burnsides did not hear Torry as he stooped over the telephone, talking fast in a low voice. Torry caught the words, ". . . they think Vescari's arriving on some charter flight connected with a church function. If he is then he should be at Westminster Cathedral at eleven tomorrow. I thought I'd better let Paul know, but I'll get you the full strength as soon as it comes in. And I want my dropsy, right? . . . Yes, okay." He recradled the handset and turned.

Burnsides's face only registered shock for a second. Torry, standing in the doorway of the booth, had shaken him, but he was prepared to bluff it out. Torry decided to do the same.

"Sorry, mate," said Torry with an easy smile.

"Just phoning my missis." Burnsides shrugged. "Didn't fancy it through any of those phones, not in public. Had to say sorry about a little difference of opinion."

"I've got exactly the same problem. Only, with me it's a bird."

"Women." Burnsides raised his eyebrows. "I'd better get back or the DCS'll wonder what's happened to me."

"I won't tell." Torry made it easy, light as a dipper's handshake.

Burnsides nodded and grinned again. "Good luck with yours."

Torry watched him crossing the road as he dialled the Kingsway office.

"I don't think he's caught on that I know," he said quietly when they put him through to Tickerman, "but that uniformed DI they call Burnsides is an inside man. Someone in the Magnus firm already has the word about Vescari's mode of entry and where he's likely to be in the morning. Suggest you check out brother Burnsides."

Tickerman was obviously not alerting whoever was in the office with him. "I'll see to it. Thank you." Brusquely, immediately closing the line.

The Dumper had buzzed Paul, then, shortly after, Crippled Eric had come through. Paul was not hanging around. He told Eric to tie up Pringle's brief. At least that way they would put one of the filth out of action for a while. Once the tape of Torry screwing Jenny Peterson was played, the filth brass would tuck the DCI away pending enquiry. But Paul Magnus was in heavy schtuck. Only one person could have put the finger on Pete: Paul's own mother, and he was not going to lumber himself with her. The

Dumper was to meet him, in a matter of minutes, at the crossroads a couple of hundred yards away.

He ran upstairs to his room, threw a couple of shirts, some socks, ties and underclothes into his pigskin overnight bag. Then he added his toilet gear and the Luger he usually kept locked away in the bedside drawer.

The Jaguar was cruising towards the crossroads as Paul Magnus approached. Bernie did a swiftish U-turn and then kept strictly to the speed limit. They would change cars at Bernie's garage within twenty minutes and then have it away fast to the farm.

A Rover and a Triumph 3500PI shot the lights at the next crossroads, going towards the Magnus house. The law in the cars were so busy they paid no attention to Dumper's Jag.

Paul felt sick. There were a lot of people about to be nicked, and Pete was in for murder. It was not a topping job any more, but Paul did not have to be a genius to know that Pete and many others would start chanting and the Magnus cousins' reign was over.

They had the various Magnus-Terrice connections well separated. Talisman, Sidney Pringle and Mary Chester were all keeping very silent at the Yard. Arnold Slater was equally silent, though truculent, at Central. Peter Magnus was there as well, under close watch. Peter Magnus was crying a lot.

The two DSs from Central had taken their haul of tapes and photographs over to the Yard where Hart was going through them with a DI from the Vice and a Legal man. From the photographs they had already identified several people—people you would not have thought would have been at it: Lord Mervyn and the MP Basil Crest were among them; also a pair of faces from show business who should have known better, except that what Mary Chester appeared to be doing to them was not normally on offer from straight girls, even in the present, enlightened times.

They were listening to the third tape—a very boring series of grunts, sighs and words—when Tickerman came in.

"Sidney Pringle's solicitor just arrived." He looked angry. "He says we've got a tape here that'll not please us. Claims it concerns a member of C1 and a material witness in the M2 bombing. You heard anything yet?"

Hart shook his head and the DI from Vice turned off the tape machine.

"He's gone to see his client, and I've got to bring him up here to identify the tape and the officer concerned," the DCS snapped.

It worried Tickerman. The only witness he could think of was the Peterson girl, and that meant that the officer could only be Torry. It was not an impossible situation, but one he would like to hold until Torry returned with the girl and they had her statement down in black and white. He also wanted words with Torry before Pringle's brief confronted them.

By now they had warrants out for a large number of Magnus people. In some ways, Tickerman told himself, they had the Americans to thank for pushing the whole thing off the cliff edge. He would have broken the Magnuses, no doubt about that. This way they had broken each other.

The telephone buzzed. Pringle's solicitor was ready. Tickerman told him that he would have to wait, replaced the handset and lit his pipe. Torry was taking his time.

Jenny Peterson came into Torry's arms as soon as he got inside the apartment.

Torry put his fingers to his lips and pointed towards the bathroom. Puzzled, Jenny followed him. He turned on the bathtaps and closed the door.

"Don't question this," Torry kissed her lightly. "Just don't talk too much. Your bedroom is bugged and I'm going to do a fast clearing operation."

"Bugged . . . ?"

"Your chum Mary. They had a tape of us . . ."

Her face wrinkled in disgust. "What? Us . . . ?"

"Yes. At it, as they say in the best circles."

"Oh, Derek. What could they have . . . ?"

"Nothing. You don't know anything about any bugging. It never happened. There is no tape any more."

"Could it have been bad for you?"

"It wouldn't have destroyed me, but they'd have had me off the case. Suspended pending an enquiry. I want to make sure there's nothing else."

He moved very quickly, knowing that if there was only one bug it would be near the bed. It took him less than ten minutes to find it, fitted into the base of one of the bedside lamps.

Torry dug the tiny radio microphone out of the woodwork and slipped it into his pocket. He would get rid of it on their way to the Yard. He turned, and was about to leave when something else caught his eye, a glint where the ventilation grill should have been, high in the wall opposite the bed. He slid a chair over and climbed up. The grill had been removed and the square where it should have been appeared to be filled with a large, heavy, domed glass paperweight. It was angled down towards the bed.

Torry reached up and pulled the paperweight out. It was a Canon $f/\cdot98$ lens on a Nikon F camera. On the side of the camera an L-shaped box was clamped a remote-control device. The pictures would be wide-angled and slightly blurred, but they would at least have got pictures with a fast film, even in bad light.

He pulled off the remote unit and unscrewed the lens, opened up the rear of the camera and took out the cassette. The whole film had been used. He put the cassette in his pocket with the mike and went out into the living room.

"You are the proud owner of a Nikon F camera."

"What?"

"No, a Nikon F." He held out the camera. "You've had it for a long time, and it was a present from Bob Terrice, if anyone asks. I've removed everything that matters. Put it away in a drawer and don't think about it again."

"You mean they were taking pictures of me . . . of us?"

"I should think there'll be a few of you and Terrice as well. Taken at his place." He looked suddenly white. "I just hope to Christ I don't have to look at them—professionally I mean."

"Derek, what kind of people . . . ?"

"Animals. Men who want to own lives and money and reputations. People who trust nobody. That's the kind of people, Jenny." Then, more softly, he whispered, "They weren't after you, love. Not unless you gave them something that would help them. I reckon they had Terrice's place well sewn up. This was an afterthought which all but paid off. Just say nothing about it."

197

He held her close, feeling himself react to the softness of her body. "We've been a long time. I have to give some excuse, like you were very upset, so go and rub water into your eyes."

"Why would I be upset with a super beautiful copper like you to look after me?"

"Maybe I gave you a bad time because of your friend Mary Chester. She's in the nick. Why in hell didn't you tell me she lived downstairs from you?"

She gave a small frown. "Frightened, I guess."

"Well, hear this, baby. If you've been hiding anything else, you have to tell me now. In half an hour it'll be too late because once you've made your statement and seen my Guv'nor, you'll be far from anybody's help."

She stayed silent for a moment. "There's nothing to tell, nothing more, nothing that matters."

"Good girl. Get your eyes good and red."

While she was in the bathroom, Torry went through to the kitchen and dropped the lens and the remote switch into the waste disposal unit.

They picked up the DC who was still patiently on duty at the door, and went down to the car.

Harriet Magnus was not taken in; Caroline Proctor was. They took her off in a Rover and left two uniformed men at the door of the Islington house. They also went on and turned over the clubs and one or two of the smaller drinkers owned by the Magnus cousins.

The accountant, Felix, was asked to go down to his local nick. Twenty minutes later the Fraud Squad arrived with a warrant and took away the books from his office.

The press were quickly on to the arrests, but nobody at the Yard gave names, except with regard to the Hughes/Fenner murders, about which they said that a man was at Central helping the police with their enquiries.

So far, Paul Magnus had not been located.

Tickerman looked more upset than angry. Torry faced him, alone in his office at the Yard.

"Derek, I want you to be very careful about this. Are you aware of any action of yours, over the past couple of days, which could make your position on this case untenable?"

Torry did not smile. It had come very fast. "I know of one thing that could, yes. But, unless I tell you what it is, nobody has a thing on me. Nobody can prove anything."

"Could it in any way be classed as a criminal action?" Tickerman was risking his own neck by asking the questions in private.

"No."

"May I ask you what that action was?"

"It was a personal matter. Some people might say it concerned morals, but I have a clear conscience, and, I repeat, there is no evidence."

"I wonder."

"I'm telling you . . . sir."

"Does it concern a woman connected with the Magnuses?"

"I'd rather not answer that, sir. Has someone made definite allegations against me?"

"No," the DCS blew smoke from the corners of his mouth. He looked like a friendly dragon. "Derek, I'm in a difficult spot. Sidney Pringle's solicitor has suggested that, amongst a series of tapes taken from Mary Chester's apartment, there is one recording which places an officer of C1 in a highly compromising situation. The woman concerned is supposed to be an important witness connected with Terrice and the M2 business. The only witness I can bring to mind is the Peterson girl. She done her statement?"

"I've been through it with her. She's here, and it's being typed up. If it's Miss Peterson and myself, sir, I can only repeat that there is no evidence."

"Derek"—a note of warning in his voice—"careful, lad. You haven't been too clever, have you?"

"I don't know what you mean, Mr. Tickerman."

"You do know what I bloody mean, and I have to tell you that Sid Pringle's bent solicitor is waiting to see those tapes and finger one of them."

"Let him finger away."

"It's your funeral, Derek."

"Funny, sir, that's exactly what Mary Chester said to me when we nicked her."

He was the one with the secret smile now. The lens, remote control switch and radio mike were safely out of the way. The only thing to worry about was the cassette of film in his pocket. He had seen villains off at their own games before and was looking forward to the look on Sidney Pringle's face.

"I hope you're right, Derek. For your sake," grunted Tickerman.

"Would I let you down, Ticker?" winked Torry.

"Come on then."

"The old double act?"

"The old one-two."

They got in touch with Crippled Eric from a telephone box about a mile from the farm. He told the Dumper to call him every hour. If he was not there, then he had been lifted and they would have to get their info direct from the Yard grass.

"What's the score?" asked Paul Magnus when Dumper returned to the car, a battered, souped-up old Zodiac.

"The filth've got us in schtuck. All hell's breaking loose." The big man turned to face Paul in the back of the car. "Look, Paul, boy. Why don't you have it away fast? We could all get out. You've got bread salted."

"You go if you want to, Dumper. Me? I'm staying. There's one score I'm going to bloody settle. So you tell me, do you stay and do it with me?"

"The Americans?"

"The Americans' head man."

"The bleedin' godfather," muttered Bernie.

"If you like it that way, yes."

"The style's going out of fashion," said Dumper. "More sensible to have it away quiet like."

"I just told you." Paul had his hard face on, and the Dumper had known him long enough to realise there was no way.

"We're with you, Paul. But Christ help us if we get our collars felt now."

"Those fucking Americans," Magnus said with quiet menace. "They're cornermen, and I've never gone down to a cornerman yet."

Wood was giving Talisman a hard time. "If I told you we have Peter Magnus at Central singing his head off . . ."

"I wouldn't believe you."

"Maybe you wouldn't, son, but you'd be dead wrong. Look, Mr. Talisman, I won't mess about. We could've had you fitted for making the M2 bomb. We could've done that yesterday. Come to that we could've done it today, but who needs it? The Magnuses are stone ginger and everybody's chirping like Harrods Zoo, so do yourself a favour. Cough and save yourself the sweat."

"There's nothing to cough."

"That's your last word?"

Talisman was frightened and near to the end. Wood had enough experience to tell. So had the DS who was leaning against the wall. There was sweat on Talisman's brow and his hands were trembling in spite of his gestures indicating innocence.

"If you insist," Wood looked sadly at the DS. "All I can tell you is that the next men in here will be the wrath of God, Boom-Boom: the whole awesome wrath of God, complete with the four beasts and the angels and the wheels within wheels. So, Mr. Talisman, I say unto you, great tribulation shall soon come upon you, and when I say tribulation, I mean bleedin' mammoth trib-u-bloody-lation, the like of which you have never seen, heard, nor even thought about, before."

Boom-Boom Talisman's brow was cold; so was his stomach, yet he could feel a distant trembling in his bowels. Detective Inspector Monty Wood was very convincing.

Sidney Pringle's solicitor was a small, fat, greasy man called Gavin. He specialised in criminal defence and was known only too well by people like Tickerman. He came into the room with Pringle and a pair of uniformed officers. Torry did not like the smile on the solicitor's face. It would be a pleasure to wipe it off. Sidney Pringle would not look so good either, once he got the message.

"You realise . . ." Gavin began, thrusting towards Ticker-man.

"We know what your client has said, Mr. Gavin, and we presume that, in saying it, he realises the charges which can be brought against him?"

"I've told him what he needs to know."

Sidney Pringle looked at the pile of tapes and photographs. "I don't know nothing about that lot," he said loudly. "All I said was that Mary Chester played a tape over to me and . . ."

"You are denying knowledge of making these tape recordings, or taking these photographs?"

"Too right. I heard a tape and Mary Chester told me who the pair was."

"Keep quiet, Mr. Pringle." From Gavin.

"Which tape is it?" asked Hart.

"How do I know? It was on the recorder when that basta—when Mr. Torry brought me down here."

Hart looked at the papers on his desk. The DI from the Vice leaned over and pointed.

"We have here," said Hart, "a statement from Arnold Frederick Slater who was arrested breaking into Mary Chester's apartment while it was being searched by Detective Sergeants Frewin and Brotherton of West End Central. Mr. Slater has told us a great deal, so have the two detective sergeants. The tape which was removed from the recording machine is marked A290."

The Vice DI sorted through the pile of tapes, found the one marked, and threaded it onto the machine, pressing the PLAY button.

There was a long silence, a hiss of static and an occasional crackle. After five minutes Pringle shouted, "Someone's cleaned the bleedin' thing off. The bastards have . . ."

"What are you trying to tell us, Mr. Pringle?" asked the officer from the Legal branch.

"It's been tampered with." Pringle was scarlet with rage.

"Not here it hasn't."

Pringle was on the edge of control. "I'll get you, you bastard, Torry. You haven't got it all, there's a camera in the ventilation grill opposite the bed . . ."

"Mary Chester's bed?" asked Hart. Torry did not like the way

202

Hart's eyes were shining. Jesus, he thought, he's after me as well.

"'Course not. That bloody slag Peterson. Terrice's bird. We was minding her to see Terrice was straight . . ."

"Take care, Mr. Pringle," warned his solicitor.

"He'd better take care, the bloody liberty-taker." Pringle's finger pointing at Torry.

"Who were you minding Miss Peterson for?" asked Tickerman quietly.

"Peter and . . ." Pringle stopped. "Torry was having it away with Peterson. Bloody slag. The filth corrupting a witness . . ."

"You say there's a camera?" Hart's eyes were still flashing.

"Am I being accused of something?" Torry spoke flatly.

Tickerman held up his hand. "In everyone's interest, I think we should see this camera."

"I insist . . ." began Gavin.

"That you go with the officers? It can be arranged."

Pringle was made to repeat the facts regarding a hidden camera in Jenny Peterson's bedroom, and Gavin was dispatched with a uniformed DI and a pair of constables after permission was obtained from Jenny.

"They got you now?" Tickerman asked when he faced Torry alone.

"No, sir. I don't see what all the fuss is about. You read Miss Peterson's statement?"

Tickerman nodded. "I'd have to take you off the case, Derek, which would be a pity."

"No chance. Looks like I've done everybody a service. Pringle's singing his head off more by accident than good advice. Chester will do the same as soon as someone tells her what's going on."

Tickerman was silent, reflectively drawing on his pipe. "Looks as though you were right about that uniformed DI."

"Burnsides?"

"Lot of money unaccounted for there. He's still up at Kingsway, but I've got eyes on him."

"Once we know about Vescari's arrival he might flush Paul Magnus for us."

"Two jumps ahead of you, Derek. When we've finished here, I

thought we might slip across and see what they've come up with. Then a bit of loose talk might cost lives."

"Preferably Magnus and Vescari."

"Mmmm." The DCS nodded, grinning, his pipe clamped firmly between his teeth. "You've played the Peterson thing coolly, it seems, Derek. I just hope there are no comebacks; the brass always had you fingered for a corner-cutter."

"They're there to be cut, sir."

"I didn't hear that. Let's go and scare the shit out of comrade Talisman, before they've got any porno pictures of you." He hesitated, catching Torry's look. "It's not serious or anything, is it?"

"I'm fond of her," Torry said stiffly.

"Hope it's not on the rebound from your schoolteacher."

"Personal, Tick. Dead personal."

At the Kingsway office they had come up with the only possible answer about the aircraft on which Vescari was travelling—an American Charter Services 707 out of JFK, scheduled for a six-hour stop in Paris to pick up ten more members of the World Council on Catholic Communication.

They had already established that the high-sounding title—World Council on Catholic Communication—was really a way for people to see something of Europe, particularly London and England, while making a contribution to their Faith and Church.

The 707 was due into Heathrow at six the following morning. The passengers would be taken to their hotel—in this case one of the new package palaces in the Cromwell Road, quite near to where Torry lived. Heads would be counted, and it seemed unlikely that Vescari, and whoever was travelling with him, would escape being shepherded to the Mass in Westminster Cathedral.

Burnsides called the Yard and spoke briefly to Tickerman, asking if they could leave it at that. Tickerman told him that he wanted everybody to wait at Kingsway. He would be over, with the other officers, in about an hour. They had to discuss the various choices open to them.

Burnsides looked apprehensively at his watch. Time was moving fast, and he needed to get the information to Crippled Eric. Even though the net was closing, the uniformed DI was determined to bleed the Magnuses of as much money as he could.

The door of the interrogation room slammed open, hard and noisily. Even Wood jumped.

"Out," barked Torry, coming on very heavy.

Both Wood and the DS made a display of leaving, their brief sentences larded with "yes, sirs," and "no, sirs" and "three bags full, sirs."

Wood looked pitifully at Talisman. "The wrath of God," his eyes said. As he turned towards the door, he gave Torry a broad wink.

Alone with Talisman, Torry lit a cigarette and looked at his watch. "In two minutes," he menaced, "my Guv'nor, Detective Chief Superintendent Tickerman, will be coming through that door. He is coming so that you can be taken up to the duty officer and charged with murder—five times: four police officers and Robert Eric Terrice who was, at the time, in their custody . . ."

"I . . ."

"I want to hear nothing from you. Not a word. You've had your chance with Mr. Wood. Now we're doing the talking and the telling . . ."

"I was nowhere near the M2. I . . ."

"You didn't have to be. You constructed the device which was the cause of those deaths . . ."

"You can't . . ."

"Prove it? You're joking, lad. We can prove it a dozen times over. The day of the Magnuses is over and everybody's getting damaged vocal chords. There's so much chat we're putting the Women's Institute out of business. You're stone ginger, Boom-bloody-Boom Talisman. They'll lock you up and feed the key to the goats."

"I wasn't in the car. That was Ben Doffman, Bernie Colts, Frank Esnam . . ."

"Ferret Frank Esnam?" asked Tickerman from the door.

"Sir." Torry stood to attention.

"I'll cough the lot." Talisman looked as though he was going to throw up. "They made me do it. Peter Magnus said they'd cut my balls off if I didn't . . ."

"You've cut 'em off yourself," snapped Torry. "I take him through it, sir?"

Tickerman was refilling his pipe. "I think Monty Wood's capable. Anyway, our friends have just come back from Richmond. Empty-handed."

Before they left for Kingsway, Torry insisted that Jenny Peterson should be given protection. She went back to Richmond in a car with a DS called Osterly, and a pretty little WDS by the name of O'Hagan. Both were armed and highly dangerous police officers; dangerous, that is, to any villains who might have wanted to see Miss Peterson tucked away.

"There's going to be a lot of awkward questions at the trial," Tickerman grunted.

"Which trial?" Torry smiled. "We've got so much going that the bit of black Pringle and Chester were pulling will seem as pure as driven . . ."

"If either Pringle or Chester are pure, I've got an arse called Rajah."

Torry chuckled, and Tickerman laughed. "The Legal are going to have their time and a half sorting the charges."

Hart, Wood, Harvey and company had arrived at Kingsway before them. The whole team was assembled expectantly. Tickerman had already warned the C1 people that some of what he was going to say might seem odd. They knew what that meant and looked grim. It was always unpleasant to know that someone on the team was bent.

The DCS talked briefly about the obvious collapse of the Magnus regime. "We want Paul Magnus," he growled, "but I'm not making a big press thing about it. I don't want to alert other people. The Magnus empire is inevitably finished, so, for the time being, we can afford to let Paul go. My own feeling is that he'll skip the country, and we've covered the usual exit points, but I'm not going to have front-page stories in the papers or on television. There's bigger game."

He went on to give some precise details regarding the arrival of

206

Giuseppe Vescari and some of his people. "If Vescari smells it at this stage he'll only find some way of turning around and heading for home. I want him in. He's going to see that the Magnuses are in chaos, and that may well mean he'll go for a straight takeover. We have the ability to watch him, and we'll nail him. In some ways it's more important for us to get Vescari. Paul we can always find later, so I want no heroics."

They showed some movie film of Peppe Vescari, provided by Washington, then a set of photographs was handed out to the whole team. A straight, and recent, picture of Peppe, together with some photofits put together to show the don in a permutation of disguises.

After that, Torry spoke, giving some added facts about Vescari's entry and the World Council on Catholic Communication. He stressed the near certainty of Peppe Vescari's being at the Mass in Westminster Cathedral at eleven the following morning.

It took just over an hour, and the various members of Tickerman's team went, either to their appointed tasks, or to get some rest prior to the strenuous time ahead.

Tickerman was sleeping at Kingsway with a few others. Torry's orders were to go home and rest, after he had lined up one important facet of the planned operation: an action, like a number of others, which had not been mentioned in the open while Burnsides was present.

Torry lingered in Tickerman's office while the DCS called the Yard Operations Room to see if they had anything new on the whereabouts of Paul Magnus. There was nothing.

"He can't even wait to get to a private phone." Torry stood by the window, looking down and across Kingsway. Burnsides was using the same telephone booth as before.

Tickerman came over. "Well, we can presume that Paul Magnus is getting the word. If this doesn't flush him out, nothing will."

"There's still a chance he might have done a moonlight." Torry stood back as Burnsides left the booth.

"True." Tickerman sucked on the eternal pipe. "A possibility, as I said in there"—inclining his head towards the main office—"but I doubt it. Paul Magnus, cornered and vindictive, will be out for Vescari's blood."

"The logic always puzzles me," said Torry. "It was the Magnuses who screwed the deal once we collared Terrice. Now he blames Vescari. Must be terrible never to be able to trust anyone."

"We don't really know who screwed the deal." Tickerman looked sombre. "Who tipped us about Terrice, Derek? Who really fitted Terrice and started the rot?"

"That bothers me, Tick. It bothers me like a persistent mosquito. The Vescaris or a Magnus man . . . ?"

"Or somebody who didn't know what they were into?"

"Could be. I doubt if we'll ever get the answer."

"Maybe. Go and get up your side of it, Derek. You'd better get tooled up from the Yard while you're at it."

Torry stood in the doorway. "I was going to do that, Tick. Who else is carrying?"

"Hart, Wood and four marksmen I'm placing."

"You?"

"Haven't made up my mind yet. There are times I think that I'm getting too old to play cowboys and indians."

Crippled Eric grabbed at the telephone as soon as it rang. He thought it would be Dumper Doffman who was due to call. Instead he heard the quiet tones of Burnsides.

"What's the strength your end?" asked Burnsides.

Eric ignored the question. "You got anything?"

"A lot, providing the price is right."

"You'll get anything you ask. Just give. We need it fast."

Burnsides told him about Talisman being charged, and one or two other things that had been happening around the Yard and West End Central. Then he came to the important part: "They're not concentrating on Paul. The Guv'nor says they can always find him later. The heat's on this American. Vescari."

"Yes."

"They figure he's coming in from New York, via Paris, on a charter flight—American Charter Services 707 arriving Heathrow at six tomorrow morning." He went on, giving Eric the full strength about the World Council on Catholic Communication, the hotel which the passengers from that flight had been booked into—

he had to repeat the flight number three times. Then he told Eric about the Mass in Westminster Cathedral.

"This geezer's going to be there? A million?"

"They think it's definite. They'll have the watchers out."

"Eleven o'clock?"

"On the dot."

"That's all?"

"No. I got a set of photos. Vescari and his possible disguises. You want those?"

"Dunno. Yes. Be on the safe side."

Burnsides arranged to drop the pictures in at a pub near Crippled Eric's gaff.

The telephone rang again, almost as soon as he put down the handset. This time it was the Dumper. Eric gave him the facts, told him that he would be out, in about an hour, for fifteen minutes, to collect the pictures.

Ben Doffman said he would call back in two hours to give Paul's instructions. Paul would be pleased to hear that the squeeze was off him for the time being.

"Couldn't you just have notice served on this Vescari shit, Paul?" The Dumper sat opposite Magnus in the small kitchen at the farm. Bernie was busy cooking bacon and eggs at the stove, and they had got through almost a whole bottle of whisky.

Paul had been pleased with the news from Burnsides. But for the wrong reasons.

"It's my job," he maintained. "If anyone gets Vescari it's not going to be the filth. I'll do it on my own if I have to—if you lot are chicken."

"I've been a Magnus man for a long time," said Bernie, flipping an egg over in the frying pan. Paul liked his eggs turned over and easy. "I'm not going to cop out on you now, Paul. I'm in."

The Dumper sighed heavily. "You know me, Paul. I've never let you down. Just tell me what you want doing. You want me to pick up those photos from Crippled Eric?"

"I don't need no pictures," Paul snarled. "I've only met Peppe Vescari once . . ."

"The New York jaunt," commented Bernie to the bacon and eggs.

". . . and I'm not likely to miss him. I think I could even smell the bastard."

"How's it to be done then, Paul?"

Paul Magnus took another long pull at his drink. "I'll tell you. What we do is . . ."

Torry drove straight to the Yard and went down to the Armourer. He was issued with a Browning Hi-Power 9mm Parabellum and four magazines holding thirteen rounds each. He threaded the holster through his belt, so that he would be carrying it above his right buttock. He inserted one magazine, pulled back the breech, putting one round up the spout, clicked the safety and holstered the weapon.

He went back to the car and drove to St. Saviour's Church.

Father Conrad was preparing for bed. Torry told him that it was terribly important and he was sorry to disturb him at this time of night. Father Conrad was polite and understanding, though he made a point of telling Torry that he had to be up early in the morning. The organisers of the World Council on Catholic Communication expected him to meet a plane coming in from India. He had to be at Gatwick by five-thirty.

"I'm hoping we might change that," said Torry. "My Guv'nor's already been on to the organisation's headquarters. I thought they might have been in touch already."

The priest asked him in and Torry sat in the familiar room sipping the coffee that Father Conrad made for him, outlining what he had in mind for tomorrow.

"I don't know if I'd be the right man for this," said Father Conrad when Torry finished telling him what they wanted.

"Wouldn't you say that the prevention of sin is better than the cure?"

"It's academic, but . . ."

The telephone rang. Father Conrad listened attentively to the caller and then said, "Yes, Father . . . of course . . . no, it's no bother at all." He put the telephone down. "They've shifted me," he said, a weary smile moving slowly across his face. "Your bishop must be a convincing man. Yes, Derek, I suppose I'll have to do as you ask, though I'm not happy about it."

Torry stayed for another three quarters of an hour, arranging details. When he left, he turned the car towards Richmond.

Jenny was about to go to bed when he arrived. The detective sergeant called Osterly was looking after things in the main living room, which meant he was lying back in a chair reading a magazine, while WDS O'Hagan was in the kitchen making a hot drink for their charge.

"Just called in to make sure everything was okay," Torry told them.

"She's been as good as gold," O'Hagan said.

Torry went over and tapped on the bedroom door.

"You decent, Jenny? It's me. Derek."

"I'm not, but you can come in."

She sat at the dressing table in her underwear, cleaning the day's make-up from her face with cotton wool. Torry went over and bent to kiss her.

"Derek, not now. Not with your people here."

"Your door's got a lock, hasn't it?"

"The lady copper's going to bring me a milky drink any minute."

"You know what they say about lady coppers," Torry grinned. "Put something on over your . . . well, over what you're wearing."

She went to the wardrobe and covered herself with a wrap. It was just in time. WDS O'Hagan came in with the drink.

"Just call for me if the Detective Chief Inspector makes a nuisance of himself," she smiled.

"There's no respect in the job any more." Torry made a face.

When the WDS left, he walked tentatively towards the door.

"Don't, darling." Jenny's face and body seemed to cry frustration. "I couldn't. The walls are too thin. They'd hear, you know what a noisy lover I am."

"Tomorrow?"

"Please, tomorrow. Please."

"It'll be all over tomorrow."

"Oh, I hope so. God I hope so. There's been so much . . ."

"I know, love. Believe me, I know."

"Do you?"

In a brief flash he did know. "I think so," he said.

"Then try to understand."

She came to him, wrapping her arms around him. When her hand touched the Browning in its holster she shrank back. "Are you going to use that?"

His eyes were vacant, impassive. "Maybe. I don't know. It depends."

"Derek, be careful, for Christ's sake be careful. I don't want to lose you when I've just found you."

"You won't. Sleep. Rest. When it's finished I'll be over, fast as a . . ."

"Bullet?"

"No more bullets, Jenny, love. Fast as Cupid's arrow."

"Lovely, sloppy romantic copper again."

"Why not?"

"It could be very good."

"It will be."

She kissed him again, long, clinging, full of wanting and wishing.

Torry went back to his place in the Cromwell Road, but he could not sleep. He hoped that it would be all over, tomorrow.

All over today.

XV

TRANSCRIPT OF TELEPHONE COMMUNICATIONS TO AND FROM SUITE 780, THE MAYFAIR HOTEL, LONDON, W1. DATE CODE: EF/23/C. HOME OFFICE PERMIT NUMBER PO/GH/COM CRIM/ 36782A. OCCUPANT: ANTHONY CHASSEN (ALSO KNOWN AS ANTHONY CHAMPION AND ANTONIO CAMPELLI).

Timed at 6.15 A.M. Note: The incoming
call is from a public telephone box.

OCCUPANT: Hello.

CALLER: I'm here, Tony.

OCCUPANT: Where?

CALLER: London. Heathrow.

OCCUPANT: Turn around and go back. It's all hell here.

CALLER: I can't turn back. Impossible. What's wrong?

OCCUPANT: The whole deal's smashed.

CALLER: How smashed?

OCCUPANT: The cousins. Their organisation's smashed. One's busted, the other's running. I don't know what the latest word is.

CALLER: What about your people?

OCCUPANT: None left.

CALLER: Enrico and . . .

OCCUPANT: Dead.

CALLER: How?

OCCUPANT: A foolish business. Call it an accident.

CALLER: I will be at the Flamingo Hotel in Cromwell Road. We should be there in about an hour. Ask for Mr. Venalls—V-E-N-A-L-L-S.

OCCUPANT: Better you should leave.
CALLER: See me.

The passengers from the American Charter Services flight from New York, via Paris, looked tired. There were several nuns among them; three priests; a number of young people, and an assorted bunch of men and women in groups or alone, looking both happy and sad.

Vescari was not wearing any disguise; only sunglasses. Tickerman and Wood watched him come through from the baggage area and noted that he seemed to have only four other men with him. All five mafiosi wore smart suits in either charcoal grey or black, and they appeared to be very much part of the general herd—each of them wearing a small tie-on label printed with their name and the fact that they were part of the World Council on Catholic Communication.

There were two priests waiting to meet them, both in the regulation black suits, clerical collars and black hats. One was an elderly, tall, thin man, the other younger, more rugged-looking, heavily built.

The priests fussed around like sheep dogs, constantly referring to lists, checking off names.

The DCS and Wood watched until the whole party was moved through the main doors into a pair of waiting coaches. Harvey and a pair of DSs would take over now. Harvey and one DS were in the back of a taxi, the other DS was driving.

Behind the dark sunglasses, Peppe Vescari's eyes constantly moved, sweeping the areas above and in front of him. His four soldiers were also alert. After making his telephone call, while they were waiting to go through to the baggage, customs and passport control areas, Don Peppe had quietly told them that things were not good.

Vescari found the two priests irritating, particularly the younger one, who was always nearby, making sure they had everything, checking they knew the name of the hotel, and issuing instructions about the routine. Once they checked into the hotel, they could rest until ten o'clock, when coaches would be ready to take them all to the Mass at Westminster Cathedral. The coaches would not leave until the whole party was aboard, so, the young priest kept reminding them, it was especially important that nobody should be late.

Vescari saw no way of avoiding the Mass, but it did not matter. He enjoyed going to Mass, it made him feel part of the larger family of God, and reminded him of his childhood, long before he knew what his father and uncles did for a living.

They got into the hotel just after seven, but it was seven-thirty before they were allocated rooms. Vescari and his bodyguard, Luigi, were in a double, the other three in single rooms near at hand.

Vescari ordered coffee and rolls from room service, also the morning papers. He stretched back on his bed and read through the news. There was scant mention of the Magnus cousins, but each paper carried short stories about a number of raids and arrests which had been made in London. They all linked these stories with a double murder, and an incident which had occurred outside a Soho club called The Graven Image in the early hours of the previous day.

Vescari knew The Graven Image was a Magnus club. He also knew the names of at least two of those killed in the incident. Giuseppe Vescari was most unhappy about the news. Tony Campelli was not one to exaggerate, and Tony sounded concerned. There was little doubt that the whole business had become difficult if not completely unstuck. He would talk to Tony. Maybe it would be best to remain simply a good member of the delegation to the World Council on Catholic Communication. See that through, and then return to New York. There would always be another time, other men in high places in London's underworld. There were always people waiting to step into the shoes of the dead or fallen. He would talk to Tony and see.

They travelled back towards London in the old Zodiac. Paul Magnus was not going to leave anything to chance. His plan would give them three bites at Vescari. He would go his own way after they got to Bernie's garage. The Dumper and Bernie would also split up, transferring into two clean cars which they would use if it seemed necessary.

Paul Magnus had the Luger, loaded in his pocket, and the two other men were also armed. When they took the cars out, they would also be taking shotguns. At least on one front the Magnus cousins would be successful.

Anthony Chassen arrived at the Flamingo Hotel a little after eight o'clock. At the desk they rang Mr. Venalls's room and told him to go straight up.

"Tony." Vescari embraced his lieutenant. "This is bad news."

"It couldn't be worse."

Tony Chassen looked around him. He had expected Luigi to be there; Peppe would never have come this far without him. The other three he knew quite well: Michele, Cesare and Settimo. All good and reliable men. The don could not have chosen more wisely.

Chassen accepted the coffee offered to him and began giving his chief the rundown on the events about which he knew. He was also vaguely aware of some of the other things going on, but a great deal was shrouded in secrecy.

"We should have made sure of someone in the Metropolitan Police before we started," he said finally.

Peppe thought for a long while. "Next time we will not make such a foolish error." His face reflected a wry cynicism. "It is a pity these Magnuses turned out to be so stupid. . . ."

"Moustache Petes," spat Luigi.

Peppe nodded in his bodyguard's direction, "As you say, my old friend. Our time is not yet. What did they used to say in that old movie series—*Zorro*—I shall return?"

"Not this time?" asked Cesare.

Peppe slowly shook his head. "Not this time. One does not take over a business which is falling into decay." He swallowed a mouthful of coffee and turned back to Chassen. "Antonio, my good friend, I want you to take the first plane you can get onto back to New York." He smiled broadly, a full and generous beam. "We will do our souls a bit of good. We will see out this World Council on Catholic Communication. After all, the Church may have a lot to teach us, it is older than we are."

216

Paul Magnus became very silent as they reached the outskirts of London. He had been buoyant for most of the trip, talking about the time to come when they would reclaim their positions in the natural criminal order of things. The Dumper and Bernie were glum. They knew the law was about, in force; that the law knew Vescari was in England and, probably, why. They had both added it up. The risk they were taking for Paul was heavy. Bernie, in fact, was wondering if it might be best to cut and run once Paul had gone after the American.

They arrived at the garage just after nine and in the back room of Bernie's place rechecked the plan, went over the weapons and drank a couple of snorts.

Paul Magnus left, still with the Luger in his pocket, a little before ten o'clock.

The law had been very thorough. Crippled Eric was picked up in his gaff early in the morning. The two DSs who went for him turned the place over and found, among other things, the Vescari photographs. They took them straight back to Kingsway and handed them over to Tickerman, who rang through to the Rubber Heels, that part of C1 whose job it is to investigate their own people.

When Burnsides arrived at Kingsway, a DCI and a DI were waiting in Tickerman's office. Tickerman was already out and about again, but Burnsides knew immediately what the DCI and the DI were after. He was a man of simple philosophy; he looked at them, nodded sadly, and went quietly down to their car with them. Later that morning, Burnsides hanged himself in a lavatory with a piece of cord the DC who was watching him had missed.

Tickerman had Westminster Cathedral sewn up as tight as a virgin in a chastity belt. Most of his people were out of sight, and he surveyed the scene, overlooking the west door, from a window in Ashley Place. He had a marksman with him, armed with a rifle and sniperscope. Tickerman was edgy, nervous, constantly sweeping the area with his field glasses. He knew how much was at stake. If anything went wrong, there would be hundreds of people

217

in the open line of fire. This was really sticking his neck out, and nobody knew it better than Tickerman.

Wood, Hart and Harvey would be in the cathedral itself, posted among the huge congregation, with eyes sharp on Vescari, and Torry was in an even more vulnerable position.

By ten o'clock, Detective Chief Superintendent Tickerman's hands were sweating.

The coaches bringing the delegates, to the World Council on Catholic Communication, to the Mass at Westminster Cathedral, began to arrive just after ten. All races, but one creed, they came quietly from the coaches, shuffling in a throng through the great west doors—black, white, yellow and brown, and a number of variants on those colours. The mixture of languages brought to mind the Tower of Babel, and the priests and other stewards were all looking harassed as they guided their respective flocks into the massive, Byzantine-style building.

Father Conrad was already tired. He had not slept well, which was hardly surprising. It was no part of an elderly priest's duties to act as watchdog to a group of dangerous gangsters. The young priest with him was a great help, but he made Father Conrad even more nervous.

They were ten minutes late getting the whole party into the coaches outside the Flamingo Hotel, and Father Conrad was concerned about their arrival at the cathedral.

He had reason to be concerned, as he saw when they reached Ashley Place. Other parties were late, and this, combined with London's eternal traffic problems, had the whole area congested. Coaches were spilling out their parties everywhere, the drivers ignoring the pleas of both coach marshals and stewards.

Father Conrad finally managed to get his large group into some kind of order, with his young assistant moving round like a stalking horse. But once on the move, it was impossible to keep everyone in check and they were soon swallowed into the great moving crowd.

Tickerman became more anxious; even with his glasses he could see little. There were so many people swelling and flowing like a human river into the building.

"It's going to be impossible," he muttered to the marksman. "We're never going to get near anyone if the balloon goes up."

Peppe Vescari did not like being jostled and pushed. It made him nervous, even though Luigi, with all his training, managed to keep very close to him. Inside, the cathedral was vast, far bigger than Vescari had imagined, and they were shuffled unceremoniously, into the pews. Vescari found himself on the Gospel side and almost at the end of a row until the young priest who had irritated him so much with his fussing pushed in whispering, "If you move up a little, I think there'll be room for me at the end."

Paul Magnus made his way, on foot, from Victoria Station to Ashley Place, and was pleased to see so many people. If the filth were about, it was not likely he would get spotted in this kind of crowd. The crush was like a football match. Paul had never realised how high God was rated among the Catholics. He finally got into the cathedral, feeling uneasy, as though watched by a million eyes. He hung about at the back trying to look as though he was one of the officials, his eyes searching the vastness for Vescari.

Wood, Hart and Harvey spotted Vescari and his four soldiers. At least they were in a position where they could be kept in view.

They also spotted Torry. Wood and Hart exchanged glances and grinned, then, as if by some unseen signal, the ceremonial began.

Torry found himself engulfed in the mystery and ritual of the Mass. He had always found it like this, since childhood; since the old time when he accepted the Faith without question, he regarded the Mass as the one unchanging act which bound the Church, its people, and God together. In spite of himself, the emotions remained the same. He might not believe it all now, but the slow ceremonial built towards the high drama of worship—the consecration of the bread and wine, the incredible mystery instituted by

God the Son at his last meal on earth, the unknowable, yet obvious, sacrifice of God: the Bread and Wine becoming the very Body and Blood of Christ.

It takes one leap, Torry thought, one leap into the darkness to grasp all this. Slowly and with dignified beauty, the Mass came to an end. The priests and acolytes departed, the choir sang its final amen, the congregation began to move.

Hart, Wood and Harvey started to close in towards Vescari and his people, pushing, rudely even, through the quietly departing worshippers. They too had been moved by the service, for it seemed to dwarf their own lives and beings with its solemnity. Even their particular fight against lawlessness appeared almost insignificant, beside this.

But it was over, and they had a job to do, a duty to protect the innocent. They came up behind Vescari and his four men, quietly in position, their hands relaxed but ready to move.

Paul Magnus had spent the time at the back of the cathedral, near the door. He waited now because he did not have to go to Peppe Vescari. Vescari was coming to him. There were several men around him, the don's soldiers, Magnus presumed. Any chance of a shot at him yet was impossible, because of the priest who blocked his line of fire, moving directly in front of the American.

Magnus decided that he would stand more chance outside, on the steps. He elbowed his way into the crowd, shouldering through until he reached the air. It would be better here, easier to make the run to the Dumper's car which by now would be parked and ready at the junction of Ashley Place and Victoria Street.

Vescari was coming out. Magnus had a brief view of some nuns to his left, then, suddenly, the young priest in front of Don Peppe glanced behind him and, in so doing, moved slightly to his left, leaving Vescari open for a shot.

Magnus brought his hand up, thrusting the Luger forward. He was only a few paces from Vescari, and as he squeezed the trigger, the young priest turned his head forward again.

Torry had found the ill-fitting black priest's suit restricting, and now as his brain registered what was happening, he could not get at the Browning with the ease he needed. He lost only a couple of vital seconds, but in that time, Paul Magnus had fired four shots.

Two of them hit Vescari in the chest, knocking him back against the crowd which began to scatter, screams building with the panic.

There was a bang close to Torry's right shoulder and he saw one of Vescari's men, gun in hand levelling for a second shot. Torry brought his Browning down hard on the man's wrist and was aware of Hart grappling with one of the other soldiers. As he looked quickly to his right, Torry saw that Wood was down, blood around his throat, among the crowd near Vescari. Other plainclothesmen were running in, but Paul Magnus had turned, threading his way quickly through the crush. Torry called out to Harvey, who he knew was armed, and pushed through after Paul Magnus.

It was like coming up from a deep dive, Torry was almost naturally holding his breath as he battered through the throng, then, suddenly, he was in the open, studded with only one or two moving figures, among them Paul Magnus running hard towards Victoria Street. Harvey was behind him, and Torry could not get a clear, quick shot. He pushed himself to the limit, knowing that he was gaining ground on Magnus. He could see the car Magnus was heading for, one man at the wheel, the door open, and, on the air, Magnus calling out, the words floating back like some weird banshee wail—"I got the bastard, Dumper . . . saw him off . . . got him . . ."

Torry was clear for one quick shot. He pulled up, legs apart and both hands over the Browning. Magnus came across his sights, and, as he was about to squeeze the trigger, there were two heavy thumps to his right. Magnus went over flailing, all arms and legs like a rag doll thrown down by a peevish child. The doll was leaking red, spreading it over the road.

Torry lifted his sights to the car, the driver had leaned over to close the door and was now bringing what appeared to be a shotgun up to his shoulder. Torry fired once, the bullet frosting the windshield. The driver dropped the shotgun and tried to get the car away, but Harvey fired twice more and there was no further movement.

Both the policemen walked slowly towards Magnus and the car; others were running up behind them.

Giuseppe Vescari was dead, as was Cesare and, unhappily, Detective Inspector Monty Wood, who had taken Magnus's third bullet in the throat. Magnus and Ben "Dumper" Doffman were also no more.

The remaining three Americans were in custody, and one innocent worshipper had been knocked unconscious during the panic following Magnus's first shots.

The rest would be paperwork and legal argument. Tickerman and his team met to begin the heavy job of getting everything down on paper. The Fraud and Vice would be busy for many weeks; so would Torry and the rest. Torry detested writing reports and these would be more difficult than usual.

During the late afternoon, he called Jenny to ask if she would like to come down to his flat in the Cromwell Road that evening. She was relieved to hear his voice, for, while Osterly and O'Hagan had kept her informed of everything, she had got hold of the evening newspapers which had not as yet named the dead policeman.

By six that evening he was bushed stupid and went through to tell Tickerman that he was going off duty.

"Thanks, Derek," the old policeman growled. "They won't be back in a hurry."

"I wish I could believe you, Tick. This lot won't be back, but there are others. Ring C11 and ask who's already climbing into the Magnuses' shoes."

The DCS shrugged. All he really wanted now was to get back to his garden and the comfort of his own home.

"I might ring them," Tickerman grinned. "Tomorrow, I might ring them."

Jenny had not been to the Cromwell Road flat before. "It's a bit bare and austere," she said. "I'll have to brighten the place up for you. If you want me to."

"I want you to. On the other hand, a house somewhere could be the answer."

"Proposals from a copper?"

"Why not? Once you've told me the truth, the whole truth and nothing but the truth."

The sparkle went out of her eyes, her mouth closing tightly.

The telephone rang. It was Father Conrad.

"I was going to call you, Father, just to make sure you were all right."

"Are you all right, Derek? It was unpleasant, most unpleasant."

"I know, Father. I'm sorry to have involved you."

"You mustn't be sorry. I'm involved already, I know that. My firm, my organisation, is the antithesis of the Magnuses' little firm or the other organisation. Holy Church fights crime as well, Derek."

Torry smiled to himself. "You're well up in it, Father."

"I don't restrict myself to the *Catholic Herald,* you know."

They spoke for a few minutes and Torry was still smiling when he replaced the handset. Jenny was sitting in one of the leather chairs, looking near to tears.

"How did you know?" she asked.

"The old copper's trick. Two and two, and a bit of intuition. The only thing I couldn't understand was your state on that Thursday, when you arrived at Bob's flat and found that he was dead. You want to tell me about it?"

She took a deep breath. "The state was real enough. I went because I didn't know what had happened. I didn't let myself know. I didn't read the papers or watch television, just like I said. I expected him to have been arrested, but not . . . not dead."

"Why did you . . . ?"

"A lot of reasons, I suppose. Oh, because I was fed up with him, fed up of feeling so much for him, loving him and not liking him. I knew he was bent, Derek, but I wasn't. I didn't know what the trip was about. Then he rang me from Paris. Rang me at the office. He told me that we were going to be very rich. That he was bringing something back which would make our fortunes. I suspected it was drugs, and I knew what it would mean. I'd never be free of him, not ever, and I'd be stuck with him making out with other women, tricking out on me. He told me he would be coming over in a couple of days, so, when the time came, I dialled 999—from a callbox, thank God—and asked to speak to somebody about drugs. I told them, and then went off and forgot about it, until the day I was due to meet him and . . ."

Torry put his arms around her. "It's all right now. It's over, and I'm here."

"Do you have to . . . ?"

"Report it? Not me, sweetheart. What? Shop my own bird? You're joking."

She reached up and kissed him, hugging him close. "Can you trust me after that?"

"We'll have to see. It shouldn't be hard."

The telephone rang again.

"You're going to have to live with this." He picked up the receiver. "A policeman's lot . . ."

"Derek?" The voice broke its way into his guts. He would always be able to tell Susan Crompton's voice.

"Yes." Flat.

"I've just seen the papers. Are you okay?"

"I'm fine."

"I was worried. Derek, I miss you. Could I come over?"

His guts and his head and heart fought one another, so he shifted position, turning back to look at Jenny. She smiled at him.

"Sorry, Sue," said Torry. "I've got my bird here. Why not come to the wedding?"

She put the phone down hard.

"Your Ex?"

"My Ex."

Jenny put on a phony American accent. "If she calls again, tell her you're under new management."

For the third time the telephone rang. It was Tickerman.

"I'm sorry, darling. It shouldn't take long." He held her very close.

"Don't worry. I'll be here when you get back. I'll always be here when you get back."

"Under new management." Torry laughed as he went to the door. "The firm's under new management."